Bittersweet Homecoming

ELIZA LENTZSKI

Copyright © 2015 Eliza Lentzski

All rights reserved.

This is a work of fiction. All names, characters, places, and incidents are the products of the author's imagination or are used fictitiously. Any resemblance to events, locales, or real persons, living or dead, other than those in the public domain, is entirely coincidental.

No part of this book may be reproduced, re-sold, or transmitted electronically or otherwise, without written permission from the author.

ISBN: 1516871286
ISBN-13: 978-1516871285

OTHER WORKS BY ELIZA LENTZSKI

Winter Jacket 3: Finding Home

Fragmented

Don't Call Me Hero

Apophis: Love Story for the End of the World

Winter Jacket 2: New Beginnings

Winter Jacket

Second Chances

Date Night

Love, Lust, & Other Mistakes

Diary of a Human

+ + +

Works as E.L. Blaisdell

Drained: The Lucid (with Nica Curt)

http://www.elizalentzski.com

CONTENTS

Prologue	1
Chapter One	4
Chapter Two	13
Chapter Three	26
Chapter Four	41
Chapter Five	58
Chapter Six	68
Chapter Seven	77
Chapter Eight	87
Chapter Nine	99
Chapter Ten	110
Chapter Eleven	124
Chapter Twelve	136
Chapter Thirteen	145
Chapter Fourteen	157
Chapter Fifteen	168
Chapter Sixteen	176
Chapter Seventeen	188
Epilogue	194

DEDICATION

To Lauven

PROLOGUE

I've been meaning to change my cell phone's ringtone for a while now. Whenever it goes off in the middle of a meeting I'm embarrassed. First, because you'd think after it happening so many times that I'd remember to put it on silent. Second, because it's some horrendous hip-hop song that's so not me. Now, deep rattling bass that instead sounds reed thin coming through the tiny speakers on my cell phone, shakes me from my sleep.

The glowing numbers on my bedside alarm clock inform me that it's just past 3:00 a.m. I can't imagine who'd be calling me at this hour, but when I see the name blinking back at me on the screen of my cell phone, it feels like my heart has stopped dead in my chest. It's 5:00 am in Minnesota. I instinctively know there will be no good news when I hit the answer button.

"Hello?" My voice is foreign to my ears, like there's cotton shoved in the canals that distorts everything I hear.

"No, it's fine," I tell her. The voice is familiar, but the sound of her tears is not. I'm transported back to our childhood. She's remained sixteen in my head, but I know she's twenty-six or twenty-seven now. I haven't seen much of her lately. Grown, graduated, married, no kids.

A slender arm moves to drape over my waist. "Baby, who is that?" Her lightly accented voice is garbled by sleep.

I put a finger up to my lips to keep her from saying anything else. Her usually unlined brow crinkles, but she obeys my wordless plea.

"Don't worry about the time," I say. I'm gripping the phone so tightly, I'm sure it'll crack under the pressure. "What's wrong?"

The voice on the line breaks. It shatters and falls apart. I can only make out every other word, which are punctuated by sharp sobs. But I understand just enough to confirm my suspicions.

Words of consolation get caught in my throat. "When's the funeral?" I ask instead.

I pause and listen to the facts.

"I'll be there." I pause again and suck in a deep breath. "I love you."

The woman next to me in bed looks startled by my words—probably because I've never said them to her, and she's been my girlfriend for nearly half a year.

Without another word, I hang up and carefully return my phone to its normal location on my bedside table. My movements are slow and deliberate. I'm numb.

"What's wrong? Who was that?" she asks me, suspicion creeping into her normally carefree tone.

"That was my sister," I say. I run my hand over my face. "Her husband died."

"Oh no," she laments with a deep sigh.

I pull myself out of bed, a full-sized mattress that takes up nearly all the floor space in my one-bedroom LA apartment. I turn on the lamp on my bedside table. The base is in the shape of Mickey Mouse and Disney characters are screen printed on the lampshade. I've had it since childhood.

I find a suitcase in my bedroom closet and begin throwing clothes into it. It's summer in LA, a season I don't think I'll ever get used to, but back in my hometown the temperatures will just be getting over seventy degrees. I pack jeans and short-sleeved shirts and throw a bathing suit in there as an afterthought—not that it's ever warm enough to swim in Lake Superior. Not that I think this trip will warrant a trip to the beach.

"You're packing *now*?" my girlfriend asks incredulously.

"The funeral's tomorrow. I have to catch a flight to Minneapolis and rent a car."

She chews on her lip and nods after a moment as if to say the math checks out. "Do you want me to come with?"

The question, whose answer should come so easily, makes me

pause my disorganized packing. "To Minnesota?" It's like she's asking me if I want her to go to the moon with me.

"No," I decide finally. "You should stay."

I don't look in her direction because I'm afraid of the hurt or the disappointment I might see on her pixie features.

"Are you sure?"

I nod vigorously, still not making eye contact. I shove a handful of underwear into the suitcase, not bothering to count out the days I'll be gone. Because I honestly don't know—I've never had to do this before. What's the proper amount of time to stay and grieve when your little sister has just lost the love of her life?

CHAPTER ONE

With the sunroof open, my long hair whips around my face. I know the wind is going to horribly tangle my already chaotic mane, but the slightly chilly breeze is refreshing. It's too hot in southern California. Air conditioning leaves me feeling refrigerated and disconnected from the outside world, so being able to drive with the windows and sunroof open is a special treat.

It's about a four-hour drive from the Minneapolis-St. Paul International Airport to my hometown. The trip takes me down a curvy, wooded county highway along the shoreline of Lake Superior, heavily traveled by semi-trucks and RV campers. I usually find the winding highway an adventure, but this is a sobering trip. I'm not on vacation; I'm going to say a final goodbye to the husband of my only sibling. Adam wasn't even thirty yet—the innocent victim in a drunk-driving accident.

I haven't seen Adam or my sister in at least ten years, minus their wedding a few years ago. I'd been the Maid of Honor, but I had no right to that job. Emily had friends in her life with whom she was infinitely closer, but my sister is a sucker for tradition and social etiquette, which means that I was the one in the pink dress giving the toast at her wedding reception.

Lost in thought, the drive goes by quickly and I find myself in my hometown: Grand Marais, Minnesota. Population just under 1500. It's summer—tourist season—so I'm forced to drive at a snail's pace through the heart of the tiny downtown district. The town has been untouched by time. Some of the storefronts look a little different—

new coats of paint and updated signs—but for the most part it's exactly as I remember. One side of the street is local businesses—T-shirt shops and ice cream parlors. The opposite side is an unobstructed view of Lake Superior. Before I was born, the city passed a zoning law that kept the lakeshore undeveloped. The city marina and a few grandfathered-in businesses dot the lakeside, but other than that, there's nothing between you and the view of the lake.

I pass my dad's store on Main Street. The hand-painted storefront sign is faded from age and sun exposure: Handyman Henry's. He's the town's handyman and our last name is Henry. It's not very original and a little on the corny side, but it gets the job done—kind of like my dad.

When my parents first got married, they lived in the apartment located above the shop. When they had me, they moved to the house where my dad still lives. The three-bedroom, one and a half bath, A-frame house is filled with memories, both good and bad. Most of my friends in Los Angeles can't fathom having lived and grown up in the same house since birth to high school graduation, but that's what small-town life is like.

Between the cross-country flight and the drive from the Twin Cities, it's late in the evening by the time I reach the long driveway to my father's house. The tires on my rental car crunch loose gravel, and the vehicle bumps in small grooves made by time and run-off water. The front porch light is on and a warm glow from other lights inside the house illuminates the walk from my car up the wooden deck and to the front door.

I still have a key and I'm sure my dad hasn't had need to change the locks since I graduated high school, but I still knock anyway.

The door swings open, and my dad stands on the other side of the door. "Where's Emily?" I ask. I drop my suitcase in the front foyer.

"Adam's parents' house. They're hosting the wake this evening."

My dad looks tired. He looks thinner than I remember him being, too. His jeans are baggy and the red flannel shirt he wears is a size too big. The man frozen in my memory banks doesn't look like this.

"Why isn't it at the funeral home?" I ask. My hometown is so small there's only one funeral home, and the funeral director and the undertaker are the one and the same.

My dad frowns. "There's no public viewing of the body."

"The car accident." My stomach sinks when the realization hits me. "Adam was . . ." I trail off.

"He was practically unidentifiable." My dad's voice drops a little, and I can tell he's working hard to keep his emotions in check. Fathers don't often like the men who marry their daughters, but I knew my dad had really liked Adam. There wasn't much not to like. "They used his dental records to identify the body."

I clench the keys to my rental car. "I should head over there. Do you want a ride?" I should probably freshen up and change into something more appropriate for a wake, but I just want to hug my sister.

"I've just come from there," he says. He grabs my suitcase before I can stop him. "I'll put your bag in your room."

I should hug him, but he's already a few steps up the staircase. I hesitate in the front foyer and watch him lug my suitcase upstairs. I've been away for too long. But now's not the time to apologize for that.

Adam's parents live only a few houses away from my dad, but the properties are so spaced out that it ends up being more efficient to drive there. The street in front of the Harvester home is lined with cars, other folks coming to pay their respects, I assume.

I find a spot to park on an adjacent street and make my way to the two-story brick colonial. The Harvesters are one of the wealthier families in town with Mr. Harvester being bank president and Mrs. Harvester perpetual president of the Parent-Teacher Association.

I don't know either of them all that well even though Adam and Emily dated forever. They'd been high school sweethearts, attended college in Duluth, and had gotten married soon after graduation. I used to joke with Emily that the best part about marrying Adam was that she didn't have to change her initials.

The house is all lit up and I can hear the muffled sounds of conversation coming from inside. I knock on the door instead of using the doorbell and am immediately greeted by someone whom I don't recognize. She's a tall woman with stick straight black hair cut just below her ears.

"Come on in," she says, ushering me inside and closing the door behind me. "Emily's in the back."

I nod my thanks. I wonder if she knows who I am.

The house is filled with people wearing some shade of grey or black. I'm decidedly not dressed for a wake. I'm wearing my most comfortable jeans, t-shirt, and hooded zip-up sweatshirt. It makes me rethink my decision to come straight over to the house. Some of the gathered mourners look in my direction as I begin to walk through the house, but after deciding that I'm no one of interest, they return to their respective conversations.

The Harvesters have a lovely home. I've never been inside, but I've driven by the house more times than I can count. My ears are filled with the quiet din of hushed, polite conversations and the scent of casserole dishes perfumes the air. Pictures of Adam throughout the years, and quite a few of Adam with my sister, crowd the walls and flat surfaces. Adam was an only child, a star athlete, and an overall nice guy, the pride of his parents.

Before I get too far into the house, I run into Adam's mother in a hallway. She's a tall, thin woman with a pronounced nose. Her black dress reaches below her knees and a black shawl is draped over narrow shoulders.

"Hello," she greets. She presses a crumpled tissue to her nose. "Thank you for coming." Her eyes are shiny and red.

I take her hand in mine. "I'm so sorry for your loss, Mrs. Harvester."

"Thank you . . ." She trails off and her eyes narrow momentarily, as though she recognizes me, but can't place a name to a face.

I had been all but invisible in high school, which is hard to pull off in a school system of less than two hundred students. I didn't play sports, and I wasn't in any after-school activities like drama, or band, or even Bible study. My closest friends had been books and the sour-faced librarian at the public library.

Emily had been the pretty and popular one. She'd had a boyfriend since she was eight years old; she'd played basketball and had run track in high school. She'd never been a great brain—that was my department—but she'd gotten solid enough grades to get into the local state college in Duluth where she and Adam had stayed after graduation. It was close enough to Grand Marais that coming home for Thanksgiving or Easter wasn't a big deal, but far enough away that they weren't back in town every weekend. She'd gotten a job as an insurance underwriter and Adam had had his own accounting firm in the small city.

I clear my throat. "I'm Abigail Henry." I don't think I look much different from when I used to live in town, but it's been a few years.

"Emily's sister," she breathes. She throws her arms around me in an unexpected hug and I freeze from the gesture. "It was so soon, so unexpected. We never got to say goodbye."

I pat the space between her shoulder blades. I can feel the bones of her back beneath my palms. She's so thin, so frail; one tight hug would have her ribs collapsing. "H-have you seen Emily?" I ask.

Mrs. Harvester pulls back from the hug and wipes under her eyes, collecting her ruined mascara on her long, boney fingers. "She's in the parlor, by the piano."

The parlor is near the front of the house, so I'm forced to change directions. Between the baby grand piano, straight-backed furniture, and a line of mourners, the room is stuffy and crowded. Over the top of people's heads, I spy my sister. She looks good. She looks calm. Strong. She gives hugs to people and consoles those who break down. I feel myself relax. Maybe this won't be so horrible. Maybe I won't cry, either. The line starts to dwindle, and I get closer to the front.

When our eyes finally meet, her face crumbles. "Hi, Abs," she says in a tiny voice.

I skip the two people waiting in front of me and wrap my arms around her. I feel her give in to body-shaking sobs, and her hot tears spill on my shoulder and neck. "Thank you for coming," she routinely mumbles through her tears.

I hug her tighter. "There's no way I wouldn't be here for you," I say in the strongest voice I can muster.

She points in the direction of the piano. "He's inside there," she sniffs, gesturing to a worn basketball sitting atop a small, raised platform. "It's what he would have wanted."

It takes me a second to realize what she's talking about. I knew Adam had been cremated because of the severity of the accident, but I didn't realize that using a sports ball as an urn was even a possibility. I guess I don't think about death too often.

There's a framed photograph of Adam's handsome, goofy, smiling face beside the unconventional urn. He's wearing one of those wacky winter hats like the characters in the movie *Fargo* wear.

"I like that picture," I remark.

"Me, too," she sighs.

I know there's others waiting for their chance with her, so I give Emily a quick squeeze and pull away. "I'll see you back at the house, okay?"

She nods wetly and wipes at her face. She takes a deep, racking breath, preparing herself for the rest of the receiving line.

+ + +

My dad's house is silent and empty when I wake up the next morning. It's a two-hour time difference between the West Coast and Minnesota, so when I wake up at 9:00 a.m., my body thinks it's only 7:00 a.m. There's a note from my sister posted on the refrigerator that she and my dad have left for the church already and that the funeral is at noon.

My cell phone has a string of missed text messages from my girlfriend, Kambria, each full of emojis and well wishes, but I don't know what to do with it. It's too early to call or even to text back so I let her messages go unanswered. Kambria is sweet—maybe a little too sweet—for a city like Los Angeles. Although a Midwesterner by blood, I've grown harder after a decade of living away from my roots, more cynical, and less eager to trust new people.

I have nothing to do until the funeral so I decide to go for a run in my old neighborhood. Along with the bathing suit I'll never wear, I had the foresight to pack running shoes and workout clothes. It's a beautiful morning, perfect jogging weather. A strong breeze blowing off Lake Superior whips around me, and it takes my breath away. I see Mr. and Mrs. Harvester driving down the road, probably on their way to the church. They both raise a hand in greeting, and I do the same as their car passes.

I clean up after breakfast and head over to the church. There's still an hour before the funeral is scheduled to begin, but the building is packed. There's a long line of grievers heading toward the altar where I see Emily and my dad. Seated in the front pew is my ninety-two year old grandmother. She immediately recognizes me even though I haven't seen her in at least a decade. Her face lights up, but there are tears in her eyes. "Abigail," she exclaims. "You're so tall!"

The Harvesters flank Emily on one side, and my dad and I cover the other. The number of mourners lined down the center aisle is even greater than the day before, and I don't know how we're going to get through them all.

"Thank you for coming," I murmur to each person as they shake my hand and express their condolences. I don't know what to do with my hands when they're not on the receiving end of a handshake or thrown around someone in an awkward hug. I flatten my hands down the front of my dress's skirt and tug at the neckline. I didn't know what to wear to the funeral. Most everything I own is black, but my dresses are of the cocktail variety since my agent Claire insisted I have them in my wardrobe for networking purposes. I'm probably dressed okay, but standing next to Mrs. Harvester, who's dripping in black gauze and pearls, makes me feel underdressed.

Death is a funny thing—not funny *ha-ha*, but funny awkward. Funny—what's the proper etiquette for this kind of thing? Funny—fuck, why can't I find the right words or get my tear ducts to produce at least a few tears so I don't look like a total, heartless robot? I'd rather be sitting with my grandma and holding her hand or not be here at all. It's a display of emotions that doesn't come naturally to me. I watch my sister out of the corner of my eye. I don't know how she has the physical or emotional energy for this. I'm drained by the time mass begins.

The funeral opens with "On Eagles Wings," which has a Pavlovian impact on everyone seated around me. You hear that song, and you immediately cry. The priest is the same officiate who married Emily and Adam in this very same church only a few years prior. When he speaks to the congregation, he talks about how hard he thought this was going to be—to give this homily. "But if you want to see hard," he says, "think about Emily." I haven't cried yet, but his words make my resolve crumble. No one should be a widow at age twenty-seven.

Every funeral in my hometown church is followed by a luncheon in the church basement, and the menu is always the same—biscuits and scrambled eggs with bits of country ham mixed in. I hate those eggs. They taste like death.

The burial is much harder than the funeral. I'm standing next to Emily. It's just the two of us. We're staring down at the tiny square hole where a camouflage-painted metal box rests. Inside is the basketball that contains Adam's ashes.

"I wish I could jump in that hole and be with him."

I hold her harder. I've never considered myself to be good with death. I don't have the words that seem to come so easily to others. I open my mouth, however, and do my best.

"He's not really down there," I murmur. "He's in the grass now. He's in the flowers. He's in the breeze. He's all around us." I kiss her temple. "I love you," I whisper into her hair.

Her body shakes harder. "I love you, too, Abs."

"You're strong, Em," I tell her emphatically.

"I don't feel very strong right now," she whimpers.

"I know," I murmur, squeezing her again. "But you are. I know you are."

After the burial we head to a local brewpub for a celebration "like Adam would have wanted." The crowd from the funeral and the burial has mostly been replaced by people closer in age to Emily and me. As I stand at the bar, a girl with whom Emily and Adam went to high school comments how the gathering feels like everyone is back together and we're getting ready to start senior year. I don't point out the fact that we're drinking at a bar. Paltry details. Everyone's high school experience was a little different, I suppose.

Emily has disappeared, and I worry that she's slipped out and gone home or back to the cemetery. At dinner my dad assures me that she'll be fine, however, so I concentrate on filling my growling stomach with planked whitefish. A storm is blowing in from the lake, but I'm not worried because the outdoor patio at the restaurant has a roof and plastic sheeting separating us from the elements. I'm thankful any inclement weather decided to wait until after the burial. Nothing would be more miserable than replaying that day's events with dark storm clouds overhead and pelting rain.

Over my dad's shoulder I spot a brief flash. I can't be sure if it's lightning or just the flashbulb on a tourist's camera. And then comes the rain. I don't know if it's actually raining hard because the patio roof is tin—to give the impression of a tropical island, I suppose—and it makes a loud racket. The wind picks up, and I can see the sheet of rainfall dancing across the surface of Lake Superior.

Our waitress comes back to ask how our food is. I give her two thumbs up—my mouth is full of coleslaw and the rain bouncing against the patio roof is so loud, I doubt she'd actually hear me.

"Wow," our waitress openly admires, staring past us toward the lake. "Look at how bright it is; you hardly ever see the purple."

I turn to look at what she's talking about. Cast across the midnight-blue clouds is the most vivid, picturesque rainbow I've seen in quite a while. In a few minutes, the entire staff is out on the patio to admire the rainbow. Passers-by stop and take photos of the sight.

Within a few minutes of the rain stopping, a second rainbow appears alongside the first. It's fainter than the first, but definitely a second rainbow. With the lighthouse, harbor, and lake in the foreground, it's awfully impressive.

It's such a small thing, this rainbow after the storm, but the words I told Emily earlier echo in my head: *He's everywhere now.*

He's in that rainbow.

And in that moment I realize that my sister has many more storms to weather. But at the end of the rain, there's always a rainbow.

CHAPTER TWO

I've been knocking on Emily's bedroom door for the past few minutes with no response from the other side. Ever since Adam's burial, my sister has cloistered herself away in her childhood bedroom, only emerging when she needs food. I suppose I should be encouraged that she's eating at all, but when she does momentarily resurface, she barely acknowledges my dad or me. She moves from one room to the next like a zombie or as if in a deep trance.

I try the doorknob and, finding it unlocked, I cautiously push open the bedroom door. The door opens only partially when it hits against a barricade on the other side.

"Em?" I call into the dark room.

When there's still no response, I shove a little harder with my shoulder pressed against the door until I'm able to gain entrance; directly behind the door is a giant pile of dirty laundry that's impeding my progress. I maneuver around the discarded pizza and take-out boxes strewn on the floor. It looks messier than a college dorm room.

I pad over to the window and yank open the curtains to allow streams of brilliant sunlight to pour into the stale bedroom for the first time in days. The flower arrangements Emily brought home from the funeral are beginning to wither. They perfume the air with a sweet, slightly rotting scent.

"Are you ever going to get up?" Annoyance creeps into my tone. "I'm going over to Grandma's in a little bit. You should come."

I place my hands on my hips, awaiting some kind of reaction from my sister, but Emily merely mumbles indistinguishably from underneath the covers.

"At least let me do your laundry," I insist. I nudge the pile of dirty clothes with my big toe. "I'm sure your sheets could use a good washing, too." I wrinkle my nose for effect. "Or thirty."

Emily suddenly sits up in bed, a look of panic in her eyes. "No!" she rasps. Her voice sounds tired and worn and her hair sticks up in places. "You can't take him away from me," she begs. "It's all I have left." She clings desperately to the cotton bedding, wrapping the sheets around her thin wrists.

I hold up my hands in retreat. "It's okay, Em. I'm not going to take him from you." I have no idea what she's talking about, but I'm not about to disturb her more than I already have. "I'm sorry. I'm- I'm just trying to help."

Emily rolls onto her side, facing away from me, and pulls the duvet over her head again. I stare at the Emily-sized lump under the comforter and sigh in defeat. After a long moment, I tiptoe back over to the window and pull the drapes closed again. I creep out of the bedroom and close the door behind me with a soft clicking noise. My sister is clearly not ready to emerge.

Downstairs, my dad is sitting at the kitchen counter with a cup of coffee and the local newspaper open in front of him.

"Good morning," I greet as I enter the room.

"Morning," he returns.

Behind him on the countertop, next to the refrigerator, is a pile of nuts and bolts and springs and other various mechanical parts.

"What happened in here?" I ask.

"Apparently the garbage disposal broke," he tells me in his even, unaffected tone. "Your sister took it upon herself to fix it while everyone was sleeping."

I pick up a piece of metal whose function is a mystery to me and inspect it. "This is what *fixed* looks like?"

"I was told I'm not to touch it. She wants to figure it out herself."

"Does Emily know how to fix garbage disposals?"

"I guess we'll wait and see," he remarks. "What are you up to today?"

I put the metal gear back on the kitchen countertop. "I thought

I'd go over and say hi to Grandma."

"You're a better person than me," he says before going back to his newspaper and coffee.

+ + +

The rhythmic ticking of a grandfather clock fills the heavy silence in my grandmother's living room. Family pictures crowd the wooden mantle above the fireplace. There's Emily and my senior portraits, Emily and Adam's junior prom picture, and a framed newspaper clipping from when the local newspaper reported on me selling my first play. The bookcases are filled with condensed *Reader's Digest* versions of classic literature, a set of encyclopedias probably older than me, and a scattering of knick-knacks. There's a thin layer of dust on everything, which is a sure sign that my grandmother is getting older. She's always been a meticulous housekeeper.

"Are you sure you don't need any help?" I call towards the closed kitchen door.

"I'm fine," comes my grandmother's voice. "You just make yourself at home."

My grandmother lives alone in a house on top of a limestone bluff that overlooks the city harbor and Lake Superior. Growing up, Emily and I had spent innumerable hours on that grassy bluff, staring up at puffy clouds and making stories about the shapes we saw in the sky. It was probably my first foray into storytelling.

Unusual for her generation, my grandmother had only had one child—my father. She and my grandfather had tried to have additional children, but it wasn't meant to be. She compensated by throwing all of her love onto my father to the point of suffocation. I only had good memories of her, however. With my dad working long, unconventional hours, our grandparents had babysat us a lot. My grandmother had become a kind of surrogate mother to Emily and me after our mother took off.

My mom left town when I was five and Emily was three. I don't remember much about her, and nearly every photograph with her in it has long since disappeared. My dad did the best he could bringing up two girls while still building his business, but it hadn't been easy for any of us. My friend and literary agent, Claire, tells me I don't tell my girlfriends I'm in love with them because of my mom. I tell Claire she needs to get a degree in psychology before she starts dishing out observations like that.

The door that separates the kitchen from the rest of the house swings open, and my grandmother emerges carrying a silver serving platter upon which I see two teacups and saucers and a plate of windmill cookies. She walks toward me with a strange gait, nearly hunchback, and with a pronounced limp.

"Let me help you with that," I immediately offer.

She makes a dismissive noise as she passes me. "I've got it. The moment I stop doing things for myself is the moment my heart stops working."

She sets the platter on a coffee table that's crowded with magazines and cookbooks. I hold my breath, expecting the precariously balanced tray to tip over, but it never does.

"Do you like this china set?" she asks as she sits down in a straight-backed chair.

"It's pretty." I bend and reach for the cup closest to me and inspect the delicate pattern of pink roses and a silver thorny vine etched across its borders. "I don't think I've ever seen it before."

"That's because you were too young to use it. It was my mother's, and I was afraid someone would break it. Might as well get some use out of it now though before I die."

I sit down on the couch and nearly lose my balance when I sink into the deep cushions.

"Need a new couch," she observes as I struggle to sit up straight. "But the moment I spend the money, I'll probably die."

I remember this about her. She talks about death and dying a lot, yet she'll probably outlive us all. My grandmother is old, but unlike the other people in this town who look subtly different than I remember, she appears frozen in time. Maybe once you reach a certain advanced age, your body simply refuses to acknowledge the passage of time.

"If you like the tea set you should put a Post-It note on it. That way when I die, the lawyers know it goes to you."

There's really no talking to her, no way to get her to stop talking about her imminent death. She's an old woman who has earned the right to speak her mind.

She sets down her teacup with amazingly steady hands. "Now what are we going to do about your sister?" she asks.

"What do you mean?"

"She'll be a dried-up old maid if she doesn't find someone new."

"You didn't remarry after Grandpa died, and you turned out alright," I point out, taking a careful sip of the hot herbal tea.

"I was in my seventies when Casmir died, Abigail."

My grandpa passed away when I was in middle school. It was the first funeral I'd ever been to. He had been a man of few words—silent but stable. I'd always found him to be a little intimidating, but it was largely unfounded. He spent most of the day in his work shed tinkering. It was probably the biggest reason why my dad had gone into the handyman business himself.

"I'm sure Emily will figure it out," I remark. "She's got time."

My grandmother isn't listening. "Don't you know any nice boys in Hollywood? Maybe someone in the movies? That would be nice."

"I'll keep working on it, Grandma," I promise.

"Good." She smiles serenely. "Now eat those cookies, Abigail," she urges. "You're too skinny."

+ + +

After spending time with my grandmother, I head downtown instead of driving back out to my dad's house. I know I should stick close to home and continue to harass my sister until she emerges from her bedroom, but I need a break from the sadness. My stomach also reminds me that cookies don't make for a satisfactory lunch, and there's hardly any food at my dad's house. He apparently lives on ham sandwiches and breakfast cereal.

Restaurant choices in Grand Marais are limited outside of fast food, so I go downtown to Roundtree's Bar & Grill. The Roundtree family and their bar has been a staple in Grand Marais for as long as I can remember. It's one of the only places that stays open year-round in the tourist-driven town, and it's become an institution, popular with locals, but not so intimidating as to scare off out-of-towners. The Roundtrees are also one of the most philanthropic families in the area. When the football field needed new stadium lights or the track needed resurfacing, it was the Roundtree family who'd been the most generous sports boosters.

The bar itself is testament to the family's support for the community. The tables are covered in old newspaper coverage of past high school team successes, and behind the bar where the high-end liquor should be displayed is a hall of fame wall—a collage of newspaper clippings about local kids' achievements. They're mostly headlines about former residents who've gone off to be sports stars at their respective colleges, but even I managed to make the wall when my first play won a newcomer playwright award. Local girl makes good and all that.

I sit at the bar by myself; it's the awkward hours between breakfast for the early risers and lunch for the working crowd. The laminated menu has the usual bar food: Burgers, deep fried pickles, chili, and beer-battered whitefish. Conspicuously absent is quinoa, tofu, or anything soy or gluten free. I love it.

A feminine voice addresses me as I inspect the menu's offerings: "What can I get you, hun?"

My lip inadvertently curls. I hate when restaurant staff calls you pet names. I hate it even more when they sit down at the table with you to take your order. I've never worked in the food industry, and I'd never want to. I loathe the idea of having to smile and flirt for your tips. I suppose I'd make a killing at those places where the waitstaff is rude to the customers on purpose.

When I look up from my laminated menu, my throat tightens and I find myself getting lost in smoky, hazel eyes. The waitress's makeup is perfect, and I'm envious of her skill with eyeliner and eye shadow. But mostly I'm just lost. Hazel-green eyes are kind of my Kryptonite.

The woman's skin is flawless, with high cheekbones and a pouty, pink mouth. Her nose is slightly crooked, which I find unspeakably adorable, and her light blonde hair is pulled up in a messy bun. She's wearing a v-neck t-shirt with the bar's name and logo scrawled across the front. The hint of modest breasts and the twin bones that connect to construct her clavicle peek out above the top of her shirt.

I clear my throat when I realize she's waiting on me. "Uh, beer?"

An amused smile falls to her lips, causing my stomach to flutter. "I'm afraid I'm going to have to card you since you ordered that with such familiarity."

I'm sure we went to high school together, but she's a few years younger than me, maybe Emily's age. We hadn't been friends, but in a school and a town so small, everyone knows everyone. I flip through my mental Rolodex to see what I can remember about her. Her name is Charlotte. Charlotte Something. I think I remember hearing that she'd gone to school at the local state university and had worked at Roundtree's during school vacations. I don't know if she graduated, but it's over a decade later and she's still working at the bar, so I make an unfair assumption that she dropped out.

"Wait." Her eyes narrow, and I can tell she might recognize me, too. "You're Emily Harvester's sister, aren't you?"

"I usually go by Abby, not 'Emily's sister,' but yeah."

"I was sorry to hear about Adam," she says. The teasing glint is now gone from her eyes. "I always thought they made a sweet couple."

My mouth twitches. "Thank you."

"How's she doing?"

"As well as can be expected, I suppose." I never know what to do with condolences except behave awkwardly. "Do you still want to card me?"

"Would you be flattered or offended if I did?"

I reach for my purse and pull my drivers license out of my wallet.

"Abigail Henry," she reads off the plastic card. "Los Angeles, California."

I love the sound of her voice—it's a lower register that's soft, not graveled, like you might expect from someone who bartends at a working-class bar.

She slides my license back across the bar top, and I slip the card back into my wallet. "You're a writer or something, right?"

"Yeah. I write plays."

I could make more money writing for a TV show or adapting someone else's novel into a movie script, but the theater was my first love. I remember getting bused to Canada in high school for a class trip to see *West Side Story*. I'd never seen a live professional production of anything before, having grown up in such an isolated area. The production, which—looking back on it now—was probably nothing more than community theater rather than a traveling Broadway company, had blown me away. I'd sat in that darkened theater, enraptured by the drama and the emotion and the beauty of it all. For weeks after, I couldn't stop humming about having just met a girl named Maria.

"Fancy," she remarks.

"Not really."

She jerks her thumb toward the Grand Marais Hall of Fame

display behind her. "You're on that wall, aren't you?"

"Yeah, but so is Mike Ballister for winning a pie-eating contest at State Fair."

"Good point," she chuckles. "Maybe we should be a little more picky about our local celebrities."

She reaches beneath the bar and produces a bottle of Labatt Blue Light. She twists the cap off and throws it a few feet where it rattles against the back of a metal garbage can.

"Nice shot," I admire.

"I've had a little practice," she returns with a sly grin.

I take a quick drink from the long-necked bottle. I haven't had a Labatt in ages; the taste instantly brings me back to hot summers in high school.

My purse begins to vibrate, followed by the obnoxious ringtone of my cell phone. "I've really got to change that," I mutter as I fish around my bag for the missing phone.

Charlotte chuckles. "It's certainly an interesting choice."

I half expect the caller to be Kambria, her girlfriend radar sensing me eyeballing an attractive woman, but instead it's my friend Anthony. I met Anthony at a fundraiser where he'd been performing in a drag queen fashion show. The man knows more about makeup application than I could ever hope for. Even though we've only known each other for a few months, I consider him one of my closest friends.

"If you need anything else, just flag me down," Charlotte offers.

"I will, thanks." I hit the answer key and press the phone to my ear. "Hello," I answer, my eyes still on the attractive bartender as she walks away to wait on another patron.

"Hey, girl," the warm voice on the line greets me. "I wasn't sure if you'd have cell reception up there in Canada."

"I'm in Minnesota."

"Same difference," Anthony defends. "All magical talking moose and Vikings, right?"

"You know it," I chuckle. I pick up my beer bottle and tip it back. I'm nearly at the bottom of my beer already. I'd have another, but then I'd have to make eye contact with Charlotte again, and that feels like a bad idea.

"I'm doing my best not to be upset that I had to find out from your *agent* that you were out of town," Anthony complains. "That's like getting your local news from TMZ."

"I had to leave in a hurry," I explain. "And it's been kind of nonstop since I got here."

"I know. But don't forget you've got people here who love and care about you."

"Have you been watching the Lifetime channel again?" I lightly tease.

"Can't a girl be a little sentimental without you getting all judgmental?"

"I'm sorry, Anthony," I apologize. "Compassion makes me a little itchy these days."

"Think there's a cream for that?" he jokes.

"Don't worry. Once I get back to LA, I'll be cured."

"Which is when?" he asks.

"I'm not sure. I'd like to hang around until my sister starts acting a little more like herself, but I don't know when that will be."

"You take all the time you need. I'll make sure your jungle doesn't die."

Anthony calls my collection of house plants a jungle. I haven't reached hoarder status, but it's pretty close. It's telling, I suppose, that I don't trust my own girlfriend to water my plants. My friends get that duty whenever I'm out of town.

When I hang up with Anthony, Charlotte makes another pass. "Can I get you another one?"

"I probably shouldn't. I'll take the bill whenever you get a minute."

"Don't worry about it," she says with a dismissive wave. "Consider it your Wall of Fame complimentary beer."

"If everyone on that wall gets a free drink, Roundtree's is gonna go out of business," I joke.

A wide smile carves across her beautiful face. "I'll be sure to let the boss know."

+ + +

Dinner that night with Emily and my dad is somber and uncomfortable. We don't talk much except to politely ask for things to be passed around the table and a mentioning of the unseasonably warm weather. It's early July and swimming in Lake Superior might actually be tolerable soon.

"May I be excused?" Emily asks when conversation has entirely fallen flat.

My dad looks in my direction, almost as if he's asking me for permission. I can only shrug.

"Yeah," he grunts out.

Emily picks up her plate and fork. She hasn't eaten much, but I don't take offense. Even though it's only spaghetti, I'm not a very good cook, and I'm sure she hasn't had much of an appetite these days.

My dad and I watch in silence as Emily drops her dirty dishes into the kitchen sink and walks out of the room. He drinks the rest of his bourbon and then begins clearing the table.

"I'll wash if you dry," I say, picking up my plate.

My dad waves me off. "You made dinner. I can handle dishes."

"Then I'll keep you company," I offer, hopping up to sit on the edge of the kitchen counter. I look up at the ceiling when I hear my sister's footsteps creaking above us. "How is she doing?" I ask. "For real." Admittedly I haven't spent much time with Emily since I left home for college so many years ago. The girl I remember is different than the woman pacing upstairs.

My dad sighs and slides the marinara-stained dishes into sudsy water. "She's been more quiet than usual," he admits. "Since she's been back it's been the same every night. An awkward dinner and afterwards, she immediately goes back to her room upstairs. It's like the World has grounded her or something."

I keep staring up at the ceiling as if I'll be able to see my sister through the floor. "I feel like I should try talking to her," I think out loud. "But I have no idea what I'd even say."

My dad shakes his head. "I don't know what's going to snap her out of this funk."

"Alcohol?" I unhelpfully supply.

My dad purses his lips. "That sounds like a horrible idea, Abby."

"I know," I nod. "Hence why I'm not the person to get her out of her room. Any ideas on who might?"

My question causes my father to fall silent and look thoughtful. The soft sound of dishes clinking and moving around in the water-filled sink fills the emptiness.

"Why do you live in this big house all by yourself?" I ask.

"What would you have me do? Get roommates?"

"No." The thought of my dad in a *Real World* scenario makes me snort. "I'm just surprised you haven't sold the house. You could always live above the store again."

"This is your and Emily's home. I could never sell it. As long as I'm alive, you'll always have this house to come home to."

"Yeah, but don't you ever get lonely?"

"I've had time to get used to it." I know he didn't mean to, but his words make me feel like crap.

"What about dating?" I ask. "Is there a special lady in your life?"

"I've already got two favorite girls in my life. You and Emily."

Oh, Dad.

"This was nice tonight," he says. "And I don't just mean me not having to make dinner for myself. I've missed you, kid."

I cast my gaze down to my hands. "I know. I should visit more."

"That wasn't meant to be a guilt trip," he says. "I was just making a comment. I know you've got your own life out there."

"But I should still come back more often," I note, shaking my head. "It shouldn't just be funerals that bring us back together."

"How long are you here for?"

"I booked a one-way ticket. I'm not here forever," I clarify, "but I'd like to stay until Emily is feeling more like herself."

"That's really nice of you, Abby," he remarks. "I was thinking about closing up the shop so I could keep an eye on her, but I don't know how much of a comfort I can be. Time heals all wounds, right?"

"So I hear."

"How's Kambria?" he asks.

I lay my hands flat on the kitchen counter. "She's good," I say, staring down at my tanned hands. "She had to work, otherwise she'd be here."

The truth is, I'd had to convince her to stay back in Los Angeles. Kambria had wanted to be there for my family, but I didn't want her here. Things had been falling apart for us in recent weeks and privately I'd thought this space, this unexpected distance, might do us good. When I returned to LA, we'd either break up or we'd take the next step in our relationship and move in together.

I'd met Kambria a handful of months ago at a party in LA. The company my agent, Claire, works for—a multi-media organization with clients in all veins of the entertainment industry—was hosting the event, and I'd begrudgingly agreed to go. I really despised those kinds of events because I wasn't traditionally famous. I'd published two plays and the royalties were enough to pay the bills, but I certainly wasn't a recognizable name or face, so small talk was hard to find. Those polite or bored enough to ask my name and what I did for a living always got confused when I'd tell them I wrote plays.

"Screenplays you mean," they'd say with some confidence. "You write for TV or the movies."

"No," I'd sigh. "I write plays for the stage."

Inevitably they'd scrunch up their brow and then leave me for more shrimp cocktail or to take covert photographs with their smart phone of real celebrities. The hint I'd received early on was not to gawk or start a small riot when you saw the hot new actress from your favorite primetime drama standing by the punch bowl. Not that there were actual punch bowls, just stacks of sugary-sweet energy drinks and unlimited bottles of whatever vodka company was sponsoring the event.

Kambria had been hanging out with a group of people, and she'd immediately caught my eye—small, pixie features and a bright, effervescent smile. She was the living incarnation of Tinkerbelle, and I'd actually wondered if she might be employed in Anaheim as a Disney Princess. I'd had no idea how to separate her from the herd—Claire loved to point out how much Game I didn't have—but when she'd broken away from her friends to stand in line for the bathroom, I'd followed. We'd made the mandatory chitchat about how lucky guys were and how there should be two women's bathrooms for every one men's restroom. It wasn't romantic or a unique meet-cute by anyone's standards. It wasn't a grand love story to tell our hypothetical grandchildren years later. But I wasn't thinking about those non-existent tykes. I was too distracted by her light accent, which I had trouble trying to place.

She'd wrinkled her cute little upturned nose when I'd guessed the United Kingdom, and she'd vowed she would stop humoring my company if I guessed Australia. I gave up too quickly for her liking, but she told me later that night when I had her pinned against an Audi TT coupe in the parking lot that she'd grown up in South Africa. Under normal circumstances I would have grilled her about Apartheid and blood diamonds and Zola Budd, but it wasn't everyday I had a gorgeous blonde challenging me, pressing her lithe body against mine. Geography was far from my mind.

"You know she's more than welcome to come and stay at the house," my dad says, albeit looking a little uncomfortable to be broaching the topic.

I can't resist toying with him even though he'd been really great when I Came Out to him over the summer of my junior year of college. "Would you let her sleep in my bed?"

"Of course," he says without hesitation. "And you'd sleep on the pull out couch in the den. I'd never make a guest sleep on that death-trap."

My jaw falls open. "Dad!"

"What?" His bushy eyebrows rise on his lined forehead. "Call me old-fashioned, but if you're not married, you sleep in separate rooms."

That night, I lay awake, staring at the single dome light above my bed. The model airplane is still there. I'd gotten into World War II history some time in middle school, and my dad had helped me build a model plane—a Curtiss P-40 Warhawk with a working engine that spins the single propeller affixed to the nose of the plane. Next to the plane and overhead light is a single glow-in-the-dark plastic star. Emily had stuck it there when we were younger to drive me crazy. Her own ceiling was an elaborate design of planetary systems my dad and she had tirelessly worked on. I had gotten a single star. It was annoying, but over the years it had transformed into a battle of wills between that solitary star and me. It's amazing that after all of this time it's still there, and that after all of this time, it still annoys me. I roll over on my side and shut my eyes to sleep.

CHAPTER THREE

I smile when I push the door open and hear the tiny bell jingle above my head. Simply by walking into my dad's store, my senses are assaulted with memories. Part hardware store, part service center, the shelves of the small shop are stacked with basic tools and home improvement accessories. Emily and I had once played Supermarket Sweep with my dad's inventory; we'd spend the good part of a week putting everything we'd dumped into our shopping carts back on the shelves.

Grand Marais is too small and too remote to ever attract a big chain store that could put my dad out of business, but even if people do the bulk of their shopping in distant Duluth, they still require my dad's expertise whenever something breaks. He does it all—plumbing, electrical, construction, even fixing the small motors on things like lawnmowers, weed whackers, and the occasional snow blower.

My dad's just coming out of the back room that serves as his office when I enter.

"Hey, Dad."

He wipes greasy hands, heavily calloused but with no signs of arthritis, on an already dirty rag. "Hey, kid. You come down for the parade?"

"They still do that?"

"Like clockwork."

"So why are you open? It's the Fourth of July."

"Just working on a project for Emma Bernstein. You remember

her, right?"

"Works at the bank?"

I pause and reflect on what I've just said. It's strange being from such a small town. Nothing gets a proper noun name except for a few restaurants and hotels—the only businesses we have more than one of.

"Why don't you grab a Popsicle from the freezer, and I'll meet you out there?" my dad suggests.

In addition to hammers and nails, he also stocks a few candy bars and summer treats. In the winter months he uses the giant icebox to store hunks of venison, purchased from local hunters. My California friends would probably be horrified to know he stores deer meat next to the popsicles and ice cream drumsticks. I grab a green Popsicle—sure to turn my tongue an interesting color—from the freezer and go outside.

I sit down on the curb in front of my dad's store and wait for the parade to start. The sidewalks are crowded with similarly minded people sitting on coolers and lawn chairs. The tornado whistle goes off, indicating the parade is about to begin. With so much water surrounding the town, tornadoes are rare. The warning siren is only ever used to announce the beginning of town-wide events like the Fourth of July parade or to proclaim that it's noon on a Sunday.

Kids cover their ears when the slow rolling police, ambulance, and fire trucks blast their sirens. The volunteer firefighters are dressed like clowns. Local politicians up for re-election in the coming months toss candy from floats, and gangs of children run into the street to claim the Tootsie Rolls and Blow Pops.

My dad makes a noise as he eases himself down to sit beside me on the curb. "Where's your sister?" he grunts.

"At the house." I pull my legs up and rest my chin on my bare knees. I had knocked a few times on her bedroom door before heading out, but she'd only yelled at me to leave her alone.

He stares straight ahead. "This used to be her favorite holiday."

I pat his knee. "It still could be."

+ + +

"Time to get up," I crow.

Emily pulls the quilt over her head in response.

I tug at the bottom of the handmade cover, but she holds fast to her end. "Come on, Em!" I practically whine. "You have to come with me to the Firemen's Picnic."

"Why?" Her voice is muffled by the comforter over her head.

"Because it's tradition!" I exclaim. "You already missed the parade, but there's still time to catch the potato sack and the three-legged races."

"You should go without me."

"But, Em," I pout, "I want to go with *my sister*. I haven't been to the picnic in like twenty years." It hasn't been *that* long, but it might as well have.

This time when I pull on the blanket, she doesn't immediately tug it back over her head and hide. Her face is red and sweaty, and her hair is slightly out of control. "Everyone's going to look at me."

"Let them. You've gotta get outside. You've gotta spend some time with the living." As soon as I say the L-word I know I've made a mistake. Emily's eyes water up, and I'm sure I've just set her back a few weeks.

"Does the volunteer fire department still host the picnic?" I ask, trying to change the subject.

She nods, and I can hear the affirming words get caught in the back of her throat.

"Hot dogs and ice cream sandwiches?"

She nods again. "And orange drink," she manages to choke out.

"The most watered-down orange drink in the state," I say. I can practically taste the powdered drink mix on my tongue. "See? Now you *have* to come with. You need your annual dosage of orange drink. It's good for the soul. Keeps you young."

She manages a watery smile. Victory is within my reach.

I grab her hand. Her skin is cold to the touch, and I intertwine my warmer fingers with her icy digits. "C'mon, Em," I coax. "Come just for a little bit."

She exhales noisily through her nose. It rattles, and I'm on the lookout for tissues. "Okay."

+ + +

Like much of my hometown, the city park looks untouched by time. There's a new jungle-gym in the center of the playground, brightly painted in red and blue and surrounded by shredded tires so if kids fall while playing, they'll bounce. The old classics are still there though—the wooden see-saw, the deathtrap merry-go-round, the hanging tire swing on a rusted chain. I feel the need to get a tetanus booster shot just looking at them.

In an empty green space no bigger than a football field, the kids' foot races are being held. From where we stand I can hear the supportive cheers coming from the surrounding crowd. I competed in those foot races every summer growing up, but always came in fourth place, trailing behind the more popular girls, never placing high enough to have my name printed in the newspaper.

A sizeable line has formed near the cluster of grills as people queue up to get their complimentary Fourth of July hot dog. I can sense Emily's discomfort; if we stand in that line she'll be surrounded by sympathetic glances without any place to hide.

"Want to go sit over there until the line gets shorter?" I ask, pointing to a vacant wooden bench. Emily nods, looking visibly relieved.

There are far fewer people in this section of the park. Most people are either at the kids' races or waiting for a hot dog.

"Not so bad, right?"

Emily makes a noncommittal noise beside me. She's always had a hard time admitting when I'm right. I'm sure it's a sister thing.

I close my eyes behind the tinted lenses of my sunglasses. It's a beautiful day, but with my sister sitting beside me, still perceptively sniffling, I feel guilty for enjoying the sun on my skin. It never really gets above the mid-70's around here, which is something I do miss about my hometown. LA is too hot for me. LA is too much of just about everything for me.

"Amelia, not so high."

I open my eyes at the sound of a vaguely familiar voice.

A little blonde cherub, pale skin despite the summer season, and a pile of curls on top of her head, scrambles down a giant wooden playground structure. I remember playing on it myself in my youth. It looks like a giant ladder made out of telephone poles.

"Is this okay?" the little girl asks. She looks around five or six years old, but I can't be sure. I know very little about kids. Her hair is an ephemeral swirl of light blonde hair. It's wild and unruly, like a delicate puff of cotton candy, or like a mound of soap bubbles that might scatter with one stiff breeze.

The woman from the bar, Charlotte, shields her eyes from the sun with her hands. "Much better," she approves.

I can't help but stare at her in profile. She's even more beautiful beneath the high afternoon sun. She splits her attention between the paperback on her lap and the jungle gym. Long, thick eyelashes curl up when she checks on the young girl. She's wearing a sleeveless sundress and strappy sandals. It's a little dressed up for a day at the city park, but she looks great. The skirt hits just above her knee, revealing tan, toned calves. The top of the dress dips low enough to show off that defined collarbone I'd been privately admiring when she first waited on me, but it's modest enough to not show off cleavage. The shoulder straps of her sundress sink seamlessly into round shoulders. Her arms are what really draw my attention—long and lean with definition in her triceps.

"Hey, Em?"

My sister makes a humming noise beside me. "Yeah?"

"Do you remember Charlotte Johansson?" Her last name suddenly comes to me.

"Uh huh. We graduated together. She's still around town, I think."

"Yeah, I saw her working at Roundtree's the other day."

"What about her?"

"Who's that kid with her?" I nod my head in their direction as unobtrusively as possible.

"I think it's hers."

"Really? Is she married?"

"I don't think she and the kid's father ever got married. I hear he was a real asshole to her."

"You hear a lot of things, don't you?"

She shrugs, nonplussed. "It's a small town. People like to talk. You know how it is."

I nod. People certainly *do* like to talk. It's one of the major reasons I had to get out of this place. Being gay in a small town is front-page news. I'm just lucky that I didn't figure it out until I was away at college so I didn't have to face these people every day.

"Why do you ask?" Emily questions.

"Asking for a friend." I'm well aware of how distracted my voice sounds. You can't blame me though—the woman's got killer legs that I hadn't seen before because they'd been hidden behind the bar.

"How's Kambria?"

The mention of my girlfriend's name is what's able to pull my attention away from Charlotte Johansson's legs. My sister looks at me with what I can only describe as a smug smile on her face. I know she's judging me and my wandering eyes, but I'll take the smugness from her any day; it's the first time I've seen anything remotely resembling a smile on her face since I got to town.

"You're horrible," Emily scolds me. "As a feminist, shouldn't you be above ogling?"

I return my gaze to the leggy blonde. "What can I tell you? I'm a bad feminist."

"How's your writing going?" Emily asks.

"Slow. But that's the glamorous lifestyle I chose for myself."

Emily's always been supportive of my creative goals and my passion for writing for the stage, but I know she's never quite approved of it being my sole income. It's too risky, too unconventional of a profession for her. But even I had worried about that; could I continue to be prolific and productive for the rest of my working life?

"Ever think you'll write for TV or maybe write a movie screenplay?"

"I'd never say never, but so far writing for the stage has been good to me."

"Why do you live in LA?" she asks me.

"What do you mean?"

"LA and television; LA and movies, sure. But I don't see the connection between Los Angeles and plays. Shouldn't you be in New York?"

"I have no aspirations to write a Broadway play if that's what you're suggesting."

"Why not?" she presses. "Don't you want more?"

"More what? Money?" I shake my head. "I like my life. More money or fame or whatever isn't going to make me happier."

"But I still don't get it. Why LA?"

"I like the weather," I quickly dismiss. "Are you hungry?"

She sighs quietly. "Not really."

"I'm sure there's a hot dog-shaped space in your stomach." I pat her leg before I stand up. "I'll be right back."

The scent of charcoal is heavy in the air. I juggle two hot dogs and their condiments in one hand and two small Dixie cups filled with orange drink in the other.

"You need some help with that?" I hear someone ask.

"No, thanks. I've got it."

I'm admittedly not watching where I'm going; I'm too focused on not dropping the orange drink, which is exactly what I do. One of the wax Dixie cups slips from my grip and hits the grass. The liquid splashes on the ground and some clings to my bare ankles.

"I guess I don't have it." I look up from the spilled cup to see Charlotte Johansson smiling at me.

"Hi."

"Oh, uh, hi."

"Charlotte," she says. "From the bar the other day?"

I nod vigorously. "I remember." As if I could have forgotten.

"Just making sure," she smiles affably. She bends to retrieve the disposable cup and tosses it into a nearby garbage can. "People tell me I look different when I'm not covered in fryer grease and Jack Daniels."

"I recognize you," I say. "I mean, you look cleaner and less sweaty, but still the same."

Her mouth twitches and her nose crinkles. "Didn't you tell me you're a writer?"

"Yeah. Why?"

"Shouldn't you—I don't know—be better with words?"

"Oh," I exclaim in understanding, "I've always been good with a pen and paper, but not so much with my mouth." I grimace as soon as the words hit my ears. "That came out all wrong."

"When's the last time you came to one of these?" Her question is meant to save me from my awkward response, and for that I like her just a little bit more.

"The firemen's picnic?" I breathe out. "God, it's been years. At least a decade, probably longer."

"I bet it's exactly as you remember it," she muses.

I nod in agreement. "Everyone's hair looks more grey, wrinkles more pronounced, but other than that everything looks the same."

She flips her long hair over one bronzed shoulder. "God, I hope you haven't lumped *me* into that category," she laughs.

"Oh! No, you look great," I insist.

"Yeah," she slyly grins, "maybe you should stick to pen and paper."

She eats the rest of her hot dog in small, precise bites, and throws away the paper coffee filter that had been wrapped around the bun. I don't want her to catch me staring, so I stare into the bottom of my orange drink instead. There's a black speck floating in the watered-down mixture, and I can't tell if it's dirt or a bug. Either way, I'm done drinking it.

"Tut, tut." Charlotte looks towards the sky. "Looks like rain."

I hold my arm out, palm up, as the first few sprinkles hit my skin. The gentle patter exponentially worsens, forcing the picnickers to run for shelter. Charlotte grabs my hand and tugs me towards the closest covered patio. It's a cement slab that serves as a platform for wooden picnic tables. Everyone else has the same idea until we're all squished together beneath the open-air canopy. I can still feel a few stray raindrops through the cracks in the shelter's roof, but it's better than standing in the pouring rain.

The rain doesn't seem to bother the children, however. If anything, it's re-energized them. While we adults are crammed beneath the roofed shelter, the party continues for them beyond the shelter's reach.

Charlotte still holds my hand even after we've reached the shelter. She feels solid and warm despite how the unforeseen rain has lowered the air temperature. I had expected her hands to be rough—calloused from opening so many beer bottles—but they're soft and smooth like I imagine the rest of her being.

She drops my hand and laughs. "Sorry. Mom instincts," she explains.

I'm too stunned to do anything but smile in return.

Fingers that had grasped my hand so tightly now rake through slightly damp hair. When I'd seen her at the bar, her hair had been up in a loose bun, messy but attractive in an effortless kind of way. Now that her hair is damp, it's begun to curl at her temples from the humidity.

"So much for that blow out," she complains.

"You still look great," I vocalize. She's more than great; she's breathtaking. The rain has caused her clothes to cling to her figure a little more.

Her fingers stop their futile task and her hands fall to her sides. "Thanks."

A shrill, high-pitched shriek snaps my attention away from the lovely bartender. Children run in zigzagging patterns around the city park with their arms stretched out as if they might sprout wings and take flight. I watch Charlotte's daughter stomp barefoot in pools of standing water.

"Do you remember ever being like that?" Charlotte speaks beside me.

"It feels like a million years ago," I admit. "Was it supposed to rain today?"

"I'm a bartender; not the local weather girl."

I tentatively stretch my foot beyond the protective covering. The light rain is cool on my sun-baked toes. I wiggle painted toenails and watch the water bead up on my skin.

Before I can step out fully into the rain, Charlotte is speaking again: "I'd better grab my kid and bring her home to dry out. Amelia," she calls out sharply. "Time to go."

I expect her daughter to put up a fight, but after one more good stomp that produces an impressive splash, she's chasing after her mom, darting between raindrops to reach their parked car. They join hands, and I hear the joyful, high-pitched shrieks and yelps.

"Are you done being a bad feminist?" Emily, looking slightly damper than the last time I saw her, is suddenly at my side.

"Where have you been?" I ask, ignoring her question.

"Taking shelter like everyone else. You and Charlotte Johansson looked cozy," she coyly observes.

"We were talking about the weather," I insist.

"You owe me a hot dog."

+ + +

I had been hopeful that maybe Emily was starting to come out of her deep depression, but as soon as we return to my dad's house after the picnic, she retreats back to her bedroom. Lying on my bed in my room across the hallway, I can hear the floor creak and groan with my sister's periodic footsteps, but beyond her haunted gait, the house is silent. There's nothing on TV and there's no wireless Internet. There's a computer downstairs in the den with dial-up Internet, but I no longer possess the patience for the slow-crawl of buffering Internet connections.

My cell phone rotates between no service and limited bars of reception. Kambria and I haven't spoken since I left Los Angeles. I sent her a text when my plane landed in Minneapolis and when I'd arrived in Grand Marais. She's sent a few texts of her own, but neither of us has attempted to actually call each other. It's the first time we've been in different area codes since we met.

With the time difference, it's still early in California. Even though it's a holiday, Kambria should just be getting off of work and probably getting ready to go out. She's an administrative assistant by day, but at night the skirt gets shorter and the makeup more dramatic. Everyone has more than one career in Hollywood. Most people I meet are some combination of waitress/model/aspiring celebrity.

During a longer stretch of connectivity, I call her number, and on the third ring, she picks up.

"Hello?"

"Kami?" There's unexpected loud music playing in the background, and I can't tell if it's even her voice because of all the noise.

"Hey, babe," she greets affably. "How is everything?"

I sigh heavily into the phone. "A mess. My sister is a wreck, not that I blame her. I managed to get her to leave the house today for the first time since the funeral though, so I guess that's a good sign."

"Abs, I can't really hear you."

I stick a finger to the ear not pressed against my phone. "Can't you go someplace where it's not so loud?" I'm having a hard time hearing her, too, even though it's silent in my bedroom.

"I'm out with some people from work. I don't want to be rude."

Well, you're being rude to me. I swallow down my annoyance.

"I'm sorry, Abs. I'll call you later, okay?"

"Yeah. Sure."

We hang up, and I toss my phone on my bed. Instead of her voice calming me or reassuring me that everything is going to be okay, it's only succeeded in aggravating me.

My relationship with Kambria isn't much different than those I've been in before, and I can almost predict what's going to happen next. Everything burns fast and hot in the beginning, but once the gestalt has worn off and someone inevitably gets bored, the relationship comes to a crash-and-burn finale. This is probably the beginning of the end.

I snap my eyes towards my bedroom door when I hear the knock. "What?" I say with probably too much heat.

My dad pokes his salt-and-peppered head inside. "I'm going down to the fireworks," he says almost apologetically. "You want to come?"

I don't feel like being social, but any excuse to get out of this house is welcomed.

I take a long, calming breath. "Yeah."

With the town boundaries hugging Lake Superior, there are few spots where you can't see the Fourth of July fireworks. The most popular place for viewing the fireworks has always been a grass-covered bluff a few hundred yards from the shoreline. It's probably the highest point in town and therefore the best spot from which to watch the fireworks. Normally the hill is overrun with wild flowers and weeds, but the city mows the lot in the last days of June in preparation of the holiday.

By the time my dad and I show up that evening in the moments before dusk, the hilltop is crawling with families. People have already staked their claim across the grassy hill with folding chairs and blankets. Children run around with sparklers that shower bright gold flecks. A few of the older kids have roman candles that they point and shoot into the sky.

I stay close to my dad as we make our way through the concentrated crowds. He stops every few feet to talk to someone he knows, and I linger in the background, smiling and silent. Small talk with people who've known me all my life makes me even more anxious than Hollywood parties. Regardless of my other accomplishments, without a diamond ring on my finger or a wallet full of pictures of my kids, I'll never feel like a real adult in this city.

"I've got to talk to Fred Patterson about a job," my dad says. "Why don't you scope out a place for us to sit?"

I nod, thankful for the task, but also dread being on my own. I do my best to survey the grassy hill for decent seats, but it's made more difficult when I'm trying to avoid making eye contact with anyone.

"Abigail Henry," a voice calls out.

It takes me a moment to scan the crowd for the owner of the lower-registered feminine voice, but then I see her sitting on a blanket in the grass. She's changed out of her sundress from earlier that day and has opted for skinny jeans and a plaid button-up shirt that's rolled up to her elbows.

I take a few steps in her direction. "Charlotte Johansson," I respond with an easy smile. "We meet again."

"I'm glad to see you didn't drown in the rain," Charlotte remarks.

"I'm resilient like that."

"No Emily tonight?" she asks.

"Nope," I say, shaking my head. "I was happy enough to get her out of the house for the picnic though. Baby steps."

Charlotte pats the space beside her. "Want to sit?"

I look around at the immediate area. Nearly all of the ground space has already been claimed, and anything left is quickly being gobbled up by families with oversized blankets. "Thanks. My dad and I didn't really come prepared."

"I've got plenty of blanket," she assures me. "And there's no way Amelia will sit still until the fireworks start, so you're both in luck."

I take up an empty spot on the blanket. "How old is she?"

"Six."

I whistle under my breath. "You have a six year old? Did you have her when you were twelve?"

"Funny," she rolls her eyes.

I do the mental math. Charlotte's the same age as my sister, which means she was around twenty-one or twenty-two when Amelia was born. To an outsider that might seem like a young age to be having children, but in my hometown, teenage births are the norm. Approaching my thirtieth birthday, I'm practically a spinster.

"Do you have any kids?"

"Me?" I'm not expecting the question. "No. I'm gay."

She doesn't blink. "That doesn't mean you can't have kids."

"Right. Sorry."

"The fireworks are supposed to be really good tonight," she notes. "Last Fourth of July the company the city hired screwed up, so they promised a show to bring down the house this year."

"How do you screw up fireworks?" I question.

"You light off the grand finale first."

A loud laugh bubbles up my throat and Charlotte looks particularly pleased at my reaction.

I'm not sure how to continue the conversation, so in the absence of having something to do, I take out my phone. I've got full reception up on the bluff, but no messages or missed calls from Kambria. There's a texted image from Anthony, however. He's set up stuffed animals among my houseplants. There's a lion and a zebra and a giraffe. I quietly laugh, but not quiet enough.

"What's that?" Charlotte asks.

"Oh, my friend Anthony is house sitting for me, and he sent a picture. We've got a running joke that my houseplants are a jungle."

She leans closer to see the screen of my phone, and the ends of her hair tickle against my bare kneecap. It's hard to smell anything over the scent of freshly cut grass, but I can make out the sweet scent of her soap.

"Cute," she remarks before sitting up again.

The sun has sunk deeper into the horizon, and the evening sky is darker. My dad has disappeared on me, but because of my current company, I'm strangely okay with that. I take a deep breath and exhale, feeling my stress escape with the long breath.

Tiny fireflies hover in the air, making their own fireworks display. The ones we have in Minnesota look like helicopters or Inspector Gadget buzzing through the air with that propeller coming out of his hat. I open my hand, palm facing the sky, and a firefly lands to take a break. It periodically glows and slowly opens and closes its wings as it perches on my hand.

"Isn't it hot?"

I look up from my cupped hand to see Charlotte's daughter, Amelia, standing in front of me. "Hot?" I repeat, not quite understanding the question.

"The bug," the young girl clarifies, "isn't it burning your hands?"

"Oh. No. The fire's inside its belly," I say.

She crouches down for a closer look. My hands remain gently curled around the insect, and its yellow-green light flashes against my skin. "Why do they light up like that?" she asks.

"It's how they talk to each other." I'm no entomologist, but fireflies had been a part of my childhood. I also know that male fireflies light up to attract females for mating and that some species are actually cannibals. I'm not about to try to explain that to a six year old though.

Amelia peers hard at my still cupped hands. When I carefully open them, the tiny bug doesn't fly away.

"What is it saying?" She speaks quietly as though afraid any loud noise might cause the insect to flee.

"I'm not sure," I say. "What do you think it's saying?"

She tilts her ear towards my hands. "I think it's trying to find someone. Like a friend, maybe."

"I should probably let it go so it can keep looking, huh?"

She nods solemnly. She looks too serious for her young age.

I open my hands the rest of the way, and the insect hovers above my palms briefly before jetting off into the night sky.

"I hope you find your friend, firefly," Amelia calls out. We both stare up into the inky black sky, which is dotted with tiny sparks of light.

"Amelia, baby, why don't you have a seat?" Charlotte suggests. "The fireworks are going to start soon."

"Can I do another sparkler?" she asks.

"*One* more and then you have to sit."

Charlotte lights the end of a metal sparkler rod and hands it to her daughter. Amelia holds it out in front of her and stares unblinking at the golden shower of sparks.

"Do you want one?" Charlotte holds the open box of sparklers in my direction.

"No thanks, I'm good."

"You're kind of a natural," she observes. "Are you sure you don't have kids?"

I'm usually even more awkward around children than I am with their parents, but like dogs that seem to sense who is allergic to them, children tend to flock to me despite my ineptitude. Sometimes I feel like I have more in common with children than I do adults.

"I'm pretty sure I would have remembered something like that."

Once the fireworks begin, Amelia obediently sits in her mom's lap, oohing and aahing at the fireworks as they explode overhead. It brings a smile to my face; I remember being that young and thinking Grand Marais's fireworks were the brightest and biggest and loudest in the world. Around me people start to cheer and clap their hands when the grand finale begins. Amelia covers her hands over her ears, but her smile isn't shaken. I periodically sneak glances at Charlotte's profile, lit up by the glow of multicolored fireworks. They have the same smile.

The cheering and applause heightens when the sky is choked with smoke and the last of the fireworks has sputtered out, and I can't help but join along. At the end, people around us begin to stand and gather their belongings. I stand up on legs made stiff from inactivity. I haven't seen my dad in a while, but I'm sure he's somewhere in the crowd, probably talking to someone about plumbing or electrical outlets.

Charlotte picks up the blanket we've been sitting on, and I help her fold it.

"It's not Los Angeles," she remarks, "but I like it."

I shake my head. "I didn't say anything."

"I know. But you were thinking it." She gives me a wistful smile that almost makes me feel like I've done something wrong. "Have a nice night, Abby. And Happy Fourth of July."

CHAPTER FOUR

The next morning I'm up later than usual. I don't know if my internal clock has gotten used to the time zone difference yet. Kambria had told me she'd call later, but besides a text from Anthony telling me that one of my plants bit him, my phone remained silent all night.

I rub my bleary eyes as I tromp down the staircase. My dad is at his usual breakfast spot at the kitchen island. It takes me a moment to realize what's missing from the counter top.

"Let me guess," I say upon entering the room. "The toaster oven was broken, too?"

My dad looks at me over the rim of his coffee mug. "Yup."

"Are you going to keep letting her break your stuff?"

He takes a sip from the steaming mug. "I'm not sure I have much of a say in this."

"You could always tell her to stop."

His eyebrows dance. "I'd have better luck locking away anything that plugs into a wall."

I've been in Grand Marais for nearly a week. So far my dad will need a new garbage disposal, a bread maker, an original Nintendo gaming system, and now a toaster oven. While the rest of the house sleeps, Emily systematically dismantles electrical devices. In the morning, a new pile of parts and broken gadgets has appeared. The pieces of various devices cover nearly every surface on the first floor, parts mixed among other parts with no hope of ever figuring out what goes with what. The moment she goes after the coffeemaker, however, I'm going to have to put a stop to it.

"What's the plan for today?" he asks.

I grab a clean mug from a cabinet and pour myself a cup of black coffee. "Writing. Or at least I'm gonna try."

Two Adirondack chairs sit near the water's edge. A worn American flag flutters lazily in the breeze. Emily's hidden away in her bedroom and my dad is cutting firewood a few hundred feet away. For as long as I can remember, he's always split his own wood for the fireplace in the living room.

I breathe in and fill my lungs with the scent of the lake—a combination of algae and earth. We have few sandy beaches in Grand Marais; the lakeshore bordering my dad's house is rocky, not that you'd ever want to go swimming. As kids, Emily and I used to go swimming all the time in Lake Superior, but at that age your body knows no limits, just like your brain knows no fear. In adulthood, I'd never been able to handle more than a few minutes of wading before my ankles went numb and my lips turned blue from the cold.

I shake out my hands at my side. It's a superstitious ritual I perform before I start writing. I'd picked up the habit in an unexpected place. I'd tried running track in seventh grade, but my stomach would twist into knots in the moments before each race. My track coach used to tell us to shake out our hands and let the nervousness fall out of our fingertips. It was the only year I tried an organized sport, but the habit of shaking out the nerves had followed me through adulthood.

It's been months since I've been able to write anything more than a few sustained lines of dialogue. I'm hopeful that the change in scenery will inspire me enough to knock me out of this writing slump.

<u>ACT 1</u>

<u>Scene 1</u>

SETTING: A small fishing boat on a slow-moving river.

AT RISE: Two women sit on opposite ends of

```
                    the boat, casting their respective
                    lines into the water.
```

"No, no, no," I mumble to myself. In the distance, my dad fires up a chainsaw. It sounds like the climax of a horror film.

```
SETTING:        A roadside rest stop in the
                middle of nowhere.

AT RISE:        Two women stare at their rental
            car and the front tire on the
         driver's side. The tire's flat.
      A loud animal calls out in the
      distance, like a wolf's howl,
      catching both women's attention.
```

Really, Abby? A horror play? I snap my notebook shut and heave out a great sigh of frustration. I'm not going to get any work done here.

+ + +

Roundtree's Bar & Grill is practically empty at this early hour. The breakfast patrons are on their last cups of coffee, and it's too early for the lunch crowd rush. Sports Center is on one of the TVs hanging over the bar, relaying the day's sporting news. I sit at a table for two, and a waitress takes my order. I have to admit it's a disappointment that the server's not Charlotte Johansson, but I order a sandwich anyway since my stomach is empty.

As I eat my lunch, I look over my spiral notebook full of failed starts and stops. I've never really experienced writer's block before. It's debilitating. My brain is usually crowded with lines of dialogue and story scenarios just waiting to be written down, but lately every time I make a concerted effort to work, I struggle to the point of frustration. I'm not panicked yet, but it's certainly worrisome.

"I think I'm mad at you."

I twist my head in the direction of the voice to see Charlotte Johansson standing in my peripheral.

I swallow down a too-large bite of my sandwich, and the toasted bread scratches down my throat. "M-Me?" I choke out. "What did I do?"

She places a hand on her hip. "Amelia has been pestering me to get her a book about fireflies. She wants to learn everything about them."

"Oh," I breathe out, my anxiety slipping away. "That doesn't seem so bad. Wouldn't you rather her be into bugs than, I don't know, dating and makeup?"

"Let's not get ahead of ourselves. She's still got more than a decade before I let that happen."

"Before you *let* that happen?" I repeat with a wry smile. "No offense, but I don't think parents have much control over when that stuff starts happening."

"You might be right. My parents had a hell of a time trying to wrangle me in. I'm afraid Amelia will be the same, like some kind of karmic payback."

As we talk, she rests her arms on my table. Every time she leans forward, she innocently offers an unobstructed peek down the front of her t-shirt. I try to stay focused on her face, but that's just as dangerous of a view. Her hazel eyes are warm and inviting and her smile reveals white, gleaming teeth. This woman is gorgeous from head to toe, and I wonder if she knows it.

"You didn't seem to turn out too bad," I observe.

She chuckles, but I don't get the joke. "How's your day going?"

I shrug. "It's okay."

"Your enthusiasm is overwhelming," she deadpans. "How's Emily doing?"

"The same," I grunt. "Still hiding out in her bedroom."

"It'll take time, but she'll get through this," Charlotte says sagely. "She doesn't have a choice."

Loud laughter coming from a far corner of the bar-restaurant pulls my attention away from Charlotte. The heads of the town's municipal departments are seated at a large table: the chief of police, the mayor, the city treasurer, the city water department head, the marina director, and even the guy who mows the grass in the city parks. They're lifelong friends having all grown-up together in Grand Marais; it's a bit of a good ol' boys club.

I can't hear the entirety of their conversation, but a few telling words and phrases reach my ears: *runaway mother, dead husband, California, writer, lesbian.*

The words themselves aren't malicious, but their laughter is unsettling. I feel my body sinking into my chair, and I stare at my half-eaten plate of food.

"Excuse me." I hear Charlotte's distracted tone. Before I realize what's happening, she's walking away in the direction of the boisterous table.

"Gentlemen," her voice carries over to where I anxiously sit, "how's it going over here?"

The city treasurer taps a finger against his coffee mug. "I could use a warm up when you get the chance."

"I'm pretty sure you guys are finished," she says.

"What?"

"Did I stutter?" She stands tall, with an icy look on her features.

The men collectively avert their eyes from her stony glare. After a tense moment, money is thrown on the table and chairs squeak against the wooden floor as they all stand.

When the last of the table has left out the front door, Charlotte returns and sits down in the empty chair across from me. "Idiots, all of them," she mumbles. "Makes me worried about this town's future."

"You didn't have to do that."

"Yes I did."

"They practically run the town." I'd hate for the Roundtrees to have lost patrons because Charlotte felt some strange obligation to stand up for my family and me.

"All the more reason for them to act like decent humans."

"Thank you, Charlotte." The words feel like an inadequate way to show my gratitude, but especially as a writer, they're all I have.

+ + +

I had arrived at Roundtree's late that morning feeling discouraged about my inability to write anything. But when I leave the bar later that afternoon, there's a noticeable bounce in my step. I'm still not eager to go back to my dad's house where Emily is no doubt dismantling the television, so I begin to walk down the main street of Grand Marais.

Two white-haired men sit on a bench in front of the barbershop. Their conversation stops when they see me, but they continue talking to each other once I've walked by. On any other day, their reaction would have me scampering down the sidewalk and ducking into the closest store to hide. Instead, I smile at them and wish them a good afternoon.

A little farther down the street is a bookstore that I don't remember from growing up. I think the building had been a video rental place or a Pizza Hut before. The only opportunity we had to buy books in town had been the Book Fair at school or when the public library had its annual book sale.

I don't recognize the woman working at the store. She looks up from the novel she's reading when I walk in. "Hello," she greets. "Can I help you find something?"

"You wouldn't happen to have any books on fireflies would you? Preferably something geared for little kids?"

The bookstore clerk frowns. "Nothing comes to mind, I'm afraid. But we could order something and have it here in a few days."

It's an impulsive, ill-advised errand. This is probably the Universe's way of telling me to back off. "No, that's okay, thanks."

I'm about to leave when I notice someone browsing the magazine rack at the front of the store. She's thinner than I remember—taller, too. Her dark brown hair hits the tops of her shoulders.

"Julie?"

Deep blue eyes turn in my direction. There's a moment of puzzlement before recognition. "Abby? Abby Henry?" Her eyebrows rise on her forehead. "It's been a while."

It *has* been a while since we've seen each other—over a decade at least. "What are you doing in town?" she asks.

"Oh, uh, Emily. Her—"

"Oh, that's right," she jumps in before I can continue. "I heard about Adam. I'm so sorry."

"Thanks."

"How is she doing?"

I don't know how many times I've been asked that question since coming back to town. My answer is always the same: "About as good as can be expected."

"I see your dad from time to time," she remarks. "He updates me on what you've been up to. Are you still in California, writing plays?"

"Yep." I bob my head. "Los Angeles." Before she can ask me another small-talk question, I ask a question of my own: "Are you hungry?"

"I can always eat. Why?"

"We should grab lunch next door," I say with a jerk of my thumb. "We can catch up for real instead of standing here awkwardly."

When she doesn't immediately reply, her delay makes me wish I hadn't put myself out there.

"Yeah, sure. I've got some time."

Next door to the bookstore is Brantley's Diner, a breakfast and lunch place popular with locals. They serve up greasy-spoon comfort food. On that day the lunch crowd is largely gone and we're two of the only diners, not counting the grey-haired men drinking coffee at the counter, all retired with nothing better to do.

Julie continues to make idle chitchat until after our waitress has taken our order. I'm still full from my sandwich at Roundtree's, but I order a grilled cheese so Julie's not the only one eating.

"You're my one big regret," I blurt out.

Julie stops pouring sugar in her coffee mug. "Me? Why?"

"You were my best friend. And then we weren't."

"And whose fault is that?"

"Mine. I know it is."

"You dropped off the planet, Abby."

"It wasn't that dramatic," I sullenly defend.

"You didn't write—e-mail or otherwise. And whenever you came home from college, you never looked me up."

"I did that to everyone though," I excuse myself. "I needed to get my head right. I needed to figure out who I was."

"And you didn't trust me enough to confide in me?"

"I know. I'm sorry. But not everyone's that evolved around here." I think about the men at Roundtree's and the two men in front of the barbershop.

"You should have had more faith in me."

She's right. I shouldn't have assumed that my best friend since preschool would suddenly shut me out of her life over something as insignificant as me being gay.

"How long are you in town for?"

I sigh and flex my fingers around my water glass. "I'm not sure. Emily ... she's a wreck. I can't abandon her."

"It wouldn't be the first time."

I suck in a sharp breath. "Ok. I deserved that."

"Sorry," she hastily apologizes. "I'll drop it now."

I roll my glass between my hands. "So what have you been up to?"

"Since high school? Nearly fifteen years ago?"

A guilty smile makes its way to my mouth. "Yeah. It has been a while."

"Well, I went to college." She takes tentative sip of her coffee before continuing. "Graduated. Came back here. Took over the family business. Not much excitement here."

"You're a dentist?"

She flashes me an overly exaggerated smile. "Well, I certainly didn't come by these pearly whites naturally."

I stare at my untouched grilled cheese. "Did you ever think about not coming back to town after you finished school?"

"Sure. All the time. But my dad was getting ready to retire. The timing was right," she shrugs. "I took over his clients, and last year I finished buying him out. The business is all mine now."

"Well, congrats. Sounds like you've done well for yourself."

"Depends on whom you ask," she says, curling her lip. "Until I get married and pop out some kids, I'm nothing but a disappointment to my mom."

I had noticed there wasn't a giant rock on her ring finger, but I hadn't put the pieces together until now. It's a force of habit to check for rings and to check out fingernails, but even then I'd been deceived by more than a few women before.

"You're doing it again."

My head snaps up so quickly I nearly give myself whiplash. "Doing what?" I ask self-consciously.

"Waiting for me while I eat."

I had known from a fairly young age that I wasn't like other girls. I felt the need to protect my girl friends as if there was something that made them more fragile than myself. Julie was a prime example of that. She was a slow eater, and even though I'd finish my lunch long before her, I waited for her every day, long after the rest of our friends had left to enjoy the break before the second half of the school day.

I don't know why I'd felt compelled to sit with her as the cafeteria emptied. I suppose I didn't want her to feel uncomfortable or embarrassed to be eating by herself. Regardless, that's the way it was every day from first grade through high school graduation; the two of us sitting in the same seats during lunch period while I waited for her to finish eating.

"I'm sorry." I'd always thought of myself as chivalrous, but maybe she'd thought it was creepy.

"Don't apologize," she says. "I always thought it was sweet."

My body parts shift and return to their proper places.

"Would you say I was your first crush?"

I raise an eyebrow. "Are you fishing for compliments?"

"Humor me," she smirks.

"I don't know, Jules," is my honest answer. "Growing up here I had no idea being gay was even an option."

Julie's features look thoughtful as she sips her coffee and contemplates the diner. "Yeah. Grand Marais's not exactly the place for sexual exploration."

I lean forward and flash my old friend a wolfish grin. "Oh, I don't know. Want to give it a try?" I tease.

She tosses her head back and laughs.

I find my way back to Roundtree's Bar & Grill later than night. I'm not particularly hungry, but I'm also not ready to go home. I'm avoiding the sole reason I came back to Grand Marais, but I'm realizing now that I'll never have the magic words to make Emily better. I keep telling people that I'm here for Emily, but in reality, we've barely said two words to each other since the firemen's picnic.

```
SETTING:        A roadside diner in the middle
                of nowhere.

AT RISE:        A woman sits on a stool at the
                counter. Behind the counter, a
                waitress tops off coffee cups
                around the U-shaped bar.
```

A friendly, familiar voice pulls me away from the pages of my notebook: "Back again?"

I manage to nod despite the urge for my eyes to linger on body parts where they don't belong. Charlotte's altered her uniform t-shirt so it's rolled up her thin, muscled arms and cut into an even lower v-cut, dipping dangerously between the twin swell of her breasts. Tonight she sports an attractive shade of red lipstick. It's new, and I discover that I like it a lot.

"I'm afraid to go back to my dad's house and see what else Emily has dissected."

She arches a questioning eyebrow at me.

"Long story," I dismiss.

She wipes her hands, strong and capable from opening so many bottles, on a small towel that's flipped over one shoulder. "You look glum," she observes, cocking her head to the side. "Well, glummer than usual."

"It's nothing: family stuff." I let out a long exhale. "I can't remember—do you have any siblings?"

"Yeah. One. My brother Max is a few years younger than me."

"Does he live in town?"

"No. He lives in St. Paul. Stayed there after college."

The bar is mostly empty, but a slump-shouldered man with stringy white hair pulled back in a ponytail sits in the vacant chair beside me. He wears a thick canvas jacket too warm for the muggy summer night. When he smiles at me, I notice he's missing a few teeth in the front.

"Buy an old man a drink?"

"Tom," Charlotte chastises from behind the bar. "You know how I feel about that."

He holds up his hands to retreat. "Sorry, Charley. Can't blame a guy for trying."

Her lips purse and she fills a glass with ice and a dark soda from the soda gun. She sets the glass on the bar and slides it in front of the man. "Don't mind Tom. He's harmless, but he can't resist sniffing around for a free drink."

"Especially when pretty young ladies are buying," he cackles.

I try to smile, but it feels like a grimace.

Charlotte notices my expression and chuckles. "I won't be offended if you leave right now and never come back."

"On the contrary, I was going to ask how you manage to resist all these fine specimens, night after night."

"Willpower," she winks.

When her back is turned away from me to fill a drink order, I allow my eyes to settle on her finely crafted backside. The denim of her cutoff shorts hugs her slight curves. She has narrow shoulders not much wider than her hips, a tapered waist, and the longest legs I've ever seen. *Damn, girl. Do those legs go all the way up?*

"You're working late tonight," I observe without thinking. "Don't you normally work first shift?"

She arches an eyebrow. "Keeping tabs on me?"

I duck my head and focus on my hands clenching the bar top. "No. Just a comment."

I take a quick breath and look up. She's still staring at me with a slightly amused look on her normally scowling mouth.

"I had to come in earlier to do some payroll; I like to take the late shift in the summer so I can spend the day with Amelia," she reveals. "My parents watch her at night while I'm at work."

"Can I buy you a beer?" I ask. I don't know when I got brave.

She licks her lips and it looks like she's thinking a little too hard about what it is I'm offering her. "You can buy me a pop."

The word sounds funny coming out of her mouth. I know people around here call soda 'pop.' I used to be one of those people, too. I guess I really am removed from life in the upper Midwest.

"It won't break the bank," I tell her. "I can afford an overpriced beer."

"I used to drink," she says. "I don't anymore."

I know there's a story, but I'm just a random, annoying customer. There's no reason for her to elaborate.

"Do you ever drink anything other than beer?" she asks.

"I used to drink Malibu and pineapple juice when I was in college," I admit, "but that seems a little too much like *Girls Gone Wild* now."

"How do you feel about bourbon?"

"I don't know," is my honest reply.

"Join me behind the bar," she says with a jerk of her head. "I'll show you how to make an Old Fashioned."

I stand from my bar stool, but hesitate from doing anything else. "Is that allowed?"

"Old Tom isn't going to tell anyone, are you?"

The man in question pretends to lock up his mouth with an imaginary key and throw it away.

"See? It'll be fine."

With her encouragement, I walk behind the bar on uneasy legs, glancing toward the front door as if expecting the owner to walk through the entrance. The Roundtrees have owned the bar for as far back as I can remember; they might have even built the place.

Charlotte dips below the bar to retrieve some items. "The classic Old Fashioned is rye whisky, bitters, and sugar, maybe a splash of club soda or water to dissolve the sugar," she recites. "We're going to do something a little different. Your fancy hipster friends would probably be appalled, but I like to use brandy instead of whisky."

"I don't have hipster friends," I protest.

"Everyone seems hipster when you live in Grand Marais," she counters with a shrug.

A single sugar cube is dropped into a glass and she hands me a silver-colored wand that looks suspiciously like a sex toy.

"You know how to use one of these?" she asks.

"That all depends. What is it?"

"It's a muddler, weirdo. What else would it be?"

I shrug and keep the other option to myself.

"Crush that sugar cube," she instructs. "The bitters will help dissolve it."

I begin my task, breaking down the sugar cube beneath the end of the sex-toy muddler. "I've always wondered. What are bitters?"

"I've heard it said before that bitters are the spices of the cocktail world. They're basically highly concentrated alcoholic herbal flavors. In the ancient world they were used as medicine to aid in digestion. Now they basically just add subtle flavors to mixed drinks or to help balance out a particularly sweet or sour drink."

"Wow," I admire. "You really know your stuff."

"Just because I didn't go to a fancy school, and I don't have letters like PhD or MFA after my name doesn't mean I don't have a working brain. In the world where I live, street smarts, hard work, and common sense will get you a lot further than a college degree."

I'm a little stunned by her outburst. "I-I didn't mean anything by it," I sputter.

"I know you didn't. I have a chip on my shoulder, that's all."

They're awfully nice shoulders, I think to myself.

She drops a dark cherry and a thin slice of orange into the bottom of the drink. "Muddle all that together."

I drop my eyes to my task and do what I'm told. I'd let her boss me around anytime.

Her hands unexpectedly come to rest on top of mine, stopping their movement. I involuntarily pull in a sharp breath at the weight and feel of her skin. "Muddle, not massacre," she softly chastises. "Just enough to release the juices from the fruit and the oils from the peel."

I nod because I don't trust my voice to not crack or waver or do something equally juvenile.

She takes the glass and muddling utensil from me. "Then you just add ice," she says, dropping a few ice cubes into the muddled mess at the bottom of the glass, "some good brandy, maybe a splash of soda if you like it pressed." She fills the glass to its brim and nudges it toward me. "And there you have it, the best brandy Old Fashioned in town."

"In the whole town, eh?" I eyeball the concoction; the drink is basically pure alcohol. "How many bars are there in Grand Marais?"

"No others worth mentioning."

"That's some company pride right there," I remark with a chuckle.

I bring the glass to my lips. The smell of the bourbon alone makes my nose hairs feel like they're on fire.

I take a tentative sip while she waits expectantly.

"Well?"

I do my best not to cough when the alcohol reaches my throat. "I think I'll stick to beer."

The bar's neon signs remain illuminated as Charlotte locks up for the night. It's a warm evening, and even though the parking lot is well lit with the yellow glow of lampposts, the night sky is filled with stars. Pebble-sized gravel crunches beneath my flats as I walk Charlotte to her car. There are a few other vehicles in the parking lot besides my rental and her green Jeep—people who took a cab home rather than risk getting pulled over for drunk driving, I suppose.

"Hey, thanks for the cocktail lesson."

"You're very welcome," she returns. "Now you can impress your Hollywood friends the next time you host a party."

I shove my hands into the back pockets of my jeans. "I think it'll take more than one drink to impress the people out there."

"Then I guess you'll have to come back for more lessons."

When she reaches the driver side door, she spins on her heel to face me. We're close—too close.

"What are you doing tomorrow?" I ask.

"Working."

"But not until later, right?"

"Yeah," she confirms. "Why?"

"Do you want to hang out?"

"I have a kid."

"I didn't forget," I say with a smile. "I just really don't want to hang out at the house all day with Hurricane Emily. I could use some company."

Her lips purse in thought. "If it's a nice day, Amelia and I will be at the beach. If it's raining, we'll be at the library."

"Why don't I text you tomorrow morning, and you can tell me where you are?" I suggest. I begin to pull my phone out of my back pocket so I can get her number.

"I don't have a cell phone."

"That's impossible," I frown. "Everyone has a cell phone. My ninety-two year old grandmother has a cell phone."

"I don't have one," she repeats. "I'm either at home or the bar. People generally know how to get a hold of me."

"You know it's not just about phone calls and texting, right? You can put e-books on your phone and read them at the beach."

"Or I can bring an actual book to the beach."

"Are you anti-technology or something? Or one of those Doomsday Preppers who lives off the grid?" I say in jest.

"I've never had a cell phone, so I don't know what I'm missing out on. I also don't have a computer at my house. I have an e-mail address, but I only check it when I'm at the library. I write personal checks, and my car is a stick shift." She props a hand on a defiant, jutting hip. "Anything else you want to know about my life in the Dark Ages?"

"No. That actually sounds really nice." I lean my hip against her car. "Refreshingly uncomplicated."

"I've got enough to deal with as a single mom. I don't need to be adding anyone else's drama to mine."

+ + +

My dad's house is silent when I return for the night. If I stay up any later though, I might catch Emily and her compulsive early morning tinkering. I still haven't heard from Kambria all day—not even a text message. I go to my dad's den at the back of the house so I don't wake up anyone. I try my girlfriend's number, but the phone rings and rings with no response.

"Hey, it's me," I say when her voicemail picks up. "You said you'd call back last night, but you never did."

I don't know what else to say in the message, so I hang up and call my friend Claire instead. Besides Anthony, my closest friend is my literary agent, Claire, another girl from the Midwest. We'd met in college and had become fast friends over our shared love of sci-fi and country music. After graduation we'd both pursued new adventures, me to San Francisco to get my MFA and she to Chicago. When I'd made the jump to Los Angeles a few years ago, she'd done the same, following her dream of becoming a talent agent.

Unlike Kambria, Claire answers my call. "Hey, I was just thinking about you. How are things?" she asks.

I sit down on the leather office chair and twist from side to side. "Weird."

"How so?"

"It's just weird being back. Like, this place is stuck in a time warp, but there's subtle differences that throw me off," I try to explain.

"It's like that when I visit my hometown, too," Claire remarks. "The landscape is basically unchanged, but no one looks like you remember them. The worst is when you run into someone you've known forever, but they're completely unrecognizable now."

I make a noise in agreement.

"How's your sister doing?"

"Not so good," I admit. "She's a ghost, walking around and rattling her chains."

"I hope you're exaggerating."

"I wish I were," I sigh deeply. "Charlotte says Emily will get through this though—says she doesn't have a choice. But I'm just not sure. She's like a shell of her former self."

"Who's Charlotte?"

"She's a bartender. She went to school with Emily. Her daughter Amelia is adorable, and I don't even like kids."

"Sounds cute."

"She is," I concur. "And her mom is smoking hot. Legs for days."

"You do remember a girl named Kambria, right?"

I know I have a girlfriend and any discussion of my attraction to Charlotte borders on emotional infidelity. But I can't help that Kambria's being a shitty girlfriend right now while Charlotte is warm and lovely and engaging.

"Of course I do. I called her tonight, but she didn't answer. And yesterday she was at a club or something so we couldn't hear each other."

"Try calling again," Claire orders.

"Yes, mom." I stick my tongue out even though I know she can't see me. It's refreshing getting to talk to someone about where my head has been these past few days. But the fact that it's with Claire and not my actual girlfriend has me annoyed.

"So what else is going on?" Claire asks. "Are you having any fun at all?"

"I guess. Charlotte showed me how to make a brandy Old Fashioned tonight."

"Oh, she did, did she?"

"Don't start on me," I complain. "It's just an innocent crush. You know how I get."

"Yeah, you of the wandering eye."

"Any bites on the new play?" I ask, desperate for a change in subject.

"Not yet, but don't let that discourage you. I've got a few more contacts who might be interested."

After I sold my first play and then my second in rapid succession, I had probably become too cocky. I couldn't fail, the voice in my head had told me; this business was easy. But finding a producer for my third play was turning out to be more of a challenge than I'd wagered.

Thankfully I hadn't blown my first royalty checks on any major purchases. I could live off of my savings for a while longer, but if I didn't sell a play or write something new, I'd have to find a job as a waitress or a barista or something equally Hollywood cliché so I didn't completely drain my nest egg.

Claire and I talk a little more before saying our good nights. When we hang up, I try Kambria's phone one more time. But like before, the call rings with no one picking up on the other end. When her recorded message ends and I hear the beep, I leave her another openly frustrated message: "Why aren't you picking up?" I complain. "We need to talk, so call me when you get this."

The sun's not up yet, and the whole house is dark. Only a limited amount of moonlight and my memory of where everything is in the house keep me from bumping into too many things on my way to my bedroom. Before I make it to the stairs, I hear noises coming in the direction of the dining room. In a city like Los Angeles, the sounds would have me calling the police, but in Grand Marais, I'm only curious.

The sounds are unrecognizable as I approach the dining room. I reach into the room and hit the light toggle. My sister, sitting at the dining room table, squints into the light. There's an assortment of tools—screwdrivers and wrenches and pliers—spread out on the table in front of her.

"What are you doing sitting in the dark?" I whisper. My dad is a light sleeper, and I don't want to wake him up.

She gestures towards the electronic circuit board in front of her. "Fixing my alarm clock."

"Was it broken?"

"It is now."

"Emily," I sigh, "what's going on with you?"

"Adam wanted to have a baby."

I freeze at her words.

"He wanted to start a family," she says sullenly, "but I wasn't ready. I told him there was no rush. I told him we had plenty of time."

I pull out a dining room chair and sit down. I remain silent; I can sense these words have been building up in her brain over the past few days. There's a leak in the dam, and it's about to break.

"I wanted children with him, but I was afraid. What do I know about being a mother? I never had one." Her bottom lip begins to tremble. "And now I'll never have his babies. It's too late."

I chew on the inside of my lip. My instinct is to pat her hand, but the movement feels trite.

Her blue eyes are heavy with tears. "Why did he have to die, Abs?"

It feels like there's a heavy weight pressing down on my chest. "I know, sweetie," I try to soothe. "I know."

CHAPTER FIVE

My dad used to tease me growing up that my nose was going to turn out pointed because it was always stuck in a book. Rules had to be made that reading wasn't allowed at the dinner table, and whenever I acted out as a child, my punishment was time away from books. Since I'd moved away from Grand Marais, the public library had been updated from a windowless, musty catacomb, to a bright, welcoming new construction with a separate room for children's literature. It's in that room where I find Charlotte and her daughter the next morning. Amelia's sitting at a low table reading aloud while Charlotte reads to herself in a rocking chair in a corner of the room. They're the only two people in the small room—in fact, besides the librarian at the circulation desk out front, we might be the only souls in the building.

"Hey," I whisper.

Charlotte smiles when she looks up from her book. "Hey. You found us."

There's no other place to sit except for the biggest beanbag chair I've ever seen. I choose a pint-sized painted wooden chair and drag it near Charlotte's rocking chair. When I sit down, my knees practically touch my chin.

Outside the day is overcast and intermittent rain has spoiled the prospect of a day at the beach. Rain splatters against the frosted windows. Charlotte looks comfortable in light washed skinny jeans that hug her calves and a University of Minnesota t-shirt. It makes me feel a little overdressed in jeans and a sleeveless shell, but I'm running out of clothes that she hasn't seen me in yet. I wasn't planning on being away for so long when I'd first thrown clothes into my suitcase.

Amelia is wearing a yellow tank top with dark blue shorts. The *tour de force*, however, are the dark green rain boots that are designed to look like turtle faces.

"She dresses herself," Charlotte remarks when she notices my amused stare. "When she turned six she no longer required mom's help."

"Ouch."

"My baby's growing up too fast," she wistfully sighs.

"I bet she learned that independent streak from you," I note.

"Maybe," she hums, "but it's going to make first grade next fall a chore if she gets the reputation as the girl who dresses weird."

"Better than her being the smelly kid. That's elementary school suicide."

"Are you speaking from experience?" she chuckles. "Were you the smelly kid?"

"Hell no," I insist. "But I was a total bookworm. That was enough social suicide."

In my hometown if you didn't participate in high school sports, you didn't matter. Charlotte had played a number of sports and had gone to college on a volleyball scholarship to the University of Minnesota. It makes me wonder if she has any old uniforms lying around. I wouldn't mind seeing her in bun-hugger shorts.

"I wish I had liked the school part of school more," she remarks. "I suppose I was having too much fun to take academics seriously. But," she says, lifting the hardcover book in her hands, "better late than never."

"What are you reading?" I ask.

"*Animal Farm*. I'm on a kick right now where I'm reading all of the books I was supposed to read in high school, but never did."

"Oh, before I forget," I say, "I saw something at my dad's store and thought of you guys." I'd been looking for a way to say thank you to Charlotte for standing up to the town's municipal hierarchy without going overboard.

She waits while I retrieve the cellophane packaged gift from my bag. "They're Chinese lanterns. You set the bottom on fire and it floats up into the sky," I explain, although I'm sure she probably knows how they work. "My dad, Emily, and I used to set them off every summer. I thought Amelia might like it. They're kind of like fireflies, I guess."

"I bet she'll love it. Thank you, Abby." Charlotte smiles at the gesture, which makes me feel less foolish for bringing the lanterns with me. "Do you want to come over and show us how it's done? Since you seem to be the expert at it."

"Uh, yeah. Yeah, that would be fine."

"I've got weird hours, but I'll let you know when my next night off is. Maybe you could come over for dinner and then we can light these things off in the yard," she suggests.

"I don't know how long I'll be in town for," I warn.

"It's okay. If we can make it happen, cool. If not, I'm sure Amelia and I can figure out the lanterns on our own."

She goes back to reading her book, and I take a notepad out of my bag and rest it on my lap. I shake out my hands at my sides and try to write.

<u>ACT 1</u>

<u>Scene 1</u>

SETTING: A high-rise in New York City overlooking Central Park. The colors on the trees are just beginning to change.

MAIN CHARACTER

Why is your play set in New York City, Abigail? You've never been there before.

Almost as soon as pen touches paper, I'm crossing out the words with agitation and trying again.

SETTING: The interior of a passenger train.

AT RISE: Two women sit across from each other, stealing glances at the

>   other over the pages of their
>   respective newspapers.

I tap my pen against my notebook. *And then what?* I put an X through the text. I stare at the blank page and will it to speak to me. Something. *Anything.*

SETTING: The moon.

Okay, maybe not *anything*.
"Is everything okay over there?"
"Sorry." I look away from my mangled notebook. "Am I writing too loudly?" I realize my pen tapping has become progressively louder and more aggressive.
"Something like that. What are you working on?" she asks, nodding toward my notebook.
"I'm supposed to be working on a new play." A displeased frown settles on my face. "But the words won't seem to come. I've got the worst writer's block."
"Is that pretty common?"
"Not for me."
"I'm sure it's only temporary," she encourages.
"I hope so." I return my attention to my notebook and the half a dozen failed starts and stops on the page. "It's worrisome though," I admit out loud. "What if the words never come? What if I'm a one-trick pony and can't sell another play?"
"Don't you have a Plan B?"
"Not really," I admit. "I put all of my eggs into this writing basket. I never really planned beyond that."
"Surest way to make God laugh," she remarks. "Make plans."
"What was your Plan A?" I ask.
An eyebrow arches. "What, you don't think being a bartender in Grand Marais was Plan A?"
"No, I-I'm sorry," I stutter out. "That was incredibly rude of me."
"It's okay. You got out of this town for a reason. I had Amelia before I could think about Plan A."
"So here's a question," I pose. "And don't answer if you don't want to ... You work at a bar, but you don't drink."
"I don't drink *anymore*," she corrects me. "After Amelia's dad ..." She closes her eyes and I watch her features struggle with a mountain

of complex emotions. "Let's just say I wasn't in a good place when he and I split. I've made a lot of mistakes in my life—things that the average person would want to forget or have the opportunity to do over. But my biggest regrets became my biggest joy."

I nod, knowing what—knowing *who*—she's referring to: Amelia.

I glance once in Amelia's direction. She appears unconcerned or uninterested in her mother's new friend. I watch her lips wordlessly move as her eyes scan the pages of a book laid out before her.

"Does she know how to read already?"

"She's got a few sight words, and she knows her letters and the sounds they make," Charlotte says. "I read to her all the time at home, but when we come to the library, she usually just wants to look at the picture books and make up her own stories."

"That's basically what I do for a living," I chuckle.

I grab one of the hardcover picture books from a nearby shelf and flip through its pages. It's one of those wordbooks that don't tell a story, but rather label the items and the people on the pages.

"This is nice," I observe.

"You really don't have to hang out with us," Charlotte gives me an out. "I'd understand if you didn't want to waste your day at the library with a six year old and her mom."

"There's no place I'd rather be."

"In the whole wide world?" she challenges.

"Okay, let me amend my previous statement: there's no place in *town* I'd rather be."

"And here I thought you were starting to become a fan of the bar."

A blush takes residency on my cheeks. I flick my gaze in Amelia's direction, but she's still quietly making up stories to herself. "Yeah, um. The beer is cold."

"And the company is pretty good, too, I hear," she smiles knowingly.

"Are you still working tonight?" I ask. I discover I want to keep hanging out.

"I'm heading over there once I drop off Little Miss Independent at the house," she confirms.

"Want some company?"

"I wouldn't say no."

+ + +

It may not seem logical, but culturally there's not much difference between small towns in the upper Midwest and in the Deep South. It's not just the politics or in the misgivings about all things foreign— it's in the alcohol they drink, the guns they covet, the music they listen to, and the four-wheel-drive trucks they drive. The scene that plays before me could be any small town in Alabama instead of northern Minnesota.

Roundtree's is busier than usual tonight because of the four-piece band covering a mix of popular country songs and classic rock. I'm turned on my stool to watch the festivities, and even though it's not my favorite kind of music anymore, my feet can't help but keep the beat. There's no proper stage, so the band performs in center of the bar with patrons playing pool or darts on either side of them. A few people have partnered up to dance on a small wooden dance floor. I vaguely recognize most of the band members; I think the bass player might have been my third grade teacher.

"Care to dance?"

I look away from the band and the dancing couples to see a man in his mid-thirties standing beside me. He's attractive in a Northwood kind of way—blond hair, square jaw, five o' clock shadow one shade darker than the hair on his head. I don't recognize him, which is a little disorienting. I don't know anyone in Los Angeles, but I thought I knew everyone in Grand Marais.

"No thanks."

"Oh, come on," he prods with an affable smile. "Just one little dance."

"Sorry," I apologize. "I'm not much of a dancer."

"Are you sure?" His voice lifts with the question. "Last chance."

"Yeah," I nod, "but thanks for asking."

The man shrugs, not visibly injured by my refusal, and moves on to someone else.

From behind the bar, Charlotte scolds me: "Abigail Henry, stop trampling on my patrons' egos."

I spin around in my chair. "Do you know that guy?"

"Not really. I think he works on one of the fishing boats. You should have given him a chance."

"I don't dance."

"What if he had been a girl?"

"I still don't dance," I insist.

"Bullshit," she calls me out. "You at least have the two-step buried away in your memory banks. We all had to learn it in junior high gym class."

"Yeah, but that was almost twenty years ago."

She wipes her hands on a clean towel and tosses it on the bar top. "Then I guess it's time for a refresher course."

She strides out from behind the bar and I watch her cross the room, over to the band. She cups her hands and speaks directly into the lead guitarist's ear. He nods once and the band is suddenly playing a different, more upbeat country song.

Charlotte stands at the edge of the dance floor with her hands at her hips, trapping me under her steely gaze. I watch her over the rim of my pint glass. My beer is empty, and I doubt I'll get a refill if I reject the bartender. I stand from the bar stool and straighten out my legs. My hands go into the front pockets of my jeans and I shuffle to where Charlotte stands, my feet dragging the whole time.

Her expression hasn't changed. "I'll be the guy," she says.

"Can't we both be the girl?"

She rolls her eyes. "Such a feminist."

"Or lesbian," I correct.

"Fine, I'll *lead*," she says with a shake of her head. She taps my right thigh. "Put your weight on your right foot because that's the foot you're going to start with. I'll lead with my left, so we're mirror images of each other."

"Okay."

"The two step is a six-count dance, and we go quick-quick, slow-slow, quick-quick, slow-slow." Her feet start to move as she speaks, and my own feet begin to mirror her movements.

"There you go," she approves. "You've got it."

While her eyes are focused on our feet, I firmly grab her right hand and my other hand swoops under her left arm to settle on her shoulder blade.

I speak directly into her ear. "Now *I'll* be the guy."

Her eyes widened slightly, but she goes with it, and soon I have her two-stepping around the small dance floor. I raise our joined hands to let her know I'm going to spin her. She steps out to the right and appropriately spins beneath our raised arms before I pull her back in, right hand settling on her shoulder blade again.

"Think you can handle a cape?" I ask. It's a pretty basic move in the two-step, but there's still a challenging lilt to my voice.

"Do your worst," she shoots back.

I raise her hand again and she spins beneath our joined arms. Instead of bringing her back to the base position, I keep my hand up and she spins a second time while I switch hands in the air. When she finally stops spinning, my arm is draped across her shoulders like a cape and our bodies are in line with each other instead of facing each other.

"For someone who claims to not know how to dance," she remarks, "you keep up pretty well."

"I never said I didn't know how to dance. I said I *don't* dance."

It's gratuitous, but every time I spin her around and we come back together, my right hand slides across the side of her ribcage before coming to a stop on her scapula. The bare skin there is soft, and the adjuster on her bra strap presses into my palm.

She humors me for a second song, but too soon she has to get back to work. "That was fun," she remarks after sliding back to her station behind the bar. "I'm guessing you don't have much opportunity to two-step in Hollywood."

"You'd be surprised. There's nothing the gay community likes more than a themed dance party." I settle back onto my bar stool with an odd sense of familiarity. "I suppose I should thank our gym teacher for the lessons."

"Do you like it out there?" She reaches into the cooler beneath the bar top and pulls out another beer for me. I didn't order it, but there's something about this woman's demeanor and mannerisms that makes it impossible for me to resist giving in to her.

I take a sip of the beer. It's crisp and light, and I could probably drink a case without feeling a thing. "I don't mind it."

She smirks. "I'm overwhelmed by your enthusiasm."

"It's big. Sometimes too big," I admit. "But I like the pace of city life. Coming back here," I gesture to the scene around us, "it's nice for vacation, like I'm hitting the reset button, but I could never live here again."

"Why not?"

"I don't know. Isn't there some saying or some book about that? You can never go home?"

"Sure. Thomas Wolfe," she nods. "It's a classic. He writes about how the place where you grew up may be frozen in time, but you yourself have changed. It's kind of like that saying how you can never step into a stream in the same place twice."

I cock my head to the side. She's so much more than a small-town bartender—so much more than a pretty face. There's substance there that I think I underestimated. "You really *do* read a lot," I remark.

"No more than you, I'm sure," she rejects.

I shake my head. "When I'm working on a new play, I can't read anything else. If I get sucked in by someone else's creative creation, it makes me second guess my own writing."

"That's too bad," she remarks. "I don't know what I'd do without my books. Reading is the great equalizer. I can be or go anywhere in my mind. Don't get me wrong—I love my life—Amelia, the bar, this town, but sometimes it's nice to have an escape like I get reading a book." She stops herself. "And, I've gotten carried away."

"I like it," I say with an encouraging smile. "Not too many people call themselves readers anymore. I've got some novelist friends, and they're always lamenting to me their loss of readership. As long as people don't stop going to plays though, I should be fine."

"I should read one of your plays."

"Oh, God. No." I shake my head hard. "Don't do that."

"Why not?"

"It's too embarrassing. Nerve-wracking. Something." My features scrunch together. "I actually considered writing under a penname so no one would know it was me."

"That's ridiculous. You should be incredibly proud of yourself, Abby. Not everyone can do what you do."

"It's one thing to have strangers read your work, but quite another to have people you actually know look over it."

"I guess that makes sense. Not a lot of sense," she quantifies with a smirk, "but just enough."

It's in the early hours of the morning by the time the last of the customers have left the bar. It's also the second night in a row that I've stayed until close, and I walk Charlotte to her car again as I've done before.

"Thanks for keeping me company today," I say.

"Thanks for the dance," she returns. She leans against the driver side door of her Jeep. "I feel pretty honored to have witnessed that once-in-a-lifetime occurrence. It was like seeing a comet or a solar eclipse."

I can't help the grin that's stuck to my face. "Think I could bump into you and Amelia at the library again tomorrow?"

"It's supposed to be sunny tomorrow," she says, "But don't quote me on that; I'm still just a bartender."

"So does that mean I'll see you at the beach?" I ask.

"If you can find us."

CHAPTER SIX

The next morning, I wake up to find the sun high in the sky. It's a cloudless, sunny day, which means no library for Charlotte and Amelia. Even though Grand Marais is situated along the shoreline of Lake Superior, hardly anyone swims downtown except for the tourists. Instead, locals pack up their vehicles and go west on County Highway 61 to find isolated patches where the rocky shoreline has been crushed into smaller pebbles. Along Minnesota's northern shores, beaches don't have sand; they have rocks.

I park my car on the side of the road behind Charlotte's Jeep. Sitting in an empty cup holder in the center consol, the screen on my silenced cell phone illuminates indicating I've got a new text message. It's only Emily asking where I am, but the glow of the phone is a reminder that I haven't really spoken to Kambria since the Fourth of July. And even then, it wasn't much of a conversation.

It hasn't escaped my notice that last night was the first night I didn't try to call Kambria. This thing, this time I'm spending with Charlotte is unlike me. I've never been unfaithful, despite my bad habit of casually crushing on women who aren't my significant other.

I call Claire, the only person I know who'll actually answer their phone at this hour.

"Do you know if Kambria's been by my apartment lately?" I ask when she says hello. "I've been trying to get a hold of her, but she's not returning any of my calls or texts."

"I've been by to water the plants, but I haven't seen her. There are dirty dishes in your sink though, so I think she's been around to eat your food."

I groan in frustration. "I hate when she does that. What's so difficult about putting dishes in the dishwasher?" I can practically picture the bugs crawling around in my sink. "You wouldn't mind taking care of that would you?"

"I'm your agent, not your maid."

"But you're also my best friend," I point out.

"Fine." She lets loose an exaggerated sigh. "But only because it's you. What are you up to today?"

"I'm at the beach."

"Must be nice. I'm stuck in meetings all morning. How's the writing going?"

I tug at my hair. "It's not. I'm woefully stuck."

"I wouldn't worry about it too much," she tries to appease me. "Your routine got interrupted. I'm sure you'll find your groove once you get back. Speaking of which, when *are* you coming home? Your plants miss you; they told me so."

"I'm not sure. My sister's still …"

"Say no more," she interrupts. "Family comes first. Do what you have to do."

"Thanks, Claire."

"Sure thing. Just make sure my paycheck doesn't bounce, okay?"

I continue to sit in my car after I hang up with Claire. Semi-trucks and RVs speed by on the county highway. I don't know why I'm still sticking around Grand Marais after all this time. It's not like I can magically cure Emily of her heartache—only time will do that. I'm pretty sure that an attractive blonde bartender is the real reason I'm dragging my feet.

I get out of my car and peer down at the lakeshore below. Charlotte and Amelia stand near the water's edge with their backs to me. They bend and pick up smooth, flat rocks to skip across the lake's rippled surface. All of Amelia's throws sink immediately, but Charlotte's rocks leap across the water. When Amelia finally makes a rock skip, her gleeful cheer reaches my ears.

"What are you doing, Abby?" I mutter to myself.

Instead of descending the wooden stairs that lead down to the beach and mother and daughter, I head back to my car to call Kambria. Predictably, her phone rings without answer.

"It's Abby. Again," I grunt when the call is sent to her voicemail. "I'm coming back in a couple of days—I don't know exactly when—but when I do, we need to talk."

I hang up and toss my phone onto the passenger seat. I'll book a flight back to Los Angeles either today or tomorrow I decide. Kambria and I will more than likely break up, and I'll get back to my life, back to my friends, and back to writing plays.

If I can ever break through this writer's block, that is.

Later that evening I'm still completely paralyzed by this writer's block—paralyzed and frightened. I've always been able to come up with new ideas or find inspiration or at least force out a few uninspired pages, but I stare at the blank page of my notebook, and I've got nothing. I can't even blame Emily and the trip back home on this wordlessness. This has been brewing for weeks, and now I'm at a dead halt.

My writer's block exacerbates my dour mood, and as quickly as I can run a brush through my hair and change out of sweatpants, I'm trampling down the stairs to the front foyer.

I reach for my purse that's hanging on a wooden knob, but my hand freezes when I hear Emily's voice: "Where are you off to?"

She's sitting in the living room, reading a glossy magazine. We haven't really talked since her breakdown in the dining room a few nights ago. I think we're both embarrassed and not sure of how to proceed.

"I'm gonna get a drink at Roundtree's. Wanna come?"

"No, thanks." She looks up from her magazine. "Isn't that like your third or fourth time this week?"

I grab my bag from its hook and check for my ID and money. "I like the ambiance."

"Uh huh," she snorts. "Or maybe you like a certain bartender."

I fling the strap of my bag over my shoulder. "I'm sure I don't know what you mean."

She closes the magazine and folds her hands on top of her lap. "You still have a girlfriend in LA, don't you?"

I take a deep breath and release it slowly to refrain from snapping at Emily. Why does everyone insist on reminding me about Kambria? We haven't talked in over a week, and I've all but thrown in the towel on our relationship. I could e-mail her a Dear John letter, but that would be crueler than a break-up voicemail. Besides, there's nothing going on between Charlotte and me. I've been a little flirty, and my eyes have probably lingered where they shouldn't more than a few times, but I've done nothing wrong.

"Technically, yes."

Emily continues that hard, disapproving look. It reminds me of what little I remember of our mother.

"Is that it?" I ask impatiently.

She remains silent, still staring. "Yeah," she says finally.

"Don't wait up," I throw over my shoulder as I leave out the front door.

+ + +

There's a scattering of patrons around Roundtree's tonight, split between the tables and the U-shaped bar. I sit at a table near the bar, but not actually at the bar itself. Most everyone is a local tonight. It's midweek in the days after the Fourth of July, so most of the tourists have gone home until the next big weekend summer festival.

Charlotte's working alone as usual, smiling and engaging the other customers, stopping every now and then to play bar dice. Each time the plastic cup slams down on the bar top, I'm jolted from my chair. It's unlikely that she hasn't noticed me, but she hasn't acknowledged me yet.

I probably should have found a different bar to go to tonight, but I feel bad enough about not showing up at the beach without disappearing entirely. And I think a part of me needs to prove to myself that this crush that's been building over the past few days is one-sided. Charlotte's a bartender; it's her job to be friendly. And the invitations to the library and to the beach were only isolated acts of kindness, nothing more.

When she steps out from behind the bar, I'm offered a view of painted-on jean shorts wrapped around long, lean legs. Her white, short-sleeved linen top contrasts attractively with her bronzed skin tone. Her cheeks have a fresh glow like she spent a lot of time in the sun today. It makes my stomach rumble with uncomfortable guilt. I wonder how long she waited for me to show up at the beach before she gave up on me coming.

She leans across a table to reach for an empty pint glasses, and my eyes betray me as they spend a second too long admiring the curve of her backside.

"We missed you at the beach today," she remarks in a conversational tone.

I quickly avert my eyes, but I'm sure she's noticed my stare. "Yeah. Sorry about that. I was writing and lost track of time," the lie slips out. "I would have called, but I didn't have your number."

"And I don't have a cell phone," she reminds me.

"Right. See? Just another reason to get a phone," I needle her.

"Or next time, don't stand me up," she counters.

"I didn't—."

"Relax, Abby," she cuts me off. "I'm just giving you a hard time." A carefree smile appears on her face, and I instantly relax. "Why don't you take a seat at the bar?" she suggests. "It makes my job easier."

I obey her words and sit down on what's become my regular seat. In the next stool, a kid emits nervous energy. He's wearing jeans, t-shirt, and a knit cap despite the muggy summer night. He can't be more than eighteen or nineteen.

Charlotte sets a beer in front of me and turns her attention to the under-aged patron. "What can I get you, hun?" She wipes down the lacquered bar top in the space in front of him and tosses a cardboard coaster down like it's a Frisbee.

"Rum and Coke." He orders the drink with cool authority, but there's no way he's of legal drinking age.

Charlotte smiles, but it doesn't reach her eyes. "ID."

The kid shifts in his chair. "Oh, I, uh, I must've left it in the car."

"Maybe you should go get it," Charlotte suggests.

The kid slaps his hand lightly on the bar. "Damn it, it's actually in my wallet in my other jeans. Don't you hate when that happens?"

"Oh, that's the worst."

She grabs a well glass and fills it with ice. A wedge of lime is placed on the rim, and when she pulls out the soda gun, I'm under the impression that she's going to serve this clearly under-aged kid. But she tops the drink with cola, leaving no room for alcohol.

The glass is set before the patron, and she smiles again. "Jonathan Walters, don't think I don't recognize you under that peach fuzz you call a beard." She yanks the knit cap from his head and his brown, shaggy hair sticks up in places. "And take off that ridiculous hat." She tosses the hat on the bar beside his soda and clucks her tongue against the roof of her mouth.

"Yes ma'am." The kid's angular shoulders slump forward and he stabs the ice cubes in his drink with the little plastic red straw.

"Jon graduated high school last year. Probably home from college for the holiday." Charlotte laughs and shakes her head. "These kids are funny thinking a year of college and they're all grown up."

"You know in my day," I can't help but remark, "we just paid someone to buy us a case of beer at the gas station."

The kid looks sideways at me. "Yeah. Whatever," he grunts. The legs of his barstool screech against the floor as he pushes away from the bar to stand up. He tosses a five-dollar bill on the bar top and leaves without having any of his soda.

"Chasing my customers away? You're worse than Old Tom," Charlotte smirks.

"Sorry," I grumble.

I make a move to leave as well, but a strong hand clamps down on my wrist before I get very far. Charlotte's arm is attached to that hand, and I follow the tan arm up to where it connects to her shoulder, across the tops of her breasts, and up to her hazel-green eyes.

"Stick around, Abby," she husks. "The night's still young."

Only when she releases me do I exhale.

Charlotte ignores me for most of the night except to bring me a second beer. When she's not topping off other people's drinks, she disappears into a back room that serves as the bar's small kitchen. I spend the remainder of the evening splitting my time between watching her and playing darts with some other locals. The rational portion of my brain tells me to pack up my things and go home, but my bruised, ignored ego has me staying long after the final customer has left.

Charlotte seems to notice. "You're determined to close down the bar again, aren't you?" she muses.

I push my empty pint glass back and forth between my hands, sliding it along the lacquered surface of the bar. My drink had gone empty hours ago, but she never asked if I wanted another one and I never bothered her for a refill. "It's good to have goals."

She makes a humming noise. "Why don't you get behind the bar and make yourself useful?"

I lift my head. "Really?"

She smiles shrewdly. "Might as well. Maybe I can get home at a decent time tonight."

I hop up from my barstool and make my way behind the bar. "What do you need me to do?"

She jerks her head toward the swinging door that leads to the kitchen. "Grab a bucket with some hot, soapy water and wipe down the bar top and tables."

When I come back from the kitchen, bucket and rag in hand, Charlotte has turned off most of the overhead lights. The neon beer signs that decorate the bar's walls are still on, giving the place a kind of eerie glow.

"Are you sure you don't mind me putting you to work?" she asks.

"Not at all," I say truthfully. It's almost a relief to have something to do. I wipe the washrag across the glossy bar top, wiping away the night's spilled beer and hard liquor. "I'm glad I can help. Besides, I like the company."

She looks at me thoughtfully. "I like the company, too."

"I can't imagine working so late and going home by myself. I know that Grand Marais is a small, safe town, but I'd still get nervous."

"I guess I'm used to it by now. Travis Spencer—you remember him from school, right?" I nod and she continues. "Well he's a cop now. He used to escort me home when he worked the night shift. But then he sent me flowers," she chuckles at the memory, "so I had to stop that; I didn't want to encourage him."

"Heartbreaker," I tease.

Despite my jest, I can't ignore the jealous tightening in my chest. It's absolutely ridiculous and unfounded, but I hate the thought of Charlotte subject to the awkward pawing of some man.

Charlotte steps behind me and pulls the rag out of my hands and tosses it back into the cleaning bucket.

"I'm not done cleaning yet," I protest.

"You're done," she informs me. "I like your company, Abby. I like you." She takes another step, and I find myself in the unexpected position of being pinned between her and the bar. Her weight is pressed against my backside.

I lick at my lips, which have become inexplicably dry in the past few seconds. "Oh, um, I like you too, Charlotte."

My palms are flat on the slightly sticky bar top and I rest my weight on them. The lean muscles of Charlotte's arm wraps around my waist, and she presses the length of her body against my back. We're about the same height, and our bodies just seem to fit.

She brushes my loose hair over my shoulder and her soft lips ghost over the back of my neck. My entire body shivers at the contract.

"Charlotte." The name is a prayer on my lips. "What are you doing?"

Fingers trail the length of my arms, down to my wrists. My hands are pinned against the bar top, and her body curves around my back. "Taking charge." Her words vibrate in my ear. "I think you're all words and no action, Ms. Writer."

I close my eyes and swallow down my arousal. I know I shouldn't be encouraging this. I should stop her. I still have a girlfriend even though I know our relationship has run its course. But when Charlotte's hand slides down the front of my denim shorts, my moral compass falls off course.

There's only so much she can do to me from this angle. My shorts are fitted and she hasn't unfastened the button or zipper, leaving very little space with which to maneuver. I arch my back and press my backside into her, my body giving in to her gentle but purposeful touch. My breath hitches when long fingers make their way beneath my underwear. She seeks out my clit, rubbing it in lazy circles, making my legs spread farther apart. Her touch is light and unrelenting. My legs begin to shake. I'm going to cum, and she hasn't even gone inside.

"Are you staying at your dad's?" she asks.

Her voice snaps me out of my lust-induced haze. "Yeah."

"Emily's there, too?" Her breath is hot in my ear.

"Uh huh."

"Sounds like a full house."

I bite my lip. It *is* a full house. And nothing's more of a mood killer than inviting someone back to your parent's place. But I don't want this evening to end, and I don't want to be presumptuous and invite myself over to her house. Plus I know she's got a kid, and I don't know how she feels about bringing people around her like that. I've never done anything with a single mom before. I'm not a lothario by any stretch of the imagination, so this is wildly out of my comfort zone.

Her hand leaves my shorts, simultaneously leaving me on the edge of orgasm. She grabs her purse from behind the bar and leaves the neon lights of bar signs still glowing. Her heavy key ring jangles in her hand, and I take that as a sign that we're done here and that she wants to lock up for the night.

We're both quiet as we walk to our respective cars in the parking lot. It's well lit by lampposts, and I can see moths fluttering around the dull yellow lights. Her green Jeep with the tan canvas top and my rental sedan are the only two cars left.

I follow her over to her car where she pauses with her hand on the driver side door.

I make a noise in the back of my throat. "So …"

"You can come over if you want." She doesn't look in my direction.

"If I want?" I echo.

She turns and shrugs, finally making eye contact again. "It doesn't have to be a big deal."

I hook my fingers through the belt loops on her jean shorts and tug her closer before she can melt away into the night. I press her up against the side of her Jeep; I love the feel of her long, lean body under mine.

When she presses her thumbs into my hipbones, my knees buckle. There's a challenging glint in her eyes. Her hand has been down my pants, but we haven't even properly kissed.

"I'll be right behind you."

CHAPTER SEVEN

It starts to drizzle on the short drive from the bar to Charlotte's place. My wipers ineffectively smear the evening mist across my rental car's windshield, which has become a graveyard for winged insects over the past few days. Charlotte lives less than a mile from the bar. It's a small house, but with it only being Amelia and herself, I suppose they don't need much space. Houses in my hometown aren't lavish in the first place. My dad's house is probably one of the biggest in town, but only because he expanded the original construction himself.

I climb out of my rental car and pick my way between the raindrops to her front stoop. It's dark out, with only a few street lamps and the overhead moon to illuminate my way. We share the space with a large planter filled with petunias and marigolds.

I rub my palms over my bare arms, feeling the goose bumps on my forearms, while I wait for her to find the key to her house on a full key ring. We don't speak or make eye contact, and I wonder if we've both lost our nerve. The bravado she'd shown in the bar is now silenced.

The porch light buzzes and erratically flickers overhead. "I've got to get that fixed." Charlotte speaks out loud, but it sounds more like a reminder to herself than her making conversation. "Must be a short or something."

She finds the right key and unlocks the front door, which opens directly into the living room. The TV is on in one corner, but it's on mute. A local news anchor recites that day's events, lips moving but producing no sound. Besides the light produced by the television, the house is dark. Charlotte lifts a single finger to her lips, and I nod my understanding: her daughter is sleeping.

"You're home early."

There's a woman sitting on the couch in the living room and her unexpected presence startles me. It takes a moment longer for me to recognize her as Charlotte's mother.

"It was dead tonight," Charlotte replies.

Unlike other adults in this town, I don't know Charlotte's parents very well. We didn't run in the same social circle in high school so there had been no reason for us to interact unless my dad had done some work on their house once upon a time.

Her mom stands from the couch and gives me a passing glance. "Everything okay?"

"Yeah. Mom, do you remember Abigail Henry? Her dad owns the hardware store downtown," Charlotte introduces. "Abby, this is my mom."

She squints at me, obviously curious as to why I'm here at such a late hour. It gives me an anxious feeling. Gossip is the bloodline of small-town America, and even though our families aren't friends, I'm pretty sure Charlotte's mom knows I'm gay. It's the kind of information that won't make it into the local newspaper, but it's somehow become common knowledge around here despite how inadequate my trips home are. I'm usually comfortable with my sexuality, but there's something silently accusatory in the way Charlotte's mom regards me.

"H-hey," I greet. The word gets stuck in my throat and my hands are similarly jammed too deep into the front pockets of my shorts to shake her hand.

If her mom has an opinion about my presence, she keeps it to herself. "Goodnight, girls."

"Night, mom," Charlotte says. "Thanks."

The front door closes, followed by the screen door with Charlotte's mother's departure.

Charlotte lingers near the door long enough to turn the lock into place.

"Free babysitter," I remark, trying to shake off the nerves. "That must be nice."

Charlotte slips out of her sandals and places them by the front door. "She's saved my ass more than a few times," she admits.

When she shuts off the TV, the room becomes blanketed by night. It's inky dark, but I can still see the outline of her silhouette as she steps a few feet closer. Her steps are silent as she walks across carpeted floor, and I'm sure she can hear the pounding of my heart, which has leapt into my throat.

"Bathroom?" I squeak.

Her predatory steps stall. "Down the hallway, second door on the right."

The covered light bulbs above the bathroom sink fill the small space with a dull, golden glow. It's not a flattering light, and my mirrored reflection looks jaundiced. I pull on my cheeks until my eyes droop, and I stick out my tongue. I don't *look* like a cheater, and yet that's exactly what I'm doing.

I pull my phone out of the tight back pocket of my jean shorts, and for the umpteenth time, I call Kambria's number. If she picks up, I have no idea what I'll say, and I assume that the walls of Charlotte's house are thin enough that anything I say in here will be projected outside of the bathroom. I'm saved though when, instead of hearing the sound of club music in the background or eventually being sent to Kambria's voicemail, the call is transferred to her voice mailbox after only the first ring.

There's a quiet knock on the bathroom door. "Everything okay in there?" comes Charlotte's subdued voice.

I immediately hang up. There's no message I can leave that will make anything I plan on doing in the next room permissible or guilt free.

I open the door and Charlotte's standing on the other side. She leans against the doorjamb, trying to look confident or seductive or some combination thereof, but her eyes tell a different story.

"Are you okay?" she asks. A glimmer of something—self-doubt perhaps—clouds her hazel eyes.

"Yeah."

"Change your mind?" Her hands fiddle with the bottom hem of my t-shirt. When her knuckles brush against my bare stomach, I feel it even lower.

"No."

My hands move of their own accord, one sliding along the side of her face and curling around her head to tangle my fingers in her hair, and the other pulls down on the center of her button-up shirt. The buttons on her linen top are only snaps, and they pop free with the firm tug. Beneath the shirt is a nude bra, functional, yet oh-so-sexy against her tanned skin. Blonde and tan, she looks practically Californian with treacherous, long legs that I can't wait to have wrapped around me.

Charlotte wobbles unsteadily from the aggressive move, and I wrap my arm around her midsection to steady her. It's amazing how natural it feels to have her in my arms. We hardly know each other, yet everything about her is familiar.

Her lips are soft and eager, and we linger in the hallway in front of the bathroom exploring each other with mouths and fingers. She touches my hands, and I feel her in my hardening nipples. Her hands grip my hips, and I feel it in my clit. My hands slide beneath the open fabric of her shirt and meet in the small of her back. I round over the warm globes of her backside and she makes a quiet moan in my mouth when I firmly squeeze.

We stumble down the hallway, both of us refusing to end the kiss. At some point she flips us around, because I don't know the layout of her house. I don't know where her bedroom is. I'm waltzed backwards into a room at the end of the hallway. Her hands are fisted in the front of my shirt, so she uses her foot to shut the bedroom door behind us.

Light from a lamppost outside filters through her bedroom window. The glow is more yellow than moonlight and casts strange shadows on the things in the room. Her bedroom is sparsely decorated. There's a rocker with an afghan tossed over the top of the chair, a wooden set of drawers, and the bed. There's nothing hanging on the walls, but I see a framed picture on top of the bureau. I can't see whose face is in the image, but I imagine it's probably Amelia's.

"I like your room," I breathe, separating myself from her mouth long enough for the compliment.

"Uh huh," she grunts, not really hearing me. Her mouth is back on mine and wandering hands cup my breasts over my bra and shirt.

I'm pushed onto the bed and the wooden frame creaks with the impact. Charlotte wastes little time in crawling on top of me and straddling my hips. She bucks into me and we both groan as our centers, still fully covered, rub together. Even with what happened at the bar, her assertiveness surprises me.

My shirt is tugged off along with her own to provide me with another unobstructed view of her stomach, tanned from the young summer. I can see the outline of her ribs directly beneath her bra. She's tight everywhere.

I reach behind her and unfasten the bra clasp at the center of her back. This too is haphazardly tossed to the floor. Her breasts are small with eager, responsive nipples. When I sit up and pull one dusky-rose colored bud between my lips, her fingers pull at my ponytail and loosen the tied-back hair from its band. Her fingers stroke through my tumbling hair, short nails lightly scraping my scalp.

With a free hand, I reach between our bodies and pop the button on her jean shorts. The zipper follows, and I'm given more room to explore beneath the elastic waistband of her underwear. My fingers travel through closely cropped curls before seeking out her clit. I cup her naked pussy in the palm of my hand, and her breath hitches in her throat.

I wonder how long it's been since anyone has touched her like this. She hasn't said as much, but I imagine she's probably nervous. But what do I know? Maybe she does this kind of thing all the time.

I position a stabilizing arm between her shoulder blades and guide her onto her back. The moment her head hits the pillow, she arches off the bed to let me remove her tight jean shorts. The sight of the classic white cotton underwear with the wide lace border has my mouth watering. It's certainly not the fanciest nor frilliest underwear I've ever seen, but there's something about the basic undergarment that I find incredibly sexy. It's like an extension of the woman herself.

Despite the eagerness with which she shed her shorts, bra, and shirt, her body stiffens when my fingers reach her underwear.

My fingertips are curled around the waistband, but I make no other movements. "I'll go slow," I promise in a quiet breath. "Or we can stop. It's up to you."

Just beneath her shallow belly button, the skin is tight but slightly marbled with small stretch marks made more visible from the sun's bronzing of the area. Unthinking, I trace my fingertips down the crooked little paths blossoming on her skin. It's then I realize I've misinterpreted her hesitancy to remove her underwear. She squirms beneath my ministrations, but I know the female psyche well enough that it's not because my touch feels too good to sit still.

When Charlotte's behind the bar, she's brash and cocky. But it's all an elaborate show; she's a woman, and therefore not immune to the cover models on the magazine that try to tell you how you too can have a firmer ass and flatter stomach in just two weeks. Not even beautiful women who live in remote parts of northern Minnesota can escape that kind of pressure.

Her hands fall on top of mine, covering up the small stretch marks. "Pretty ugly, right?" she says, making a disappointed face.

"Stop," I gently chastise. "You're beautiful. You're amazing."

I pull her hands away and press a soft, reverent kiss to the squiggly white lines in her skin. They're battle scars of a life lived and tangible evidence of her strength. She made another human being. The weight of that knowledge is heavy.

Her top teeth seek out her lower lip. "Keep going," she urges.

At her words, I slowly pull the front of her panties down and press a feather soft kiss to her already protruding clit. Her hips jerk up, but expecting the reaction, I move with her to avoid a broken nose. I slide her underwear the rest of the way off her body, kissing her hips, thighs, and legs as the cotton material passes each body part. Tan lines from a tiny bikini remain, giving the impression that her undergarments still remain on her body, but they've been cast to the floor with the rest of her clothes and my tank top.

Positioned between her parted thighs, I place my hands on either side of her sex and separate her outer lips before lightly blowing on her clit. I flick the sensitive bud back and forth a few times with the tip of my tongue, and her hips undulate, seeking more contact.

A quiet sigh reaches my ears when I lick the length of her sex and collect her mounting arousal on my tongue. Her eyes are closed, with her head tilted back. Her hand is at the back of my head, fingers buried deep in my hair, and I love it.

I slowly push a single finger between her pussy lips and sink into her heat to the second knuckle. She's like a warm, wet pillow surrounding my finger. I pull my finger all the way out until just my fingertip remains before burying myself back inside.

My finger retreats again, and I rub my now coated digit around her clit and between her folds, spreading around her arousal. Her pussy burns even hotter and wetter than before.

More quiet sounds and words of encouragement tumble from her parted lips. Her body is active on the mattress and I work to match the rhythm her hips have set.

My ring finger joins my middle finger and I curl the pads of my fingertips up against the rippled area.

"Oh my God!" she quietly exclaims. I repeat the motion and her body jolts upright. "Shit," she calls out in a strained voice. "I'm cumming."

I continue to rub the spongy area and suck on her clit while her thighs quiver and shake around my ears.

She falls back onto the pillow and the down material plumps up around her head. She looks exhausted, but wired. I know the feeling well.

"Jesus." She drapes her arm across her forehead and lets out one long breath. "What was that?"

I roll onto my back beside her. "Your G-spot."

"Is it always like that?" she asks.

I stare at the ceiling and drum my fingers on my abdomen. "Usually."

"Damn it," she exhales. "If I'd known that, I would have gotten with a woman sooner."

I remain on my back, unable to look at her. I'm not embarrassed about what we just did, but now that it's been done, I don't know what to do. *Do I stay or do I go?*

I turn my head towards her when I feel her touch my shoulder. She lightly fiddles with my bra strap. "So ..." I can tell she's thinking the same thing.

I sit up in bed and look for my discarded tank top.

"Where are you going?" she asks.

"I figured I'd head home."

"But you didn't ... I didn't ..."

"It's okay," I give her a pass. "I know it's not for everyone."

Her hand comes to rest on my upper thigh and stays there. "I kind of wanted to try." She gives me a half smile. "If you don't mind, that is."

Her words have my backside glued to the mattress when I had once been eager to leave. "Oh, um, no. I-I don't mind."

Her pink tongue darts out, and she licks her lips. I can feel her heated gaze everywhere. "Should you lay back down?"

"I-I suppose I can do that."

She resumes her previous position of straddling my hips, but this time she's completely naked and I'm more than a little distracted. I know she wants a turn, but I don't want to be done with mine yet. I try to flip us over again, but she's too strong. Her hands clamp around my wrists and she pins me to the mattress.

"Don't."

She's a mom, and years of picking up a small child has given her arm strength that I simply don't possess.

My shorts have somehow stayed on to this point, but a button and zipper later and they're tossed onto the floor with my tank top. She cups my panty-covered sex, and I can't hold back when my hips buck against her hand.

I continue to help move things along by reaching behind my back and unfastening the back clasp of my bra. She helps the rest of the way when she slides the twin straps off of my shoulders and tosses my beige bra toward the bottom of the bed.

I wait anxiously as keen eyes drink in my body. I consider myself in shape, but I'm not anywhere as chiseled as she is. I also haven't had enough to drink to not be self-conscious about my half-naked body, but when her knee slips between my thighs, worries about how my body looks in a darkened room scatter from my mind.

Her fingers slide the crotch of my panties to the side. "Is this okay?"

"Seriously okay," I gulp.

She swirls her finger around my clit without dipping inside.

"Jesus," I cry out.

"Shhh . . ." she hushes me. "Or am I going to have to gag you?"

"Oh, God," I quietly groan. It's awkward, but also kind of a turn on. I haven't had to temper my noises in years, not since I had a roommate in college over a decade ago.

Her fingertips trail over my shaved pussy lips, and I can feel myself becoming wetter as the seconds tick by. Her touch is light and exploratory but mostly conservative as she avoids my clit and my slit entirely.

I can't help my groan of frustration. I've been on the edge of orgasm since we left the bar.

She lowers herself on the bed, positioning her upper body between my parted thighs. The mattress springs squeak as she rearranges herself, and I might die if she doesn't touch me soon. But at the same time, I'm trying not to be impatient and to go at a pace with which she feels comfortable.

I can only really see the top of her blonde head before she presses her mouth against my panty-covered mons. She kisses me over my underwear and lightly tongues my clit through the material. The way she rolls my sensitive clit back and forth feels delicious, even without direct contact, and my eyes flutter close.

Eventually, when she's grown tired of that, she tugs on the elastic leg band of my underwear. "I need these off," she huffs in frustration.

I immediately lift my backside off the mattress, and the undergarment is ripped down my hips and legs. The night air is cool, and I love the way it feels against my overheated, overstimulated pussy.

Even though I'm completely naked, she still avoids my most intimate place. I can't tell if she's nervous or simply making me wait out of sheer torture. She nibbles on my inner thigh while her fingers walk up my abdomen. My teeth sink into my lower lip when she takes a detour to trace a fingertip around one of my nipples, which instantly hardens under her touch. She pinches the sensitive nub between her thumb and forefinger and gives it a light tug. Her mouth continues to suck and lick the tender flesh of my inner thigh. She's not where I need her most, but I'm also not hating this unhurried exploration of what my body likes.

Her breath is hot against me as she kisses her way closer to my clit. I watch with mounting anticipation as the distance between the flat of her tongue and my sex is eliminated.

"Oh fuck," I quietly groan when her tongue finally wiggles against my clit. She flicks it back and forth with just the tip of her tongue. Her hands squeeze my bare thighs and travel up to my hips where they remain.

She licks me, slow and tentatively, down my center. She smacks her lips as though deciding if she approves of my flavor.

"Stick a finger in me," I urge in a whispered command.

Her touch is light against my already damp slit. She trails a short fingernail the length of my sex before rubbing the underside of my clit. I can feel the pressure of her fingertip against my entrance before she pushes a single finger against me, so slowly, so gentle.

"Yes," I hiss.

She pulls her finger almost all the way out before pushing back in. I'm wetter now and my inner muscles work to accommodate her.

"It feels different than I do," she whispers in near reverence.

"I guess vaginas are like snowflakes."

Her finger flexes and wiggles inside me experimentally.

"Try another one. I won't break," I pant. "Promise."

A second finger diligently follows the first, and my mouth falls open. "Oh God," I whisper. "Right there."

Her mouth attaches to my clit the moment she bottoms out. Her tongue flutters perfectly against my clit, and her fingers continue their dedicated assault between my thighs. I throw my arm across my face and bite into my own forearm to keep from making too much noise. It's all I can do not to claw her back or scream her praises.

"Just like that," I cry in a pained whisper. "Please don't stop."

She pulls herself up on her knees, a movement that gives her more leverage. Her fingers quicken inside me. I watch the tightened muscles of her right bicep flex and harden with each thrust. Her two fingers are like a blur, and the other fingers on her hand smash into my pelvic bone and inner thighs. It's inelegant and clumsy, but it's working.

My hand falls between her shoulder blades, just beneath her neck. Her skin feels inflamed, and I'm sweating, too.

"I'm close," I breathe. "Oh fuck, Charlotte. Oh, God. You're gonna make me ..." I feel the beginnings of the mounting orgasm tightening in my stomach and travel lower. "Oh fuck, yes. I'm gonna cum."

I throw my head back and slam my eyes shut as the intense sensation radiates through my body. My lower body arches off the bed, but she stays on task as I ride out the orgasm.

My center is still throbbing with the aftereffects of orgasm, but I'm up and flipping our spots so she's on her back again.

She looks up at me with wide, dreamy hazel eyes. "More?" she asks, wonderment in her tone.

I dip my head and kiss her soundly on the mouth, tasting my arousal on her lips. "We're just getting started."

BITTERSWEET HOMECOMING

CHAPTER EIGHT

The bedroom window is open, and I can hear the sounds of traffic in the distance and of mixed birds erratically chirping outside. The woman beside me is long and warm, and based on the evenness of her breathing, still sleeping. Eyes closed, I inhale the scent of the room. It's a combination of fabric softener and something clean and fresh, the northern air, no doubt.

My eyes flutter open when I hear a squeaky door hinge. Charlotte's bedroom door is slowly opening. I slept in my contacts so my vision is slightly blurred, but there's definitely a small figure running toward the bed. Before I can squawk out a warning, the duvet cover is billowing around me and small limbs are crawling across the mattress. High-pitched giggling sounds off in my ear, and all I can think about is *Where Are My Pants?*

I'm naked beneath these blankets, and I know Charlotte is as well. She's awake now and playfully wrestling with her daughter while I remain rigid beside her, clinging to the underside of the sheets as though they're my only life source.

Amelia stops jumping on the bed when she realizes that her mother is not alone. Her nose wrinkles and she cocks her head to the side. "Who are you?" she asks.

I open my mouth, not sure of what to say, but Charlotte answers for me. "She's a friend of mommy's. We had a sleepover party last night," she says. "Why don't you go brush your teeth and I'll make us some breakfast?"

"Okay!" As quickly as the little girl had appeared, she hops off the bed with a solid thud and scampers out of the room.

I stare at the doorway, which has remained open. "Sleepover party?" I repeat.

Charlotte shrugs. "She's six."

"Do you have sleepover parties often?" I pose.

"Would you be jealous if I did?"

"Uh . . ." I don't know how to answer the question.

Thankfully, she lets me off the hook. "No. I try not to bring people home because of Amelia."

"Then . . . why me?"

Her hazel eyes stare back at me. "Because I wanted to," she says as though it's the most obvious answer in the world.

Without waiting around for my response, she throws the blankets back and gets out of bed. She walks across the room to her clothes bureau, unperturbed by her nakedness. I don't mind watching, and she doesn't look like she minds having an audience.

"Do you want to stay for breakfast?" she asks over her shoulder. "I was thinking waffles or eggs." She pulls a tank top and sweatpants out of two separate drawers.

I prop myself up on my elbows and continue to watch as she dresses. "Will you let me help?"

"Can you cook either one of those?"

"I'm sure I can burn both of them."

Her wide mouth twists into a knowing smirk. "How about I put you on orange juice duty?"

I pretend to think it over. "I think I can handle that."

I hop out of bed myself and grab her around the waist. The floor is a rough carpet beneath my feet. "I had a lot of fun last night," I murmur into her ear. I give the outer shell a quick lick and something surges inside me when I feel her shudder.

"Me, too," she says quietly.

She spins around and her nose knocks against mine. We're about the same height in our bare feet. "Do you have plans today?" she asks.

"I should probably try to get some writing done," I sigh. I lean forward so our foreheads touch. "I'm seriously stuck, but I should at least try."

She sneaks a quick kiss, too chaste and fleeting for my liking. "Let's get some food in you so you're not working on an empty stomach." She taps her pointer finger against my forehead. Once. Twice. "You need some brain food."

"You're kind of great, you know that?"

"I have my moments," she muses. "I'll start breakfast. You can take your time in here, but if I don't come out soon, Amelia will be back."

My jean shorts are in a heap on the floor. When I retrieve them, my phone slips out of the back pocket and bounces off the carpet. My phone is nearly out of battery. Reception is spotty at best in this town, and when the device is roaming for a signal, it drains the battery. There's no missed messages, no phone calls, no text messages. Nothing from Kambria. I suppose I should feel justified, or at least relieved that she hadn't tried to call me back at the exact moment that I was in bed with another woman, but feelings of guilt creep up on me, nonetheless.

Charlotte's house looks different in the light of day. It's airy and clean and flooded with ample natural light. The house had seemed small and crowded with old floors and low ceilings, but now everything feels fresh and renewed. But maybe the house hasn't changed; maybe I have.

I follow my nose toward the distinctive scent of bacon. I find Charlotte cooking breakfast in the narrow galley kitchen. On the other side of the Formica countertop is a dining room table where Amelia sits with a fistful of crayons and a piece of paper. She's humming, carefree.

I've had my share of one-night stands over the years, but not enough to become an expert in morning-after protocol. Breakfast is very rare, let alone breakfast with my partner's six year old.

Charlotte is torturing me with her white tank top and sweatpants rolled at the ankles. Her upturned breasts and nipples are just visible through the near-sheer material and she's wearing the hell out of those dark grey sweatpants. The black-framed glasses are a surprise, but incredibly hot. If her daughter weren't in the room, chattering about a friend who's allergic to oranges, I'd have Charlotte pinned against the kitchen counter, tonguing her sensitive nipples through the material of her tank top.

Through my lust-filled haze, I'm vaguely aware that someone is talking, and I think they're speaking to me: "Sorry, what?"

Charlotte twirls a spatula in one hand. "Amelia asked you a question."

"Oh, sorry, Amelia," I apologize, shaking my head hard. "What's up?"

Amelia's hair is curlier than usual, and when she smiles at me I notice for the first time the gap between her two front teeth. Her wide, blinking eyes are the same color as her mother's. She's about the same age as I was when my mother left. It's a sobering thought.

"Do you have any food allergies?" she asks.

"Nothing that I know of."

"Good. Mom can make you a peanut butter sandwich when we go to the beach today."

Charlotte stumbles over her words before I can respond. "Sweetie, Abby can't stay. She has to work."

"On a Sunday?" Amelia questions, looking visibly displeased.

"I could, um, meet you guys at the beach after I get done?" I propose.

"You don't have to do that," Charlotte quickly dismisses. "It's okay."

"What if I want to?"

"Yeah?" There's a ghost of a smile at her lips.

I look between mother and child. "Yeah."

"There's orange juice in the fridge," Charlotte says. "Help yourself."

I open a few upper cabinets before I find the glasses. "Amelia, would you like some juice?"

She doesn't look up from her drawing. "Yes, please." Her legs swing under the table. "But none for Reggie. He's allergic."

"Who's Reggie?" I ask. I look to the floor, half expecting to see a dog waiting for food scraps.

Charlotte divides fluffy scrambled eggs onto three plates, the smallest plate and portion for Amelia. Bacon gets transported from the frying pan to a plate lined with paper towel to soak up the grease. "Reggie's a friend of the invisible variety."

"Ohhh," I nod in understanding.

"Crayons away, Picasso. Breakfast time." Charlotte's voice is warm but direct. I can tell she's a good mom; she carries herself with a quiet confidence that I find extremely sexy. "Have a seat, Abby."

I reach for one of the empty chairs, but Amelia makes a noise. "That's Mommy's seat," she informs me.

"Oh." I touch my fingers to the top of a different chair. "How about this one?"

"That can be yours," she allows. Charlotte catches my eye and raises an amused eyebrow. I wipe my hand across my forehead and pantomime an overly relieved motion.

Charlotte sets a plate in front of Amelia and then one in front of me before returning to the counter to get the third plate for herself. Amelia doles out a portion of her scrambled eggs to the empty place setting beside her.

"Amelia Bedelia!" Charlotte sharply scolds when she turns back to the table and sees what her daughter has done. "What have I told you about that?"

"But, Mom! Reggie's hungry!"

"I have to agree," I chime in. "Reggie shouldn't miss out. These might be the best damn eggs I've ever had." I glance in Amelia's direction when the curse word inadvertently slips out. "Sorry."

"It's okay," Charlotte allows with a small smile. "She's heard worse."

"But seriously, this is really good." I motion at my plate with my fork. "Do you ever cook at the bar?"

"Only when we're shorthanded." Charlotte sets her plate at the table and finally sits down. "I do better behind the bar than in the kitchen."

If there wasn't a six year old with wide eyes and open ears at the table, I would have made a remark about her skill in the bedroom, but I keep those remarks to myself.

It's strangely comfortable having breakfast with Charlotte and her daughter. It's clear they have a close rapport and that breakfast on a Sunday morning is part of their routine, but I feel like I'm a part of that, too, not an intruder. Amelia tells me all about Reggie and how excited she is for school in the fall. I sneak periodic glances at her mother as Amelia talks without taking a breath. The indulgent smile on Charlotte's face makes my stomach flutter. Even the way she holds a coffee cup is sexy—long, thin fingers curled around the ceramic mug.

After breakfast, Charlotte disappears to fix Amelia's untamable hair. In their absence, I fill the kitchen sink with hot, sudsy water. I'm not much of a cook, but I'm awfully skilled at washing dishes. Growing up, my sister and I had been responsible for all dirty dishes—I washed and rinsed and she dried and put them away. We used to bug our dad about buying a proper dishwasher but he'd seen no point, knowing he had our free labor readily available. The hardware store had been like that as well, child-labor laws be damned. But while I'd been more satisfied to sit with my head in a book and blindly hand my father the tools he needed at a job, Emily had been a far more apt student.

"You don't have to do that," Charlotte censures when she walks back into the kitchen.

"I don't mind," I insist. "I like earning my keep."

"At least let me rinse."

"Nope," I refuse. "You cooked, so I have clean up duty. That's the rules in the Henry family."

She comes to stand next to me. I don't look in her direction—my focus is on not breaking the juice glasses I'm cleaning—but I can feel her beside me. The sound of ceramic plates clunking around in soapy dishwater punctuates the silence.

Her hands join mine in the kitchen sink, submerged in the water. Beneath the sudsy water, she covers her hands over mine, causing me to momentarily pause in my task. She speaks in a low, quiet tone. "You really don't have to come to the beach later. Amelia will be disappointed, but she'll get over it."

I pull away, frowning. "Do you not want me to come?"

"It's a free country," she shrugs. "You can do what you want. I don't own the beach."

"No. The Harvesters probably do," I joke without humor. "But you know what I mean."

"I don't want you to think that I'm expecting anything after last night."

I twist away from the sink to face her. I don't know what to say or how to react to her words. Instead, I touch a finger to the side of the frames of her glasses. "These are cute."

"I normally wear contacts."

"I like them. But they hide those gorgeous eyes."

My hands are wet from the dishwater, but I carefully remove her glasses. When I've taken them off, she stares at me, blinking and unfocused.

"That's not fair," she complains. "Now I can't see you at all."

"Do you need to see me to do this?" I swoop my head low and press a quick, fleeting kiss to her pouting mouth.

She licks her lips. "I guess not."

Her fingers take residency in the front of my tank top as they'd done the previous night. She leans her weight into me and her braless breasts press into own chest. I'm pinned between her body and the kitchen sink. The countertop is wet and my shorts soak up the mess, but I don't mind at all.

"Mommy!" The sound of tiny feet pounding down the hallway registers in some part of my brain while the rest of my person is distracted by the color of Charlotte's eyes. "I can't find my swim suit!"

Charlotte jerks away like my body is covered in barbs. "Did you check the laundry room?" Her voice is high and tight. "There should be one hanging up in there."

Amelia smiles brightly and races back down the hallway. Despite her small body, her feet beat loudly on the floor.

Charlotte releases a long breath.

"You okay?" I try not to feel too offended by her reaction.

"Yeah." She rakes a shaky hand through her long blonde hair. "Sorry about that. I'm just not sure I'm ready to have that conversation with her yet."

"The gay one?" I guess.

"No. The Abigail Henry one."

+ + +

The days are starting to melt together, which makes me feel like I'm on vacation, but I know it's the weekend when I see my dad sitting at the kitchen island with a thick stack of newspapers in front of him. Sundays at the Henry household were all about football and fighting over who got to read the comic strip first.

"Morning," I greet.

My dad looks up from the sports section. His eyes scan my outfit—the clothes I wore yesterday. "Did you come home last night? Not that I'm keeping tabs on you," he clarifies.

"No, uh," I stand awkwardly in the archway. "I stayed at a friend's house. I didn't want to drive all the way out here after I'd been drinking at Roundtree's."

"Good thinking," he hums. "I'm glad you're being safe."

I'd nursed two beers all night—not nearly enough to justify following Charlotte home and falling into bed with her.

It's only when I step into the spray of a hot shower in the upstairs bathroom that I take full measure of what happened the previous night. There are small bruises on my collarbone that I didn't notice before and a distinct soreness between my legs.

I cheated on my girlfriend with Charlotte.

After my shower I try contacting Kambria again. I don't prepare anything to say because by now, I know she's not going to answer her phone. Like the previous night, my call is forwarded straight to her voicemail. I turn my phone over and over in my hands after hanging up. If I hadn't spoken to Claire and Anthony I would have thought there was something wrong with my phone or cell service in Grand Marais. I can only begin to imagine why I haven't heard from Kambria in over a week.

I told Charlotte I would try to write today, and feeling obligated to honor my word to at least one person, I sit at the desk in my old bedroom where I used to do my homework. The corners of the desk are rounded and worn and there are deep grooves on the writing surface from years of use. I open up my notebook to a clean page. I shake out my hands at my sides. And I write.

<u>ACT 1</u>

<u>Scene 1</u>

SETTING: A grove of willow trees. It's dusk and the sun has set.

AT RISE: A young girl hides behind the long, draping branches of a willow tree. Other children play beyond its protective shelter. They run around and shout and laugh, unaware of the young girl just out of their view. A firefly sits in the wings, watching the scene play out.

A few hours later, I spy Charlotte's green Jeep parked on the side of the county highway. Below the elevated road is the pebbled shoreline. The day is hot—about as hot as summer ever gets this far north—and the smooth rocks burn the bottoms of my bare feet as I make my way down to the lake where Charlotte waits on an oversized beach blanket.

Amelia wades in the water up to her knees, squealing every time a whitecap crashes against her. In the Pacific Ocean the waves would be sucking her out to sea, but the current and riptide are less fierce here.

Charlotte's swimsuit leaves little to the imagination, a single scrap of white fabric horizontal across her chest and matching tiny white boi shorts. The white material of her suit contrasts deeply with her bronzed skin. She peers at me over the rims of her sunglasses, and her pink lips curl up on one side. "Nice suit."

I self-consciously tug my bikini top higher on my chest. It's one of those suits that's more decorative than functional. I've only worn it a few times, and it's never been in the water. "When I packed my suitcase, I wasn't really expecting to go to the beach."

The tip of her tongue skims across her top teeth as she continues to regard me. She's seen me completely naked, but that was in her darkened bedroom. I feel like there's a spotlight on me now. "I like it."

I unfasten a button and work my linen shorts past my hips. "How's the water?" I ask.

"Freezing. But Amelia doesn't seem to mind."

I can feel her continued gaze as I strip down to my bikini bottoms. "You guys go to the beach a lot, huh?"

"Almost every day in summer," she confirms. "Amelia plays in the water, and I read until it's time to head back into town for a quick rinse before my shift at the bar."

I sit beside her on the blanket and rub my arms. It's not cold, but I'm not sure what to do with my hands.

She digs into a canvas bag beside her and pulls out a sandwich wrapped in a plastic bag. "Eat," she orders, shoving the food in my direction. "It's peanut butter and jelly."

"Such a mom," I tease, but I gladly take it. My stomach reminds me that I worked straight through lunch, afraid that if I took a break

I might lose my writing momentum.

Seagulls squawk around us, annoyed that I won't share my sandwich. I'm not a rookie though—I know what'll happen if I give up even a crust. I catch myself happily humming around each bite.

"You're in a good mood," Charlotte observes.

"I had a really good writing day," I admit.

A small smile, full of wisdom and mirth plays on her lips. "I wonder what has you feeling so inspired?"

"I think you probably know."

I lean across the blanket to steal a kiss. Her lips are warm and slightly salty. It's an instinctive action, one that I don't toss around in my head for too long and risk the moment passing. She presses her lips back against mine, but I realize, too late, that she might not be so comfortable kissing me out in the open. We're fairly isolated on the long shorelines of Lake Superior with few prying eyes beyond a scattering of tourists, but there's still Amelia to consider.

"What did you write about?" she asks.

"It's a secret," I smile around my mouthful of sandwich.

"Do I get to read it?"

"Maybe, but not until it's finished. I don't let anyone read rough drafts, not even my agent, Claire."

She whistles under her breath. "You actually have one of those?"

"I'm not important enough to really need one," I shrug, "but she gives me a great deal because we've been friends since college."

"Where did you go to school?" she asks.

"U of M. Same as you."

"Really? I'm surprised."

"And then I went to San Francisco State to get my MFA."

"I wonder if I'd like California," she muses aloud. "I've never been anywhere. I thought Minneapolis was the big city when I was in college. And before I could do any real traveling, Amelia happened."

"They're just cities. Tall buildings. Honking cars." I grab a fist full of sand and let the gritty material slide through my fingers. "There's nothing like this in LA."

"I thought southern California was lousy with beaches?"

I hazard a glance in her direction. "Maybe I was talking about you."

She gives me a shrewd look in return. "I'm almost convinced."

"Of what?"

"That you're a writer."

"Mommy!" Amelia bellows from the lake. She scoops water into her hands and splashes it around. "Come into the water!"

"In a little while, sweetie," Charlotte calls back.

"She's a great kid," I remark in earnest. "You did a good job with that one."

"You think so?" She holds her hand up to her forehead like a visor to block out the high afternoon sun as she watches Amelia on the pebbled shoreline. "I worry about her sometimes."

"Don't all parents worry? Isn't that your job?"

"I suppose so," she frowns, still staring. "But the unorthodox outfits and Reggie are just the tip of the iceberg. I would never want to squash her creativity, but it can be so hard in this town if you're different."

I make a humming noise. "Preaching to the choir."

She shifts on the beach blanket and regards me again. "When did you know you were gay?"

"Not until college, actually. But when I finally figured it out, a lot about my childhood suddenly made sense. I thought every straight girl had the same thoughts and feelings as I did, but it turns out there's a reason why I never had a boyfriend that lasted longer than a weekend and why I held doors open for my girl friends."

"Last night," I begin with trepidation. "What was that? Curiosity? Boredom?"

She licks her lips. "Attraction?"

I swallow down the last mouthful of my sandwich with difficulty. "Has that ever happened before?"

"A few times," she admits. "But I never acted on it."

"Why now? Why me?"

Her eyes narrow as she continues to contemplate me and my question. The moment is interrupted by a high-pitched squeal and the sensation of cold water dipping on my face and legs.

"Mommy!" Amelia's grown impatient and has abandoned the lake and returned to the beach blanket. Sand clings to her ankles and Lake Superior drips from her hair. "Are you coming in the water?" she asks.

Charlotte smiles at me. "You game?" she challenges.

I scramble to my feet. "Last one in's a rotten egg."

When the sun has dipped a little lower in the sky, I walk Charlotte to her car and help her load their beach bags into the back of her vehicle. Amelia is big enough to not need a car seat, but she still sits in the backseat with her Invisible Friend. Through the car windows I see her help Reggie with his seatbelt.

Charlotte lingers near the driver side door. "What are you up to tonight?" she asks.

I shove my hands into the front pockets of my linen shorts. "No plans yet."

"I have to work tonight, but do you want to come over after I close the bar?"

I don't have time to consider the question before she's second guessing herself.

"I'm being clingy, aren't I?" she vocalizes. "One night in my bed and I'm already expecting another. And I don't even know what this is—this thing we're doing." She's getting more agitated the longer she talks. "And it's not like you're sticking around town for much longer."

"Hey, relax." I snatch the hand that's nervously raking through her wind-tussled hair. My free arm curls around her waist, and she doesn't resist when I pull her close until I feel the press of her hipbones against me. "This doesn't have to be anything if you don't want it to be." My lips brush against her temple. "Whatever you want to do though, I'm game."

Her top teeth dig into her bottom lip. "I don't know what I want, Abby. But these past few days have been fun. Is it selfish of me to want to keep having fun?"

I shake my head. She's not the selfish one. That's me.

CHAPTER NINE

A few feet down the shoreline on my dad's property is a fire pit that Emily and I constructed when I was eight or nine. We'd spent the summer day collecting fist-sized rocks and arranging them in a neat little circle. When my dad had gotten home from work that day, we couldn't wait to show him what we'd made. His enthusiasm had paled in comparison to our own, and I remember going to bed that night feeling disappointed that our hard work had gone under appreciation. The next morning, I went down to the beach, determined to cast each rock back into the lake, only to discover that the rocks had been mortared together. My dad never spoke of what must have taken him hours to complete and neither did we. He wasn't an openly demonstrative man, but he showed his love for us in quiet, yet profound ways.

"I can't believe that thing is still together."

I look away from the bonfire to see the shadowy silhouette of my sister. The tide is high and waves crash noisily against the normally subdued shoreline.

"I brought you a blanket," she says. "I thought maybe California living had thinned your blood." Even though Emily is younger than me, in many ways she behaves like she's the older sister. It had always been like that though. Even when she was young she'd been an old lady, cautious and conservative.

I turn my eyes back to the crackling fire. "Mark Twain said once that the coldest winter he'd ever spent was summer in San Francisco."

Emily sits down on a log across the fire from me. "I thought he didn't really say that."

"He didn't."

"Speaking of Twain, how's the writing going?"

I pick up a short stick and begin poking at the burning fire. Ashes shoot into the sky. "It's laborious and disheartening and makes me wonder why I ever thought I could do this for a living."

"You'll figure it out."

I stare at the orange-red glow of the embers deep in the fire. "As much as I thought I was coming back to help you, I think I needed this trip home for myself," I speak aloud.

"How so?"

"Don't you ever need to stop and re-evaluate everything you've been doing? Kind of like an out-of-body experience where you can be reflective about life choices."

"Everything seems to have worked out for you though," Emily remarks with no malice. "You've made a career doing what you love. I know I've probably given you a hard time about it over the years, but it was probably just jealousy."

"Jealous? Of me?"

"Sure. Why not? You might have done the risky thing by deciding to become a fulltime playwright, but what do I have to show for years of being cautious and practical? A job in Duluth, Minnesota that I couldn't care less about."

"You had love though. That's a lot better than me."

"Whatever," she readily dismisses. "You've dated plenty."

"That's the key word: *plenty*. I've got numbers on my side, but no great love story. No one of substance in my life."

"This girl you're with right now—Kambria, right? You don't think she's *The One*?"

"No."

"Wow. No hesitation," she remarks, eyebrows rising to her hairline. "So if she's not *The One*, then why are you still together?"

"Because I'm terrified of being alone?"

"That's terrible, Abby," she clucks.

"I know," I say with a grimace.

"That's not fair to either of you if you're just biding your time until something or someone better comes along."

"I know. And I plan on doing something about it as soon as I go back," I vow.

"Which is when?" she asks. "You haven't said."

"I'm not sure. I haven't booked my return ticket yet."

"Are you procrastinating going back because you don't want to face Kambria?"

"No. Maybe. I don't know." I breathe out a great sigh. "I thought I was sticking around for some noble reason, like you needing me. But now I don't know."

"We're Henry's," she says, staring deep into the fire. "We're survivors."

"Yeah, and we also bottle up emotions and let them fester instead of letting them breathe," I counter.

"That might be true. But I'm doing the best I know how."

"Has Dad dated anyone since Mom?" I ask.

"I don't know why you still refer to her as that," Emily says sharply. "What kind of mom abandons her husband and two small children?"

"Fine," I back peddle. "Has he dated anyone since *Linda* left?"

"Not that I know of."

I pull my phone out and type in the security code to unlock the first screen.

"Can we have a civilized conversation without you playing on your phone?" Emily says in an annoyed tone. "I'm trying to open up to you."

"Hold up. There's something I have to do."

"What can't wait?"

"Breaking up with my girlfriend."

"Right now?" Emily squeaks. "Over the phone?"

"You were right," I say, pulling up Kambria's number. "It's not fair to either of us to keep dragging this out."

The phone rings and like so many times before, Kambria doesn't pick up. When her recorded message finishes, I leave a message of my own:

"Hey, it's me. Listen, I've been trying to get a hold of you for days now; it's like you've dropped off the planet. It's pretty annoying, especially since I'm here for a funeral and you haven't once called to see how I am. Anyway," I say before I can become too tangential, "I'm calling to tell you that this relationship isn't working out—I can't do this anymore. When you get this, I don't know, call me or don't. I guess it doesn't matter anymore."

It's imperfect, and I owe her more than a voicemail, but I feel lighter once I've done it. I would have preferred talking to her face to face, but it's the best I can do under my current circumstances.

Emily is still staring at me when I hang up the phone. "What?" I ask, feeling self-conscious.

She shakes her head. I'm sure she has a lecture for me, but for now, she keeps it to herself and we continue to sit and stare at the fire in silence.

After we've piled a few more logs onto the fire, my phone rings. My heart leaps in my chest, thinking it might be Kambria, finally calling me after getting this most recent voice mail. But it's an unknown number with a Grand Marais area code.

"Hello?" I answer.

"Hey," the voice on the other end greets. "It's Charlotte."

"From the bar." I smile into the phone. "I remember."

"I, um, I'm all done with work now." There's slight hesitation in her voice. "I'm leaving for home in a few minutes."

"Still feel like company?" I ask.

"I wouldn't say no."

We hang up, and I stand from the fire. "You gonna stay down here or should I bury the fire?"

Emily looks up after me. "Where are you going?"

"To Charlotte's house."

"At this hour?"

I glance at the time on my phone. It's a little after midnight. "I guess I am."

For the second time that night I see my sister's cheeks hollow as she holds back her judgment. Her glare moves away from me to regard the slowly dying fire.

Standing on Charlotte's front porch half an hour later, I feel underprepared. I should have picked a bouquet of wild flowers in my dad's yard or brought her a book or something. After I knock quietly on her front door, I also realize that I reek of campfire smoke. Before I can scurry away, however, the door opens. Charlotte smiles at me through the screen door.

"Hey," I greet. I point to the flickering light bulb above me.

"Your light's still broken."

"Are you offering to fix it for me?"

"My dad's the handyman, not me."

"I thought all lesbians owned tool belts."

"Don't rat me out," I smile. "They'll kick me out of the club."

Her lips twist into a smirk. "Are you coming in or are you gonna stand on the front stoop all night?"

"Definitely coming in."

It's only been a handful of hours since I saw her at the beach, but it feels like much longer. She's changed out of her work clothes and into jeans and a t-shirt.

I slide out of my shoes and leave them by the front door. "Did your mom leave already?" I ask, looking around the seemingly empty living room.

"Uh huh."

I breathe a little easier. "I'm sure she's great, but I'm kind of relieved to have escaped the Evil Eye two nights in a row."

"I owe my parents a great debt," she defends. "They basically raised Amelia after her dad and I split. I was too messed up to be a decent person, let alone a decent parent."

"What happened with you and Amelia's dad? If you don't mind me asking," I qualify.

She shakes her head. "I'd rather not talk about it. Have you eaten?" she asks, redirecting our conversation. "Are you hungry? Can I get you something to drink?"

"How about you stop being a waitress for a minute and just hang out with me?" I propose.

"Old habits," she smiles sheepishly.

"I don't mind the hospitality," I clarify, "but you clocked out for the night already. Let's just enjoy each other's company."

"I think I can handle that."

The TV is on in the living room with the volume turned low. A few table lamps brighten the room, but just enough. There's a homemade afghan flung over the back of the couch.

Charlotte grabs the remote off the coffee table and flips through a few channels. "Do you want to watch a movie or something?"

I place my hands over hers and gently pry the remote out of her hands. "You seem ... a little nervous." I observe. It's a stark difference from the confident, aggressive woman who had me in her bed the previous night.

I lean forward and cup one hand against the side of her face. Her eyelashes flutter at the touch. I draw her in, slowly, sweetly, cupping my hands on either side of her face. I press my mouth to hers for a soft kiss. Her breath tastes fresh and minty like she brushed her teeth moments before I arrived.

I kiss her again, this time capturing her lower lip and nipping at it with my teeth. Her tongue slides against mine and she makes a quiet, approving noise in my mouth.

"Is that better?" I ask, pulling away.

"Mmhm," she murmurs, eyes still closed. Her smile relaxes and so does the rest of her body. "Sorry if I'm being weird. I guess I didn't know what it would be like, seeing you a second time."

"I feel like I need a shower," I say, picking at my hair. "Emily and I were having a bonfire when you called."

"I hope I wasn't interrupting."

"No. You actually had perfect timing. I don't know how Emily and I ever lived under the same roof for so long."

"Ahh, yes." She nods sagely. "Siblings. No matter how old we are or how much time has passed, whenever my brother Max and I are around each other, we revert to children."

"And the walls are starting to close in on me," I add. "I know I should be around my dad's house more, but there's only so much of my family I can take."

Charlotte's features take on a pinched look. "I'm trying to remember your mom. I'm at your dad's store all the time. What does she do?"

"Besides run away?" When Charlotte looks even more confused, I elaborate: "She took off when I was really little. Left a note saying this life was too small for her."

"I'm sorry, Abby."

"Like mother, like daughter," I mumble.

"What do you mean?"

"She left Grand Marais because she wanted more than small-town life had to offer. I guess you could say the same about me."

"Almost everyone wants that for themselves, Abby. It's why we leave town to go to college."

"*You* came back," I point out.

"I didn't have much of a choice. I had a newborn and my

boyfriend was an abusive tyrant. Coming back to Grand Marais probably saved my life."

I discover I'm digging my fingernails into my palms. "He-he hurt you?" The thought makes me ill.

"Physically, no. He never laid a hand on me. But I don't know how many times I heard how stupid and inadequate I was. After swallowing down so many hurtful words all the time, you start to accept them as your truth."

I don't have words. I clench and unclench my jaw.

"I got pregnant my senior year of college. I lost my athletic scholarship because of it, but my parents had a little money saved away for a rainy day, and it was pouring." She shakes her head a little sadly. "Amelia's dad wanted to get his MBA, but we didn't have the money to pay for baby formula let alone graduate school. I think he resented us for cutting short his grand life plans."

"You're really amazing, Charlotte. Beautiful *and* resilient."

"It's not a big deal," she brushes off.

"No, really. I don't know what I would have done in your position. I don't think I've ever had any real life trial or struggle. Everything has always come easy for me."

"We're only dished out what we can handle."

"Are you not very good at taking compliments?" I lightly tease.

"They're just words. I'm a bigger advocate for action."

"As a writer, I'm going to have to respectfully disagree. Words have amazing power."

"Oh, I don't disagree with you. Empty promises, assurances that have no follow through—they all have the power to hurt."

I hollow out my cheeks, unsure of how to respond to such serious words.

"You're not a bad person for leaving Grand Marais, Abby," she says. "Your mom though, no offense, but what a bitch."

"Can't argue with that logic."

There's a hole in the knee of her jeans, and I absentmindedly play with the frayed material. Beneath the jeans is bronzed skin that my fingers skim over.

"I really like this," I think aloud. "You and me getting to talk with no outside distractions. Like really talk. About things that matter. I can't remember the last time I had a serious conversation."

She makes a humming sound. "It's strange. I'm normally not a big sharer. Especially not about this kind of stuff."

"With someone you've only known a week," I add.

"Technically we've known each other all of our lives," she points out.

I continue to stroke her knee. "Just not like this."

"No," she agrees. "Not like this."

It's a long time between eye blinks. When I shut my eyes, a replay of the local nightly news is on. The next time I open them, the closing credits of a rerun of *Saturday Night Live* are scrolling down the TV screen. I'm acutely aware that I'm leaning heavily on another body.

The fingers stroking my hair come to a stop. "And you're back," Charlotte quietly murmurs.

I gingerly sit up on the couch. My neck is sore from sleeping at an awkward angle. "Geez, sorry. I didn't mean to fall asleep on you—like literally *on* you."

"It's okay. You're cute when you sleep," she remarks. "Even with all that drooling."

I hastily wipe the back of my hand across my face, but there's nothing there. "You're mean," I say, sticking out my tongue.

"Even Amelia doesn't stick out her tongue anymore."

"You must bring out the best in me," I quip. I don't know what time it is, but I know it's got to be late. "I should probably go."

"I'm not kicking you out."

"I know. But I don't want to wear out my welcome."

She's silent for a long moment as if she's trying to decipher the real reason I'm taking off instead of spending the night with her again. "This happened fast."

"It did," I confirm.

"And I know you have no intention of staying in Grand Marais."

I shake my head.

"Then why do you have to go tonight?"

"I'm just trying to do the right thing." That's the truth, but she still doesn't know about Kambria, which the more time we spend together, the more heavily I'm burdened with unresolved guilt.

"I'm a big girl," she says. "Why don't you let me worry about myself?"

I don't have the willpower to deny her.

I don't want to think about the fact that I'm going back to Los Angeles in the immediate future. The knowledge is too heavy and complicated and that's the last thing I want to think about right now. All I want to fill my eyes and brain with is the vision of Charlotte's perfect breasts and how well they fit in the palms of my hands.

I tug lightly on her hair to direct her where I need her most. "God, right there," I quietly pant when the up and down movement of her tongue makes my eyes roll backwards. "That's so fucking good. Don't stop."

She lifts her head and does the very thing I begged her not to do. She stops.

"Why did you do that?"

Her face is serious. "You said to stop."

"No I didn't. I said *don't* stop."

She rests her hands on my inner thighs and squeezes. "You should speak a little more clearly."

"I would, but I'm afraid of a six year old hearing us and walking in."

"Maybe Amelia could have a sleepover at Grandma and Grandpa's tomorrow night," she proposes.

A frustrated, pained whimper reaches my ears and it's a moment before I realize the noise came from me. "That doesn't help me out right now," I can't help but pout.

I reach out and twist a long, blonde tendril around my finger. "Are you sure you've never done this before?"

"I'm sure," she answers me. Delicate kisses are placed on the soft inner flesh of my inner thighs. "But I've had enough practice on myself."

The imagery of Charlotte on her back, legs splayed open, fingers running through sweet folds and arching into her own touch flashes through my head. It's a curse to be so visual sometimes.

It's late, and I'm sure she's exhausted from a long day of being a single mom and a bartender, but her body doesn't surrender to sleep until we're both fully sated. It's like she's found water after wandering the desert for years and can't get her fill. I know because I feel that way, too.

+ + +

I've found paradise within the four walls of Charlotte's bedroom. A long, naked limb peeks out from beneath the white cotton sheets of the bed. The furniture and wall decorations are sparse. There's no TV or computer; the only real technology in the room is a digital alarm clock and the cell phone in the back pocket of my jeans. The entire room is filled with sunshine, but nothing is more golden than Charlotte's hair or brighter than her sleepy smile.

"Good morning," I murmur. I stretch my arms above my head. I've had only a handful of hours of sleep over the past few nights, but I feel amazingly rested and relaxed.

"Morning," she returns.

Her long hair is tussled, and the combination of sex and a humid night has caused her hair to curl even more. I reach out to tame a particularly wild flyaway near her temple. "Now I see where Amelia gets her hair."

She makes a humming noise. "The magic of hair products."

I slip the baby fine hair over the pads of my fingers. "It's like corn silk," I think aloud. "Or cotton candy."

"Hungry?" she teases.

"A little," I admit.

She sits up in bed and the covers slide down her tan, naked form. She pulls them tight around her chest before they reveal any more. It's cliché, but I think the sight of a naked woman beneath crisp, white bed sheets is the most beautiful view in the world.

"I feel cheated."

Her words cause my throat to constrict, and the languid feeling of slowly rousing from sleep is replaced with dread. Somehow, she knows.

"You what?"

"Two sleepover parties, and no one's braided my hair or painted my toenails," she smiles.

I relax into the pillow. "What time do you have to be at the bar today?" I ask. My hand fits snug among her long fingers—fingers that only hours ago were exploring my body with dedicated curiosity.

"The late shift again."

"Think I can take you out before then?"

"Depends."

"On?"

"I've got a kid."

"I haven't forgotten. I was hoping the three of us could spend the day together."

Charlotte chews on her lower lip. It's clear neither of us have really thought much beyond what would happen when we woke up. A one-night stand can be written off. But two? She's got Amelia, and I've got ... my own stuff.

"I've got some errands this morning, and later on—"

"No, it's okay," I interrupt, suddenly embarrassed by my suggestion. "I get it."

I slide out of bed and begin to pull on my clothes from the previous day. They smell like campfire smoke, but it's all I've got.

"I would, Abby," she apologizes from bed. "But Amelia—"

"It's okay," I cut her off again. "I'll see you later."

CHAPTER TEN

"Anthony."

Mindful of the time difference, I wait for a respectable hour to call my friend in the morning.

"Well, hello, Miss Abby," he greets after a long yawn. "Long time no chat. How are things in the land of lumberjacks and lesbians?"

"I need some advice," I tell him.

"You've come to the right place." His voice instantly sounds more alert. "What can Miss Fabulous help you with, child?"

Miss Fabulous is Anthony's alias when he's performing in drag. She's a little bit hip-hop, a little bit beauty pageant, and all sass.

"If a person breaks up with someone over voicemail, but they never respond to the message, are you really broken up?"

"Is this one of those trees falling in the forest kind of hypothetical questions? Or is this a page taken from your disastrous dating life?"

I groan into the phone.

"What's going on, sugar?" Anthony presses.

"I broke up with Kambria in a voicemail, and I haven't heard from her, so I don't know if she got it, which means I don't know if we're really broken up."

"Number one, I can't believe you'd break up with someone in a voicemail. I thought you were better than that."

"I know. It was totally juvenile," I agree.

"And why are you so anxious to be suddenly single? Don't tell me you've already found your next girlfriend in the land of milk and cheese," he laughs.

"That's Wisconsin."

"Same difference. Don't ignore the question."

"There's-there's a girl," I admit with some hesitation.

"You dog!" Anthony practically squeals. "You're worse than me!"

I tap my phone against my forehead a few times.

"I want all the dirty details," Anthony prods. "Ooh, where's my popcorn?"

"Her name is Charlotte." Simply saying her name aloud twists my stomach into knots. "She's funny and charismatic and so incredibly sexy. Like, I never want to stop looking at her."

"Is she smart?"

Anthony knows my biggest issue with Kambria is that beyond the beautiful exterior, there isn't much substance. I've complained to him more than once about it.

"She's really smart," I confirm. "She reads all the time, but it's not like a nerdy, introverted thing. She's actually kind of sneaky smart, like you wouldn't expect it."

"And does Miss Perfect like you, too?"

"Well, we had sex."

Anthony gasps. "Was this before or after you broke up with your girlfriend in a voicemail?"

"In between?" I grimace at my answer.

"So you cheated on Kambria, broke up with her over the phone, and then had guilt-free sex?"

I run my hand over my face. "I guess so."

"I'm so mad that I'm just hearing about this now."

"I'm sorry. I've been a little wrapped up with all of this."

"I understand. So you totally like this girl, she likes you back, and you're single through the help of technology. So what's the problem?"

"Well, there's obviously the distance thing. I don't know what's going to happen when I come back to Los Angeles."

"What do you want to happen?"

"Long distance sucks. And I don't even know if she'd be into it."

"Forget about geography. That's a paltry detail. What else is there to worry about?"

"She's got a kid. Her name is Amelia. She's six and she's got an imaginary friend named Reggie."

"Single mom? Oh, honey. You really know how to pick 'em. Be

careful," he warns. "You can't casually date single moms. There's a whole different rule book for those ladies."

"Do I tell her about Kambria?" I worry aloud.

"She didn't know?"

"No. I didn't say anything about having a girlfriend."

Anthony whistles, long and low. "That's messy."

"You're telling me," I grunt. "What do I do?"

"If you like this girl—like if you see a future where she and you are a thing—you tell her the truth. The complete truth and nothing but the truth. If it's just a summer fling though, you'd still better make sure the two of you are on the same page."

"I was afraid you'd say that."

"You know what you have to do, Abby. So go do it."

"Yes, ma'am," I sluggishly concur.

"Take care, girl. Miss your face."

"I miss you, too, Anthony."

I'm only back at my dad's house for a few hours before I'm feeling antsy and in need of a reprieve from my family. "I'm going for a drive," I announce. I grab my key ring from a glass bowl on a cabinet near the entryway.

I've always enjoyed driving. Growing up in a remote part of the country required a road trip for just about everything. Driving without congested traffic was not an option first in San Francisco and now in Los Angeles, however. I drive around Grand Marais and the surrounding area seeking clarity. I drive for hours without destination, ruminating about the future and listening to country music on the radio. The sun is warm, and I've got no place to be.

I like Charlotte. A lot—certainly more than I should after such a brief time. It's more than a passing fancy or one of my stupid crushes. But I know my *modus operandi*; everything new is shiny and more desirable than what's familiar and comfortable. But that's what makes Charlotte so intriguing. She's new *and* familiar at the same time. I want to discover everything about her, and yet she's as comfortable as a favorite pair of jeans. It's a troublesome combination, and I don't know how to proceed with her. I'm going back to Los Angeles at some point—that's where my friends and career reside—and she'll remain in Grand Marais. And I don't know what that means for us.

We haven't talked much about this thing we've been doing. She says she's having fun, and I'm inclined to agree. But I do know that I need to be transparent before anyone gets hurt. I need to tell Charlotte about Kambria.

My travels bring me out to the school where I attended kindergarten through high school. It's a long, ranch-style building that had been dropped in the middle of an open plot of land sometime in the 1960s. The parking lot is filled despite it being summer due to a baseball game being played on the field behind the school.

I park my car and walk up to the field. The intermittent cheers grow louder as I approach. My fingers curl around the chain length fence that protects fans from foul balls. I don't know any of the kids playing, but there's something familiar and comforting about the unchanged baseball field and the sports uniforms. I remember the polyester outfits from my own years playing summer youth softball. I have a suspicion that they're the very same jerseys I wore more than twenty years ago. Same grey stretch pants. Same yellow and black jerseys with the word "Angels" screen-printed across the chest. When I had been on the team, someone had misspelled the team's name to be "Angles." I'm happy to see nothing but yellow Angels now clumsily fielding their respective positions.

Someone in the bleachers whistles. It's loud and shrill like a wolf whistle. My head turns away from the playing field to appraise the culprit, only to discover that it's Charlotte. Our eyes meet, and I quickly take mental inventory of myself. She doesn't wave, but she smiles, which is enough to make my stomach do flip-flops. I touch my hand to my hair. I've been driving around for hours with the sun roof open, and my hair is probably wilder than a banshee's. She's seen me though, so I can't very well run away.

I climb up the bleachers to where she sits.

"Should I be worried about having a stalker?" she casually remarks when I take the vacant space beside her.

"I was just driving around, and I saw the game," I explain. "What's your excuse?"

She nods toward the field. "I've actually got a kid playing."

Amelia's a tiny yellow dot in right field, surrounded by dandelions the same color as her jersey. Her unruly blonde hair has been contained at least for the moment beneath a black baseball cap.

Someone makes the final out of the inning, and the parents sitting around us politely clap as the fielders change positions from defense to offense. Amelia jogs into the dugout with the rest of her teammates.

"You got her out of the rain boots," I observe.

"Small victories," Charlotte smiles. "I pointed out to her that she'd run faster with proper cleats on. My girl might be weird, but she's also fiercely competitive."

Amelia wobbles up to home plate wielding a metal bat that probably weighs as much as she does. There are black streaks beneath her eyes like a football player.

"Your daughter also looks pretty fierce," I say with a chuckle.

"It's the only eyeliner she gets to wear until she's in high school."

"What are the rules?" I ask.

Charlotte watches the playing field. "Three strikes and you're out."

"Wow," I remark. "Even at this age?"

"We're not raising entitled misfits who get participation trophies just for showing up."

"Tell me how you really feel," I laugh.

The coach on the augmented pitching mound softly tosses the ball towards home plate. Amelia takes a mighty swing, but misses.

"Choke up, sweetie," Charlotte calls from the stands.

Miniature hands move up the handle of the baseball bat. She swings a second time, but the pitch is too high, and she swings underneath it.

"Keep your eye on the ball, Amelia. You've got this," her mother calls.

Amelia's cleated feet dig deeper into the batter's box and her tongue pokes out the side of her mouth. On her third swing, she connects. The aluminum bat sings as the ball hits the barrel of the bat. The ball doesn't travel very far, but it stays fair, and Amelia takes off for first base. The entire stands come alive, everyone cheering Amelia on or the players trying to field the ball.

The fielding player is a young boy, maybe seven or eight years old who throws a wobbly ball to first base only seconds before Amelia's foot stomps on the bag.

"Out," the home plate umpire shouts. There's a combination of applause and groans from the people in the stands.

"Should I go slash his tires?" I mumble out of the side of my mouth.

"I think the ump rides a bicycle," Charlotte returns with a smile.

Amelia trots back to her team's dugout.

Charlotte claps her hands and calls out words of encouragement. "Good job, Amelia. Nice try."

So hot.

"You and I might have differing opinions about what's attractive," she murmurs for my ears only.

I feel the heat of embarrassment on my cheeks. I hadn't intended to speak out loud. I stare at Charlotte's hand, innocently set on the metal bleacher. I ache to grab her hand and pull it on my lap—to sit with her relaxed and familiar, not rigid and uncomfortable.

"I know," I hear her say.

I snap my eyes away from her hand. "You know what?" I ask, throat tightening.

"It's killing me not to touch you, too." She reaches over and gives my fingers a quick squeeze before returning her hands to her lap. "Follow me," she commands.

I look up after her when she stands up from the metal risers. She straightens her long legs and picks her way through the other Little League parents. When she reaches the grass, her hands go to her hips and she stares up expectantly at me in the bleachers.

I hop up as well, and with a little less finesse, I make my way down the bleachers, mumbling my apologies each time I nearly trip over someone. Before I can even reach the ground, Charlotte is already stalking off away from the baseball field. I hazard one fleeting glance in the direction of the field where Amelia's team is playing before following in the direction where Charlotte headed.

I somehow manage to lose her somewhere between the bleachers and the grassy alleyway I currently find myself in. The recreational park isn't very large and most everyone is gathered around the two adjacent baseball fields.

"Charlotte?" I quietly call out.

"In here." Her head pokes out of a large metal shed before disappearing again.

I tentatively follow, not sure what I'm getting myself into.

The large tool shed is filled with smaller, compartmentalized metal cages. The cement slab beneath my feet is cold and damp, and the air smells musty. Charlotte stands in the middle of the shed, wringing her hands in front of her.

"What is this place?" I ask.

"It's where they store the summer baseball equipment," she explains. "I used to smoke in here during high school track practice. I picked up a lot of nasty habits in high school." Her rounded shoulders rise and fall. "I've straightened my life out a lot since then."

"Interesting choice of words," I remark. "Luckily for me not everything in your life is so straight."

Her lips quirk into a knowing grin. "Yeah. Lucky you." Her hands slide roughly beneath the bottom hem of my t-shirt, forcing me to suck in a sharp breath when short nails rake down my abdomen.

"I'm sorry about this morning," she starts.

"You don't have to apologize," I insist.

"No, I do. You didn't do anything wrong. I'm the one who made the moves on you, and then I made it weird this morning when you were only being kind."

She kisses me then, and I'm left breathless from the force of it. My hands clutch tightly to her waist and slip down to her hips. I pull her against me and we simultaneously groan when our centers connect. It feels very much like high school, slipping away to make out on school property, fumbling over and under the other person's clothes.

"I have to get back soon," she says, teeth tugging on my earlobe. "Amelia gets to play first base after the sixth inning."

"And we've barely gotten to second."

"Tonight," she promises as she pulls away from me. She fixes the bottom of my tank top and flattens the material over my abdomen. "Tonight, I'm predicting a grand slam."

+ + +

I can tell Charlotte's in a good mood. The music playing on the jukebox is loud and she's half-dancing, half-walking behind the bar, making sure everyone's drinks are topped off. Her tank top shows off round, bronzed shoulders, and her backside looks utterly squeezable in the tight jeans she wears. It takes an admirable amount of willpower on my part not to jump behind the bar and have my way with her in front of half the town's drinking population. It also makes my decision to tell her about Kambria difficult, but even more prudent. I can't anticipate how she'll take the news, but I've been weak-willed and selfish for too long. That stops tonight.

I'm perched on my usual bar top making conversation with Old Tom. I buy him a soda with lime and he tells me his philosophy on life. Charlotte drops by when she's not serving other customers and we share private, knowing grins.

"You're awfully important," Tom remarks.

"Huh?" I've been staring at Charlotte again and don't know what he's talking about.

"Your phone keeps lighting up." He nods to the cell phone on the bar top that I've been ignoring all night.

My phone is set to silent so I haven't noticed the missed calls from my sister. I should probably call her back, but if it had been an emergency, she would have at least left a voicemail.

Warm hands clasp around my head to cover my eyes, and my phone goes out of view. "Guess who?" a familiar voice says.

The bottom drops out of my stomach. *Oh no.* This is not going to end well.

The hands fall away, and I turn around slowly on the barstool. "You … I…" I shake my head, hoping it will rattle my brain back into commission, hoping I might wake up from this soon-to-be nightmare. "What are you doing here?"

Kambria is beaming at me. "I missed you, silly."

I say the first words that come to my mind: "I've been trying to get a hold of you for over a week."

"I lost my phone." She sticks out her lower lip. "It's probably spare parts by now or lodged between the cushions of a booth at some club never to be seen again."

She lost her phone. That would explain why her phone has recently gone from ringing without answer to her voicemail immediately picking up. The battery was dead.

I swallow hard. "So you didn't get any of my messages?"

She shakes her head. "No. Why?"

I hear someone clear her throat. Charlotte stands behind the bar with a peculiar smile planted on her face. "Who's your friend, Abby?"

"Oh, uh …"

Kambria sticks out an eager hand before I can utter more than a few unintelligible syllables. "Hi, I'm Kambria." They shake hands across the bar. "I'm Abigail's girlfriend."

The handshake abruptly ends, and I make an involuntary noise.

Kambria frowns at our reaction. "I'm sorry. Did I just Out you to the bartender? I thought everyone in your hometown knew."

Charlotte's hazel eyes are trained on me. I don't like how it feels—like a bug under a magnifying glass. I'm sure I'm going to combust into flames. "No, you're fine," she says. "Everyone knows."

I grab Kambria's elbow and gently try to pull her away from the bar. "We should be going." With my free hand, I dig money out of my back pocket and toss the bill on the bar.

Charlotte pins the twenty-dollar bill to the bar top and slides the crumpled money back in my direction. "Your money's no good here." Her tone and face are unreadable.

I clear my throat uncomfortably. "No, I insist," I say as I start to push the money back towards her.

Charlotte clamps her hand around my wrist, and I expect the worst. "No," she says slowly and also noticeably chillier. "*I* insist. In fact, let me buy both of you a drink."

"Oh, that's so sweet," Kambria coos beside me. "I love American small town hospitality."

She doesn't know Charlotte, and she doesn't know the sound of her voice. She doesn't know that I'm seconds away from being crushed like a bug. Charlotte still hasn't let go of my wrist. I'm afraid to move or even to protest the free alcohol. She isn't hurting me; she just continues to hold me in place as if she knows the moment she lets go I'll scamper away, proverbial tail between my legs.

"Kambria was it?" Charlotte asks.

Her head bounces affirmatively like a bobble doll.

Charlotte finally releases me. "Sit down, Abby," she says, making purposeful eye contact. She uses what I can only describe as a Mom-tone, even though I don't remember much of my own mother. She pulls another Labatt from the cooler and sets it in front of me.

"What can I get you to drink, hun?" she asks in Kambria's direction.

Kambria bellies up to the bar and perches on an empty stool beside me. "What do you have for white wines?"

"I've got a chardonnay and a pinot grigio."

"I'll try the pinot."

Charlotte fills the drink order, pouring a generous serving of white wine, and sets the long-stemmed glass in front of Kambria. "Your accent—South African?" she guesses.

Kambria practically squeals in delight. "Most people don't guess that. This one," she says, playfully nudging me in the ribs, "thought I was Australian when we first met."

I try to smile, but I know it probably looks like a grimace. I desperately need to get Kambria out of here.

"How long ago was that?" Charlotte grabs an empty beer bottle and tosses it into the recycling bin behind the bar with enough force that I can hear the glass shatter.

Kambria sets a pink-painted fingernail to her mouth in thought. "About five months now, I think. Boy, time flies, huh?"

Charlotte continues the casual conversation. "How long are you in town for?" I picture her a dangerous predator, luring Kambria into her web of hospitality and kindness before attacking us both.

"Only a few days. Unlike some people," she jerks her head in my direction, "I actually have a job and an office I need to get back to."

My hands wrap around my long-necked beer bottle like I'm strangling it. "I have a job."

"Of course you do, sweetie," Kambria replies.

I lift my head to appraise Charlotte. I can see her working the back muscles of her jaw like she's chewing on an oversized piece of gum. "Let me know if you need anything else," she says in a mumbled rush. "Welcome to Grand Marais."

She spins on her heel and walks directly for the door that leads to the kitchen.

The swinging door is still moving back and forth with Charlotte's exit when I turn to Kambria. "How did you find me?" The question sounds like dialogue from a cop drama, and in this situation, I'm the criminal on the lam.

"Your sister said you were down here. You guys don't look alike at all."

"No, we don't."

She doesn't elaborate on how she found my dad's house, but I suppose in this world of over-sharing and saturation of information, those details are readily found.

"I feel like you're not happy to see me," she frowns.

I anxiously shred the paper label on my bottle of beer and cast furtive glances in the direction of the kitchen door. Charlotte has yet to return. "I am," I weakly insist. "You surprised me, that's all."

Her hand comes to rest on my bobbing knee and she gives my leg a gentle squeeze. My leg jerks violently at the touch, and her hand is dislodged.

"I can't do that," I quietly hiss. "Not here."

"I thought you were Out."

"I am. But it's one thing to know that I'm gay and something else entirely for them to *see* me be gay."

Her bottom lip pops out. "Okay. Do you want to go?"

I hop up from the stool like my pants are on fire. "Yes."

My eyes fall to the closed door again. There's a circular window at the top, but I've seen no movement or sign of Charlotte since she disappeared into the kitchen.

Despite what Charlotte had said about buying us drinks, I leave the original twenty-dollar bill on the bar. Kambria's eyebrows scrunch together and she stares at the money, but she doesn't say anything about it. She leaves her wine glass on the bar, its contents largely untouched. My beer remains unconsumed as well, and we leave.

In the parking lot outside of the bar, the night air is insufferably humid. I don't remember it being so oppressive when I first arrived. I know Kambria is eager to get back to my dad's house, but I can't leave without trying to talk to Charlotte first.

"I have to go back," I blurt out.

Kambria turns to me. "What?"

My brain runs rampant, trying to come up with a reason why I can't leave just yet. I make a big show of patting the pockets of my pants. "I, uh, I left my keys in the bar."

"Want me to wait for you?" she asks.

"No." My reply is suspiciously quick even to my ears, and I'm sure she heard it, too. "It'll just be a second," I insist. "I'll see you back at my dad's house."

She hesitates, and for a moment I worry I've blown my cover. I'm not cut out for this double life of deception. But finally she nods and gets into her rental car. I walk back to the bar, doing my best not to look too desperate to get back inside as quickly as I can.

Inside the bar, Charlotte is still missing, and it's clear from the empty glasses and bottles stacking up on the bar top that she hasn't come back from the kitchen since I left. No one gives me a second glance when I walk behind the bar and knock on the swinging door that leads to the kitchen. There's no response from the other side, so I take a deep breath and push the door open.

The kitchen is small. The bar menu is limited and most people come for the alcohol, not for the food. There's a deep fryer and a large cooktop that produces adequate cheeseburgers and grilled cheese.

The room smells strongly of fish. Charlotte is by herself in the kitchen, breaking down the catch of the day. Scales and guts remain on the cutting board, and I eyeball the filleting knife that she wields with uncomfortable dexterity. I wonder if she's imaging slicing off my skin instead.

I clear my throat so as not to startle her.

She looks up from the butcher block, wide-eyed and wild. "What?" she demands.

I jerk my thumb towards the bar behind the closed kitchen door. "I think your patrons are getting thirsty out there."

"There's other bars in town if they don't like the wait. They're free to leave and so are you."

"Can we talk?"

"No." Her tone tells me she's in no mood to negotiate.

"Please, Charlotte."

I wince when she hacks off the head of a large fish. The knife is impressive and she wields it like an axe.

She continues to avoid eye contact as she filets the next fish. "In case you haven't noticed, I'm at work and I'm busy."

A curse word slips out and she sticks her index finger into her mouth.

I take an involuntary step forward. "Are you okay? Did you cut yourself?"

"Are you a doctor now?" Charlotte coolly asks. "Did you lie about being a writer, too?"

My arms flap uselessly at my sides. "Charlotte—"

"Go, Abby." She tucks her head into her chest and continues to butcher the fish.

When she continues to ignore me, I finally leave, heartsick and repentant.

The first floor of my dad's house is lit up when my car pulls up the long driveway. Kambria's rental is parked next to my sister's car. A feeling of foreboding sits heavily on my chest as I climb the four steps that lead to the front porch and use my house key to enter.

I hear the low murmur of voices inside. Emily and Kambria are in the living room. I don't see my dad, but it's late, so he's probably asleep. Their conversation stops when they see me in the front foyer.

"Hey," I announce my arrival.

I look between my sister and Kambria, but nothing in their faces reveals what they've been talking about. Kambria smiles at me, but Emily looks less than impressed.

"I'm going to sleep." Emily stands from the couch and tugs on the front of her plaid pajama pants. "I'm sure you two have a lot to talk about." She stares me down as she turns the corner and ascends the stairs to her upstairs bedroom.

I know exactly what Emily wants us to talk about. I haven't explicitly told her what happened between Charlotte and me, but from my spotty hours at home, I'm sure she's been able to guess.

"Your sister seems nice," Kambria remarks.

"What were you guys talking about?" I ask.

"Nothing much," Kambria shrugs. "Girl stuff." She pats the couch cushion beside her, inviting me to sit.

I continue to stand in the living room archway, my key ring clenched in my hand. I want to go back to the bar and try to talk to Charlotte again, but I know nothing will be accomplished tonight. Emotions are too raw and too fresh. "I'm really tired," I say, which isn't a lie.

"Okay." She bounces up from the couch. "Let's go to bed."

She walks past me and begins to climb the stairs. She moves around my dad's house with an uneasy familiarity. "Your bedroom is adorable," she calls over her shoulder as she mounts the staircase. "The military posters were a bit of a surprise though." When she notices I'm not following her up the stairs, she stops and turns. "You coming?"

"We're not married." My voice is devoid of all emotion. "I sleep in the den."

She blinks once. "Are you being serious?"

"My dad has rules."

"But I came all this way," she frowns. Her fingers curl lightly around the banister. "I haven't seen you in over a week."

"I'm sorry." The words are useless and empty at this point. "I'll see you in the morning."

I'm like a robot removing the cushions from the couch in the den and pulling the foldable bed out of its hatch. The mattress springs and underused metal joints of the bed frame squeak and groan. I find a set of sheets, musty smelling but serviceable. The den smells like cedar and my dad's cologne. Growing up we rarely used the room, and it had become a catchall for furniture that didn't fit elsewhere and storage space for things that in other houses would have gone in a basement.

It's a restless night. Every squeak and creak from upstairs jolts me awake, and after bar time, I wait for the phone call or the knock on the front door that never comes.

CHAPTER ELEVEN

My dad and Emily are having coffee in the kitchen when I finally roll out of bed. I've been awake for hours, but I stay in the den, procrastinating on starting the day and facing the consequences of my bad decisions. My lower back hurts from the uncomfortable pull out couch. There's a support bar down the center of the bed frame that dug into me all night. Regardless, I wouldn't have gotten much sleep. My brain was too cluttered with should haves and what ifs.

The kitchen counters are still littered with unidentifiable electronic pieces, but none of them look new, and I don't notice anything else missing from the countertop. Kambria's visit shattered the make believe life I'd been living with Charlotte, but maybe it's put a stop to Emily's appliance destruction, if only temporarily.

My dad pours coffee into a clean ceramic cup and silently passes it to me. Both he and Emily are reading the newspaper and their avoidance of the elephant in the room—namely me—is obnoxious.

"Will one of you say something?" I huff.

Emily looks over the top of the local news. "What would you like us to say?"

"I don't know—*I told you so?*"

"I've got to get to work." My dad drains the rest of his coffee and folds his portion of the newspaper.

"Really?" I practically yell.

My reaction has my dad looking wildly uncomfortable. He's never been good with excessive emotions, which is problematic when raising two girls on your own. "You girls talk," he says. "You'll figure this out."

He leaves Emily and me in the kitchen without another word. The front door opens and closes, followed by the sound of his old pickup truck's engine starting.

Emily stands and begins to clear her breakfast dishes. "We're obviously disappointed, Abby, but you're a grown up. You make your own decisions, even if they suck."

I close my eyes and pinch the bridge of my nose. "I don't know what I'm supposed to do."

"Do you still want to break up with her?" Emily asks.

I look toward the staircase and the silent second floor. Unless I wake her up, Kambria won't be awake for hours. Even without the time zone difference, she's never been an early riser. "Yes. But how? And when?"

"As shitty as it would be to break up with her right now after she's come all this way to see you, it would be even more cruel to pretend that everything is okay only to break her heart when you get back to Los Angeles."

I release a long, exhausted sigh. "I know you're right. But it's not going to be easy, regardless of when I tell her. God," I lament. "Why couldn't she have just gotten my voicemails?"

"Are you going to tell her about Charlotte?"

I regard my sister. I haven't told her the details of what's transpired between Charlotte and me these past few days. I've been more absent than usual around the house though, combined with my late-night visit, so she's probably put the pieces together. I don't mind that as much, but thinking that my dad might know is embarrassing.

"I don't know. Would you want to know?"

Emily pauses, thoughtful and reflective. "No," she decides. "I don't think I'd want to know. And I don't think it really matters; it's not like you and Charlotte have a future together."

Emily's words provoke a knee-jerk reaction. "You don't know that."

"Be reasonable, Abby. She has a kid. You don't mess around with single moms. Even I know that."

I leave Emily in the kitchen before we can start a fight and climb the stairs to the second floor. The door to my bedroom is closed. I slowly turn the handle until I hear the latch click open. The door mercifully opens without sound. One of the advantages of living in a craftsman's house is that door hinges are always well oiled and screws and nails are securely fastened.

Kambria sleeps on her stomach in my childhood bedroom. It's strange seeing her in this setting, surrounded by the material objects of my past. She doesn't belong here.

I turn to leave, but the wooden floorboards give me away.

Kambria's breathing changes and she makes a low noise. Heavy eyelashes flutter open and piercing blue eyes settle on me.

"Hey. I didn't mean to wake you. Go back to sleep," I quietly urge. "It's still early."

"Will you come to bed with me?" She pulls the covers back.

"I'm sorry. I can't. Dad's house, Dad's rules." He's gone for the day and probably wouldn't care even if he was home, but Emily's right; I can't pretend like everything is okay. I have to yank off the Band-Aid.

After I've had my breakfast.

When I come back downstairs, Emily remains seated at the kitchen island, surrounded by the broken pieces of a toaster oven and a bread maker. I can feel her eyes on me, but I head directly for the refrigerator.

"If you're looking for the milk, I used the last of it."

"I'll go get more," I offer.

Emily regards me with clear skepticism. "You're not trying to avoid someone upstairs, are you?"

"Yes, I am." I'm not going to deny it. "Before I get a lecture, I'm going to talk to her," I vow. "But she's still sleeping, so there's no need for me to be around until she gets up."

Emily shakes her head, looking displeased. "If you say so."

I leave the house with a promise to my sister that I'll be right back. I'm only supposed to be gone long enough to pick up a gallon of milk, but it's not my fault that dairy products are at the back of the grocery store and that I'm tempted to throw other things into my cart that we don't really need—at least that's the lie I tell myself as I leisurely stroll up and down each aisle of the downtown grocery store.

I'm so focused on avoiding Kambria that it never crosses my

mind that Grand Marais only has one grocery store. Everyone in the area does their food shopping here—including Charlotte Johansson.

I see her when I'm standing in front of the bakery counter. She's talking to the man who works in the meat department. Her oversized tank top nearly hides her cutoff jean shorts, and I have a sinking feeling that I might be the reason for the sunglasses she wears inside.

Amelia pushes their shopping cart, even though she can barely see over the cart's handle. She's clearly dressed herself this morning—a puffy pink skirt that looks like a ballet tutu and an orange tank top paired with her favorite green rain boots. The color combination reminds me of rainbow sherbet.

When Charlotte turns away from the bratwurst and ground chuck, I duck behind a display rack stacked high with hot dog and hamburger buns.

"Who are you hiding from?" a voice asks me. I look away from mother and daughter to see my old friend Julie staring at me. A grocery basket hangs from her arm. "Or is there an incredible sale on bread that I'm missing?"

I stand a little straighter, but I don't come out completely from behind the bread display. "Charlotte Johansson." There's no point in trying to deny what I'm doing.

When Julie scans the store, I snag her by the elbow and pull her behind the bakery rolls with me. "Don't stare," I hiss.

There's an amused smile on my friend's face. "Why are you hiding from her? Did you give a bad review of her bar on Yelp?"

"Worse," I say through gritted teeth.

There's a puzzled look on Julie's face before realization settles on her features. "You and she didn't—"

I nod grimly.

"I didn't know she—"

"Neither did I."

"But don't you have a—"

"Who showed up unannounced last night at Roundtree's."

Julie whistles, long and low. "That's enough heat to keep the town gossips warm all winter long."

I feel suddenly panicked. "You can't tell anyone, Jules. Not a soul."

I don't worry about my own reputation in Grand Marais, but Charlotte's got enough to deal with without the whispers and disapproving stares.

She holds up her hands in retreat. "Okay, okay," she insists. "Not a word."

My shoulders sag under the weight of guilt. "I really screwed up. I like her *so* much. I should have been honest with her from day one."

"Charlotte's tough. She's been through worse than you."

"That's what makes it even worse. Now I'm just another jerk on a long list of jerks."

Julie pats my shoulder, albeit rather awkwardly. "It's kind of refreshing to know that lesbians can be just as bad as men."

"You're welcome," I deadpan.

Emily's still sitting at the kitchen counter when I get back to the house, and there's no sign of Kambria yet.

"Have you moved since I left?" I ask.

"Did you forget the milk?" she counters.

My hands are empty. Not wanting to risk running into Charlotte in the checkout line, I abandoned my shopping cart and the food inside of it.

"They were all out."

Emily gives me one of her patented disapproving stares. She purses her lips and lifts one eyebrow. Thankfully, before she can launch into the lecture that I'm sure she's been holding back all morning, my dad's landline rings.

Emily picks up the cordless phone in the kitchen. "Hello?"

"Who is it?" I ask. For some reason, the phone call makes me nervous. Maybe Charlotte saw me at the grocery store. I doubt she would call the house since she has my cell number, but I can't keep from both hoping and dreading that she'll eventually reach out to me.

"It's Dad," she says, hand over the receiver. "He's at Emma Bernstein's house and needs a tool from the shop."

"I'll get it," I immediately volunteer.

"Do you even know what an air compressor looks like?"

"I'll Google it."

Emma Bernstein lives near my dad's house, but it takes some time to drive into town to the hardware store and then back out to the worksite. As I park in the long concrete driveway in front of Mrs. Bernstein's house, I get a call from my dad's landline. It's probably Emily, and I'm not in the mood for one of her lectures or reminders that Kambria is at the house. I'm well aware of that fact. I answer the call anyway though in case my dad forgot he needed something else.

"Where are you?" It's Kambria, not my sister. "I just got up, and your sister said you'd left."

"My dad needed me to pick up a tool for him." I don't mention that it's the second time of the young morning that I've left on an errand.

"When will you be back?" she asks.

"I don't know. My dad might need me to stick around or go get more tools for him."

"I was hoping you'd give me the grand tour today. I want to see where you grew up."

"There's really not much to see," I insist. "A few stores downtown and the lake; that's about it."

"That bar last night seemed fun. We should go back tonight."

Worst idea ever. I make a noncommittal noise.

"What am I supposed to do while you're going?"

"I don't know."

"Why are you acting like this? I came all this way to see you."

"I never asked you to do that. This isn't a vacation for me."

"But I missed you. And I didn't know when you were coming home."

"All you needed to do was pick up the phone and call me."

"I told you I lost my phone," she huffs.

"You couldn't buy a new one? You couldn't borrow a friend's phone long enough to call me and let me know what was happening?"

I'm irrationally angry and taking out my frustration with myself on her. It's not fair, and I know it.

She hangs up on me or my cell phone loses reception, but whichever one it is, I don't call her back.

I find my dad in Mrs. Bernstein's garage. He's using a turned over five-gallon bucket as a chair.

"I got your air compressor doohickey," I announce as I walk in.

"Thanks. You find it okay?"

"Yup."

He stands and begins moving things around, tools and sheets of pink insulation and drywall.

"Can I help you with something?"

He gives me a quick glance. "Shouldn't you be hanging out with your girlfriend?"

"Maybe I'd rather spend time with you," I deflect. "I can see Kambria all the time when we're back in Los Angeles."

"I thought you two were breaking up."

"We—I ... yeah." There's a stray construction nail on the concrete and I kick at it.

"I'm not good at this sort of thing."

"Me either."

"I've gotta do some finishing work in the garage's attic space. Why don't you hold the ladder for me and hand me tools when I ask for them?"

"I can do that," I say, happy for the task. "What does the air compressor do?"

My dad climbs up a tall ladder and disappears through a small square opening in the ceiling. "It powers the nail gun so I don't have to be plugged into a wall. Emma doesn't have power out here."

I stand at the base of the ladder and stare up through the cutout in the ceiling. "Mrs. Bernstein seems nice," I remark. She had been a bank teller at the bank for as long as I could remember. Her husband died of an early heart attack a number of years ago and she'd never remarried. "Is she dating anyone?" I'd often thought she and my dad would make a cute couple, but I'm no matchmaker. I can't even handle my own love life.

"How would I know?" my dad's disembodied voice replies.

I lean against the ladder, resting my weight on it. "Doesn't everybody know everybody else's business in this town?"

"I do my best to keep out of that. Not worth the time or the trouble. Son of a ... Mother puss bucket."

My dad doesn't swear. So when I hear the string of near expletives, I know something's wrong.

"Dad?" I call up the ladder. "Everything okay?"

"Yeah. Just put a nail through my hand." His voice is so calm and matter-of-fact that I think he's kidding.

The ladder shakes as my dad gingerly descends from the attic. When he's near the bottom rung, I notice he's holding his right hand close to his chest.

"Holy shit, Dad. There's a nail in your hand!" I exclaim.

"That's what I said." Same no nonsense tone.

I usually do okay with the sight of blood and minor injuries, but there's something about the way the carpenter's nail looks protruding from my dad's hand that turns my stomach.

"What do you need me to do?" I ask with heightened urgency.

"Well, I suppose you can drive me to the doctor."

Grand Marais is tiny, but the drive from Emma Bernstein's house to the walk-in clinic on the far side of town feels like it takes forever. Periodic glances towards my father who sits in the passenger side of my rental car has me swerving erratically across the center median.

My father's mouth forms a permanent grimace and the color has drained from his face. Beads of sweat collect at his temples and near his hairline. "I'd like to make it to the doctor's in one peace, Abby," he says in an overly calm voice.

"Right. Sorry."

I park out front and rush into the clinic before my dad. "I need some help," I announce to anyone who'll listen. "My dad's got a nail in his hand."

The hospital staff at the reception desk, all two of them, slowly look in my direction. Everything feels like it's going in slow motion, but also too fast. The automatic doors open behind me, and my dad lumbers inside the hospital, holding his injured hand close to his chest.

A woman in light blue scrubs steps out from behind the front desk. "What's the problem, Jerry?"

"Eh, wasn't paying attention," he says meekly. "Got myself in the hand pretty good."

There's such a lack of urgency from either of them, I'm appalled.

The woman brings the reading glasses hanging by a chain around her neck up to the bridge of her nose. "Let's take a look."

"Shouldn't you take him back to a room or something?" My voice has become high-pitched. "He'll probably need a tetanus shot."

"Mary, you remember my oldest—Abigail—don't you?" my dad drawls.

The woman regards me. "Sure do. You're the writer, right?"

I nod tightly.

"Then why don't you take a seat in the waiting room and leave the health care to me."

I'm filled with a kind of indignation, but I bite my tongue and do what she says.

As I wait for my dad to return, I fiddle with my phone. It's probably a good thing Charlotte doesn't have a cell phone, otherwise I would have gotten myself into more trouble. I'm tempted to call Roundtree's regardless, but it's too early for her shift and I really shouldn't be making any phone calls in a hospital waiting room, even if it's only Grand Marais. I text Emily to let her know what's going on and ask her to relay the message to Kambria. It's horrible, but I'm actually thankful for the accident. It gives me more time to mentally process what's happened over the past twenty-four hours. I need to break up with Kambria. Properly. And I need to find a way to make this up to Charlotte.

I'm no closer to coming to a resolution when my dad finally re-emerges, his injured hand heavily swaddled in bandages. He's given a prescription for painkillers that I'm sure he'll never take and directions from the doctor to take it easy, whose advice he'll disregard. As evidence of his hardheaded stubbornness, as soon as we leave the clinic, he wants me to drive him back to Mrs. Bernstein's so he can get his work truck and tools. When I protest him doing anything more strenuous than using a remote control, he reminds me that God gave him two hands and that he only needs one of them to drive his truck.

He does, however, let me bring his tools back to the hardware store so he can go straight home from Mrs. Bernstein's house and rest. My trip back through town has me driving past the neon signage of Roundtree's Bar & Grill. A few cars dot the parking lot at this hour, but none of them are Charlotte's green Jeep.

I slam my hand against the steering wheel. "Damn it."

With a sharp tug on the wheel, I'm turning my car around and driving down the street where Charlotte lives.

I raise my closed fist, but the door to the ranch-style home lurches open before I can knock. Charlotte stands in the threshold, hair looking wild and unbrushed, and her eyes angry and red. I can hear Bessie Smith blasting in the background, lambasting a man who's done her wrong.

"Don't you know when to stop?" she snarls. She balls up her fists at her sides. If she had hit me, I wouldn't have been surprised. And I would have definitely deserved it.

I hold up my hands to surrender. "I need to explain."

Her body practically shakes with anger. "Explain?" she spits out. "Like how you have a girlfriend? How you cheated on some poor, unsuspecting girl with another unsuspecting girl? I don't see what else there is to explain." She grabs the edge of the front door, and I can tell she's going to slam it shut in my face.

I shove my foot forward so when she does throw the door closed, it bounces off of my shoe and re-opens. She clearly isn't happy I've forced the door back open, but I need to make her hear me.

"I have a girlfriend." I brush my tongue over dry lips. "Her name is Kambria."

Technically I broke up with Kambria, but if she didn't get my voicemails, I suppose that means we're still together. When a tree falls in an empty forest, I guess it doesn't make a sound.

Charlotte's eyes narrow. "I don't need the details."

"Maybe not, but I still need to explain myself."

"Let me save you the trouble. You're only explaining so you can feel better about yourself—so you don't feel so guilty about leading on two women. But nothing you can say right now is going to make me feel any better." Charlotte crosses her arms across her chest. "So why don't you do something noble for once and just go?"

I drop my eyes to the concrete. She's absolutely right.

"Where's Amelia?" I ask.

"She's at my parents' house," Charlotte says dully. "I needed time to work this out by myself, so my mom picked her up."

"Did you tell her—."

"I don't want to talk about this anymore," she interrupts. "Go back to your girlfriend, Abby," she tells me. "Go back to California where you belong."

Where she'd been nothing but fight and vinegar when I'd first shown up, now she looks and sounds drained. I want to invite myself in and hold her and whisper away the pain, but you can't console someone when you're the cause of the heartache.

This time, when she shuts the door, I don't stop her.

It's late by the time I make it back to my dad's house. The sun has set and the moon hangs full in the midnight-blue sky. My brain and heart are filled with a cacophony of thoughts and emotions.

Kambria's sitting on the couch in the living room when I return. Her hands are in her lap and her wheeled suitcase is packed and upright beside her. Her right knee bounces with pent-up energy. The house is silent, but it's late, so my dad and Emily are probably asleep in their rooms.

The front door shuts behind me, and the noise it makes sounds like an explosion.

"I'm back," I announce.

She doesn't look in my direction. "Where were you? Your dad got home awhile ago."

"I had to get gas," the lie slips out.

"Did you know your dad's store sells cell phones?"

"It does?"

She slowly nods. "Your sister let me know. So I went there and bought a new phone." Her mouth twitches. "I got your messages. Your many, many messages."

My throat tightens. *Damn you, technology.*

"You broke up with me in a voicemail."

I swallow hard. "Yeah, I did."

"Do you want to tell me what happened?"

No, not really. "Coming back here, to this place, it made me realize how very different you and I are. I'm sorry, Kami. I just don't think you and I have a future together."

"It couldn't wait until you got back to LA?" Her voice waivers with emotion. "You couldn't stand the thought of dating me so much that you had to break up with me in a voicemail?"

She's spiraling down a hole of self-doubt and loathing, and I'm powerless to stop it. "No, that's not it at all."

I don't bother taking off my shoes. I sit beside her on the couch. The fabric smells like my dad's cologne—Old Spice. We sit beside each other in silence, neither of us brave enough to talk or to even look at each other.

"I'm sorry." The syllables get caught in my throat and I try again. "I'm sorry you came all this way."

When I feel the couch cushions begin to shake, I hazard a glance in her direction. Her head is bent forward and tears roll silently down her cheeks. "The bartender?" She's more perceptive than she gives herself credit for. "I could tell something was off with you two."

"I didn't mean for it to happen," I say helplessly.

"But it did."

"But it did," I acknowledge.

"I feel like an idiot. I wanted to surprise you, but you never wanted me here. You never wanted *me*."

"That's not true," I weakly protest.

There's a wet sobbing noise and then Kambria's standing up and extending the handle on her suitcase.

I look up after her. "Where are you going?"

"The airport. This was a mistake."

I couldn't agree with her more, but it's too late for her to be driving all the way to Minneapolis.

"Stay the night at least," I urge. "The airport will still be there in the morning."

By some miracle, she agrees to spend another night. I sleep on the pull out bed in the den and she once again takes my childhood bedroom. Kambria leaves in the morning after a stiff and awkward goodbye to my family and me. I don't try to see Charlotte after that night. I stop going to the bar, the beach, and the library—the three places I'm sure to see her. I avoid most other places as well, afraid that I might bump into her at the grocery store or the video rental place. I want to give her space, but I'm also afraid. Seeing her is a tangible reminder of the terrible thing I've done.

At least Emily has started to come around, otherwise my dad would have had both of his daughters haunting his house. The roles now reversed, Emily leaves food outside of my bedroom door while I hide out. Pain is one of life's great motivators. Right up there with love, heartache and disappointment has always activated my pen. I write a lot. I pour out my emotions into a new play. My ink-stained hands resemble the kind of work my dad does for a living. Maybe that's why I had been so stuck before—I had been too content with my life. But without the extremes of passion and angst, my emotional gas tank had been running on empty. I owe both Kambria and Charlotte penance, so I do it the only way I know how—I write.

CHAPTER TWELVE

Surrounded by the familiar silhouettes of my childhood bedroom, it should be easy to fall asleep. The stack of stuffed animals on my steamer chest. The bookshelf packed with novels. The outline of movie and band posters on the walls. Beyond my bedroom window, Lake Superior crashes against the rocky shoreline, more soothing than any white noise recording.

I had had such big goals for myself when this room had been my home. I was going to graduate top of my high school class and go to a fancy university in the Twin Cities. And after college, I'd move out-of-state to an exotic, exciting city where I'd make a name for myself. I hadn't known yet that I wanted to be a writer, but I'd been confident that whatever career I pursued, I would be the best at it.

A rewarding, long-lasting relationship had never figured into those grandiose plans. I'd only ever dreamt about my future career and the big city where I'd live. And as little as I had thought about what my future significant other might be like, having children figured even less into the equation. Maybe because my dad didn't date, having a relationship as an adult hadn't been high on my list of priorities.

I thought about my dad living in this big house all by himself. I didn't want that for me. I could buy houseplants to fill every room, but in the end it was human touch and companionship that I craved. Was I ever going to find someone to grow old with? Or would I continue to self-sabotage my own happiness?

A gentle knock on the door to my bedroom has me rousing from troubled thoughts. The door opens partway, and I hear my sister's quiet voice: "Abby? Are you awake?"

The door opens the rest of the way.

I wipe at my eyes and clear away the frog that's taken residency in my throat. "What's wrong, Em?"

"I can't sleep."

I pull the sheets back. "Get in."

Her steps are light as she scampers across the room as if she's worried I'll rescind my invitation. She wiggles her body into the empty space beside me. My bed is only a twin-sized mattress, and I consider it a small miracle that we're both able to fit. Even when I was in high school and she was in junior high, she'd sleep in my bed whenever we were hit with a particularly brutal storm. She's always been afraid of thunder and lightning. It's not storming tonight though.

"Your girlfriend didn't stay very long," she says into the dark room.

"She didn't stay my girlfriend for very long either," I remark.

"I tried calling to give you a heads up, but you didn't answer the phone."

"I know. I've got no one to blame but myself. I never should have encouraged Charlotte or I at least should have been able to keep it in my pants until I got back to Los Angeles and broke up with Kambria properly."

"Probably would have been a good idea."

I know that sometimes I live inside my head. I become a character in one of my stories where there are no consequences and everything works out by the end of the play. But real life doesn't work like that—and even the best told stories don't always end happily with a tidy bow.

I breathe out heavily and stare at the single glow-in-the-dark star stuck to the ceiling. "I messed up, Em. And now Charlotte hates me."

"Did you really think you wouldn't get caught?"

"I wasn't thinking, period. That was my problem."

We don't talk the rest of the night. Soon enough I hear the sound of her quietly snoring. I don't expect to get any sleep, but after a few hours of staring at the glowing star on the ceiling, I finally pass out.

When I wake up in the morning, Emily is gone. I hear the sounds of pots and pans slamming around downstairs, so I know she hasn't gone far.

Walking past my sister's bedroom, I pause in her doorway when I notice that the room is flooded with sunlight. The blinds have been opened and the curtains pulled apart. The sheets on the bed have been stripped to be laundered and the top quilt is folded at the end of the mattress.

I trudge down the stairs. "You're awfully loud this morning," I grumble upon entering the kitchen.

"Good morning to you, too," Emily sweetly chirps. She's wearing clothes—real clothes—jeans and a button-up shirt. It's the first time I've seen her in something other than ratty old t-shirts and pajama pants since the Fourth of July picnic.

The kitchen looks clean, less cluttered. The various electrical components that have become a part of the landscape are gone. I run my fingers through sleep-tangled hair. "Did you finally give up and throw those parts away?"

"No. I put everything back together this morning."

As if to punctuate her point, I hear a quiet chime and the toaster-oven door flips open to produce two perfectly toasted pieces of whole grain bread.

"Did you make bread, too?" I wonder.

"The bread maker wasn't really broken."

"You're kind of creeping me out."

"Sometimes things have to fall apart completely before they can be put back together."

"Are we still talking about the toaster?"

"I could always put those things back together," she says with a dismissive wave of her hand. "But I wasn't ready to."

"What changed?"

"I decided to stop feeling sorry for myself," she says. "It's time to go on living my life. Adam would have wanted me to."

A small smile plays at my lips. "That's really great, Em."

I'm happy for her, naturally, but I can't help but have my misgivings. Is it too soon? Is she forcing it? Will she have a setback that will only plunge her back into depression? She's always been practical. I'm sure processing and dealing with all of these emotions has been disorienting for her. Full-steam ahead is her comfort zone.

I sit at a stool at the kitchen island. "Have you made plans for your life beyond fixing Dad's stuff and making breakfast?"

"I can't go back to Duluth. There's nothing there for me except for an apartment full of memories."

"What about your job?"

"It was just a job," she says. "I never really liked it. It paid the bills, nothing more."

I lay my hands flat on the counter's surface. "Okay, no Duluth, no insurance underwriting. What are you going to do instead?"

"I thought I'd fix up the apartment over Dad's store. I could help him out until I figure out the next step."

"So your grand plan is to live above the hardware store and stay in Grand Marais? That doesn't sound like moving on, Em. That sounds like going back in time."

"Dad's renting a truck this weekend and we're going to Duluth to pick up my stuff and bring it back here. Do you want to come with us? It could be a Henry Family road trip."

"It's like college all over again," I remark.

"If you have something to say to me, Abby," she states sharply, "go ahead and say it."

"Is this really home anymore? Isn't Duluth where you and Adam built a life? Your job? Your friends?"

"You wouldn't understand. You said it yourself—you've never been in love."

"I never said that," I protest. "I've loved before."

"Try going back to a place where everything reminds you of your dead husband," she snips. "And all of our friends were Adam's friends. I can't go back to all those sad faces, to all those people who'll only ever see me as Adam's widow. At least in Grand Marais I have an identity. I was Emily Henry before I was Emily Harvester."

"You've put some thought into this."

She nods somberly. "I've had nothing but time."

"I need to get back to my life, too," I think out loud. "I should probably book a flight."

"I still don't understand why you're in Los Angeles," Emily says. "I know you like living in big cities, but LA seems excessive."

I reach for the toast from the oven and take a bite. "I have my reasons."

+ + +

The day before my return flight to Los Angeles, I drive out to the beach. It's a beautiful, cloudless day and I know I'll find Charlotte's Jeep parked along the highway. I spot Amelia in the water. Her head is a tiny blonde speck on the horizon, bobbing up and down in water that reaches her neck.

Gusts of wind ruffle my hair as I cautiously pick my way down a sand dune. Green shoots of dune grass stick up through the compact sand. The edges of the blades of grass are sharp and they knick my feet.

Charlotte sits in the center of a beach blanket on the shoreline. Her hair is tied up in a loose bun, and a long white tank top covers a deep blue bikini. Her head is tilted down, eyes focused on the book in her lap.

The sound of waves knocking against the shoreline and the squealing cry of seagulls is too loud, and she doesn't notice or hear my approach until I'm standing in front of her and my body casts a long shadow across her blanket.

She doesn't say anything, but the deep frown on her beautiful face lets me know she isn't pleased to see me.

"Amelia!" she suddenly calls out. Her voice is so loud and so unexpected, it makes me flinch. "Pick up your stuff; we're heading back in."

"Wait. Don't. I'm not staying," I say. "I didn't come out here to ruin your day."

Her eyes are hidden behind the dark lenses of her sunglasses. "Then why did you come out here?"

"I'm going back to California tomorrow, but I wanted you to have something before I left." I reach inside my canvas bag and pull out a flimsy cardboard box used to store a ream of computer paper.

She takes the box from me, but her forehead is lined with confusion. "I don't need printer paper. I don't have a computer."

"I know."

"What is this?" she asks. She turns the box over in her hands, but doesn't open it.

"An apology."

I leave without looking back or another word of explanation. I've got to get back to my life, and she doesn't follow. I consider it a miracle that she actually took the box. What she does with it later though, I'll never know.

+ + +

My return flight to Los Angeles is over two weeks after coming back to Grand Marais for Adam's funeral. During that time, I've witnessed my sister's personal dismantling like one of those electronic gadgets she took apart. She gave the impression that she was starting to heal, but only time will reveal if she would ever be the same. One can repair a broken mirror, but you can still see the cracks.

I had not been untouched or unaffected by this trip either. Being back in my hometown reconnected me with my family and my dear friend Julie, but it had done so much more than that.

My dad and sister see me off as far as Duluth where they're going to rent a moving truck and bring Emily's belongings back to Grand Marais. My sister was serious about removing herself from the city where she and Adam had gone to college and had begun to build a life together. I make the rest of the trip to the Minneapolis airport on my own.

My workbag digs into my shoulder as I wait in the long security line at the airport. The line creeps forward slowly, one passenger at a time. In a few short hours I'll be back in Los Angeles and back to my life.

There's the white noise din of other people's conversations happening around me, the periodic announcements about flight delays and departures, but somehow above the noise, I hear someone calling my name: "Abby! Abigail Henry!"

I twist and turn my head this way and that to look for the voice's source until I see *her* across the airport atrium. It's Charlotte. Charlotte Johansson is standing on a crowded staircase in the Minneapolis Airport. Her long blonde hair falls in a wavy cascade down her shoulders. She wears a long tank top and loose flowing skirt that reaches just below her knees. The strap of a knit messenger bag crosses her chest. Her features are pinched in concern as she scans the security line.

It's like I'm starring in my very own romantic melodrama.

ACT 2

BITTERSWEET HOMECOMING

<u>Scene 3</u>

SETTING: At the Minneapolis-St. Paul International Airport.

AT RISE: ABIGAIL HENRY waits in a long line to get through airport security. CHARLOTTE JOHANSSON shoulders her way through the crowds.

(The two women walk purposefully toward each other. Their smiles grow bigger the closer they get.)

CHARLOTTE

I can't let you leave like this.

ABIGAIL

Then don't let me leave. Or better yet, come with me.

Dramatic music swells as the two women embrace. Fade to black.

How many romantic comedies have ended in that very way? But my life isn't the movies. It's not one of my plays either.

I apologize to the passengers around me and duck beneath the black, retractable line corral. "Excuse me. Sorry."

The airport is crowded and other travelers knock into my shoulders as I try to weave through the people. My luggage makes it harder to maneuver. Charlotte still hasn't spotted me moving through the crowds and I'm tempted to call out to her, but I don't trust my voice to make it to her ears.

The concerned look on her face relaxes when she sees me climbing the stairs with haste. But then her features unexpectedly harden and sour. She reaches into her bag and pulls out a thick stack of papers. I barely have time to recognize it as the text from my play before she's shoving the manuscript into my chest. The wind is nearly knocked out of me from the force behind it.

"Is this supposed to be about me?" she demands.

My hands curl around the papers' edges, and I feel the bite of a dozen little paper-cuts on my palms and fingers. "It's not entirely about you, but I was certainly inspired."

"Do you do this a lot? Fuck people and then use their life story to get more famous?"

"I don't—I'm not—" I sputter. "I wasn't going to publish it. I wrote it for you."

I return the stack of papers to her, pressing the script more delicately than she had into her chest. "Take it, please."

"I don't want it, Abby," she protests. "I don't want any of it."

"Then why are you here?" I softly implore. "Why did you drive four and a half hours on the off-chance that you'd catch me before I went through airport security?"

"To throw these papers in your face."

"Well, you've done that," I say. "Now what?"

"Now I go back to Grand Marais."

"How about a vacation instead?" I know I'm pushing my luck. "You're already here, and I'm betting Amelia is with your parents. Why don't you come to LA with me? And if LA doesn't sound fun, we can go anywhere you want."

"Don't be ridiculous," she dismisses me without hesitation. "Even if I forgave you—which I definitely do not—I couldn't do that."

"If you're worried about the money, don't. I've got frequent flyer miles I can cash in. Don't say no. Don't over think this, please."

"It's not that simple," she shakes her head. "There's payroll to do, and truck deliveries to supervise, and the Gustafsons are coming in for a tasting for their fortieth wedding anniversary that we're catering," she lists off. Her shoulders slump a little more from the weight of it.

"That's a lot of duties for a bartender," I innocently remark. "I hope the Roundtrees are paying you well."

"The Roundtrees don't pay me anything." Her eyebrows bunch together. "I don't work at the bar, Abby. I *own* the bar."

"Oh, I-I didn't know."

The anger and indignation returns. "You just assumed I'd come running after you—the Big Shot Writer. A girl like me would be lucky to get a girl like you, right? Well I won't be your charity case, Abby. You don't have to save me because I don't need saving."

"I wasn't trying to—"

"I like Grand Marais just fine," she snaps.

There's no time for me to formulate my defense because after her rant, Charlotte immediately hustles away, escaping and becoming just another body on her way to a new destination. I can't even watch her leave because she blends into the crowds so well that she disappears. She has no cell phone, so I can't even call or text her to give me another chance to explain. There's nothing left for me to do but go through security and board my plane.

The security line has more than doubled since I left it. I won't miss my flight, but I'm sure this is some kind of karmic justice. A forced smile is on my lips when I hand the TSA agent my license and boarding pass.

CHAPTER THIRTEEN

I don't know what to expect when I get back to Los Angeles, specifically the condition of my apartment. Kambria's not the first girlfriend with a key to my place to have ended with an ugly breakup, and experience tells me to expect the worst.

When I open my front door, I breathe out a sigh of relief. It's clear that Kambria has been by to pick up her things, but everything else is unaltered. Most importantly, my houseplants are alive and well.

Claire's voice is directly behind me. "It looks empty in here."

"Kambria had a lot of stuff."

"Yeah, next time you and a girlfriend split up, give me a little heads up. I came to water the plants and thought you'd been robbed."

I'm too tired to put up a fight. "Sure thing," I agree. My one-hour layover in Denver turned into three, and I hadn't been able to sleep on the plane to Los Angeles thanks to the seat kicker in the row behind me. I'd considered it karmic retribution for my bad behavior in Grand Marais.

"So what happened out there?" she asks me.

I had called Claire for a ride from the airport, but I'd left out most of the details about my extended visit.

"Nothing good."

Claire frowns. "Do you regret going back for the funeral?"

"Maybe."

I had too much time on the airplane to process my trip home. I'm not sure I helped Emily grieve, and I know for a fact that Charlotte would have been better off if I hadn't been in town. The only thing I had succeeded in doing was breaking up Kambria when there was really nothing wrong with our relationship. It was a little routine and boring, but maybe I was expecting too much.

"You're being awfully verbose," Claire observes. "Did Minnesota break you?"

"Just saving all my words for my next play, Boss," I say.

Claire looks unconvinced, but she knows better than to pressure me to talk when I'm not feeling like sharing. I'll come to her when I'm ready.

A phone call interrupts our awkward interaction. My phone flashes a number I don't recognize, but it's a southern California area code, so it could be work related or totally random. I normally let unknown numbers go to voicemail, but I'm happy for the distraction.

"Hello?" I answer.

"Ms. Henry, this is Daniel Hanson," the voice on the phone introduces.

It takes me a second to recall how I know that name. "Oh, hey. How are you?"

"I found her."

My stomach drops at his announcement. "You did?" My voice raises an octave in surprise. Hearing the change in my tone, Claire looks on curiously.

"If it's convenient, I'd like to meet with you at my office to discuss the details."

"Yes, yes. That will be fine." My travel fatigue is momentarily forgotten with this news. "Is right now too soon?"

"That will be fine. See you soon."

When I hang up, Claire continues to regard me with curiosity. "Who was that?"

"Think you can give me a ride to the Valley?" I ask.

"Why? Running low on porn?"

I ignore her attempt at humor. "No. A few months back, I hired a private investigator. That was him on the phone." I take a deep breath. "He says he found my mom."

Hanson Private Investigators is located in a small office at the end of a strip mall in the San Fernando Valley. Daniel Hanson, the man who's been working on my case for the past few months, sits at a desk in front of me. He's young, maybe even younger than me, with a medium build and sandy blond hair. Daniel's the fourth private contractor I've hired over the years to find my mom. The first two had come up empty, and honestly I'd given up on the task until Private Eye number three, a woman named Kinsey, had tracked my mom to southern California. A family health emergency had kept Kinsey from following up on her leads, but before leaving, she'd given the case to the man seated across the room from me.

"Can I get you something? Coffee? Water?"

There's a mini-fridge behind him stacked with bottled waters that I remember from our first meeting. A single-cup coffeemaker—the kind you might find in a hotel—is perched on one of the metal filing cabinets that crowd the room. It's mid-summer in July and an oscillating fan rotates and splits its time between us.

"No, thank you," I decline. I'm eager to learn what he's found, and any distractions or delays are unwanted.

Daniel opens the top drawer of his desk and produces a plain manila envelope. He pushes it across the desk toward me with the tips of his fingers. Inside the envelope are glossy black and white images of a woman going through a daily routine: drinking coffee in a shop by herself, pushing a grocery cart down an aisle, filling her car with gas from a pump. I stop on one image; she's at a park, playing with a young girl.

"That's her granddaughter," Daniel says, noticing what or who has captured my attention.

"She ..."

"Remarried," he supplies. "Has a son. His name is Samuel. The little girl's name is Emily."

A cry gets caught in my throat. Is the name a coincidence I wonder?

"Your mother gets coffee at a little place in Bunker Hill on Tuesday mornings. I'd say that's your best bet to bump into her. I have her home address, but the most successful confrontations usually occur in public."

I nod my understanding. "How did you find her?"

"Trade secret," he winks. "Actually, Kinsey did all the real work. I just kind of connected the dots she'd already laid out."

I clutch the envelope containing the surveillance photos. "Thank you for this."

He runs his fingers through his hair. "I'd save that Thank You if I were you."

I give him a puzzled look.

"Yours isn't the first missing person case I've worked on," he explains. "This doesn't always end with the happy reunion most people are looking for. Your mom made herself damn near impossible to find. There might have been a reason for that."

+ + +

The next time Tuesday shows up on my calendar, I find myself taking a cab out to Bunker Hill. The coffee shop that my mother frequents is actually an independent bookstore. I keep my distance and try to observe her without being noticed. She hasn't seen me since I was five, so there's probably no chance she'll recognize me. Without the images the private investigator had given me, I probably wouldn't have recognized her either. She's dressed conservatively in a sleeveless blue silk shell with a fashion scarf tied around her neck. She's a brunette with a few lighter streaks that could be blonde highlights, or they could be grey hair. I can't tell from this distance. Between hiding from Charlotte at the grocery store or from my mom, I'm getting better at this unobtrusive staring thing, but I've got some work to do.

There's a worn photograph in my hand, not one from the private detective, but one that I've kept in my wallet for a dozen years. I run my finger over the deep fold in the center of the image. It's a picture of my mom and dad. She's lying in a hospital bed, face sweaty and exhausted looking. My dad sits on the edge of the bed, holding a tiny bundled newborn in his arms—Emily. I'm in the picture, too. I'm two or three with a mouth full of tiny white teeth, hair fashioned into uneven pigtails, courtesy of my dad, no doubt.

My dad had once kept pictures of my mom around the house, but once Emily was old enough to know what they were, she'd thrown them all away, including the picture frames they'd been displayed in, but I'd been able to salvage a few. One of my favorites is of my mom and me on a blue sled. We're stacked in a row with her seated behind my smaller frame. The picture is tight on our faces, like an original selfie. My cheeks are rosy from the cold weather, and my dark brunette hair is tucked under a knit cap with just the ends of my bangs sticking out across my forehead. I'm probably four or five, not far away from when she left us. I used to wonder, as I stared at that image of a moment from my childhood that I could no longer remember, if she had already known she was going to take off when the picture had been taken.

I've thought about this moment for most of my adult life. I haven't made up my mind up yet if I'm going to approach her today or not. Daniel Hanson commented that she's a creature of habit, so as long as I continue to live in the area, every Tuesday morning holds the possibility of a reunion. Maybe today will only be surveillance before I'm brave enough to actually talk to her. Maybe we'll join the same book club and become friends. Maybe someday I'll tell her who I really am.

I didn't always want to seek her out, but as I grew older, particularly as I approached and passed the age at which she'd left Grand Marais in search of a different life, I started to wonder about her and what had become of her. I never imagined that she would have remarried and had had new children to replace the two daughters she'd left behind, but I suppose it was naive of me to not consider it a possibility.

I glance once more in her direction. She reads a book, unaware of my stare. I don't think I can do this. Not yet, at least.

She looks up from her novel to take a sip of her drink, and I immediately avert my eyes and pretend to be browsing the bookshelves. I'm in the children's literature section, non-fiction. Despite the high-pressure situation, the words on the binding of a slim hardcover book catch my attention. It's a children's book about fireflies. I take a moment to flip through its glossy pages, momentarily distracted from the purpose of my stakeout. It's mostly science and fun facts about the insect. It's perfect.

I clutch the book in my hands, and as if on autopilot, I bring the book to the cashier at the front of the store. He's a middle-aged man who's beginning to go bald.

"Hi," I greet. I set the book on the countertop. "I'm wondering if I could have this shipped to someone's house."

"Sure thing. What's the address?"

My confidence falters. I have no idea what her house number is, but I know the name of the street. "Amelia Johansson. Two s's. She lives on Prospect Street in Grand Marais, Minnesota."

"And what would you like the note to say?"

I see movement in my peripheral vision. The woman whom I'm told is my estranged mother is gathering up her things and getting ready to leave, but I'm mid-transaction.

The man behind the register tries to garner my attention. "Ma'am?"

My mother is pushing in her chair. She buses her own coffee cup and a small ceramic plate, dusted with crumbs.

I whip my head back in his direction. "Sorry?"

"The note," he repeats. "We typically put a card inside the packaging so the recipient knows who the book is from."

I realize I'm standing right next to the front entrance. In order to leave the store, my mother will have to walk past me.

"Oh. No note," I say distractedly. "She'll know who it's from."

I hear someone clear his or her throat. I look in the direction of the sound and see my mother, standing nearby and smiling warmly in my direction. I stop breathing.

"Have a nice day," she says.

I open my mouth to speak, but the words won't come out.

"Thanks. You, too, Linda," the man working the register returns.

The bell above the coffee shop's entrance jingles, and I watch my mother leave.

"That'll be twenty-three, sixty two."

My eyes jerk once again in the direction of the store clerk. I'm going to give myself whiplash. "What?"

The man blinks. "The book. Do you still want it?"

"Oh. Right." I dig my wallet out of my bag and hand him a credit card. "When will it be delivered?"

"Morning orders go out the very same day, so either tomorrow or the next day."

"So soon?" I squeak. I start to second-guess the impulse buy even though the man has already run my credit card.

His face scrunches. "Is that a problem?"

"No, that will be fine." I bite my lower lip. "Do you know the woman who just left?"

"Sure," he says, finishing up the transaction. "She's in here a couple of times a month. Always gets a coffee and an apple tart."

"Does she usually come in on Tuesdays?"

"I guess I've never noticed. Why?"

"Oh, n-no reason."

The man regards me for a long, silent moment. I can't blame him. Between my bumbling about the book and asking questions about one of his regular customers, I'm sure my behavior has raised several red flags. I leave the coffee shop without further incident and return to my apartment. It's one of those days I wish I could start over. With no proper office to go to and no meetings or conference calls to attend, I relish the opportunity to go back to sleep.

Hours later, I'm awoken by the sound of plastic blinds being yanked open, and I'm assaulted by late afternoon sunshine. I hold my hand over my brow to shield my light-sensitive eyes from the blinding sun.

"What the fuck, dude?" I groan into the light.

"Change your locks if you don't like me barging in."

"Consider it done."

"Please, girl," Anthony scoffs. "You should consider yourself lucky."

"Why?" I would call myself a lot of things based on the events of the past few days, but "lucky" is not one of them.

"Because you got me in the divorce, obviously."

"You don't have to do that, Anthony," I say with a frown. "Why can't you still be friends with both of us?"

"I don't know if I should even be telling you this, but I spotted Kambria at Club Charlie last night getting friendly with a red-headed glamazon. Didn't take her long to move on," he sniffs archly.

"Everyone deals with breakups in their own way." I've got no moral legs to stand on. I can't even muster a crumb of indignation.

"Well, whatever. I can't stand anyone who looks better than I do in a dress. I only became friends with you two because you averaged the couple out. "

"I'll pretend that wasn't a veiled insult," I deadpan.

"Your apartment is disgusting, by the way," he remarks.

"It's really nice of you to stop by, Anthony. You should do it more often."

Since returning to Los Angeles, my diet has been a lethal combination of delivery food and fruit rollups. My bed is littered with plastic wrappers and my floors are a blanket of pizza and Chinese delivery boxes. It's starting to look a little like that garbage island the size of Texas that floats around the ocean, but I don't have the energy or desire to clean it up.

Anthony perches a hand on one hip. "Sorry if I'm just a little concerned about my good friend." His face doesn't look like he's sorry at all. "Are you planning on sleeping your life away? When's the last time you got any sun? You're looking pale, even for you."

"It's too hot for sun," I complain, flopping my head back onto my pillow. "And don't give me that nonsense about it being a dry heat. One hundred degrees is still one hundred degrees."

"If you don't like the heat, you're living in the wrong part of the country."

"Well maybe I'll move," I stubbornly threaten.

"To where? Back to Minnesota?" he clucks.

"It wouldn't be so bad," I defend.

"Oh honey, I know it's bad if you're actually considering going back to the farm."

"I didn't grow up on a farm," I huff. "I keep telling you it's northern Minnesota, not Iowa or Wisconsin."

He arches a painstakingly manicured eyebrow. "Is there really a difference? And what is this?"

Before I realize what's going on, Anthony snatches my notebook off of the ground. I'm surprised he could even see it underneath the dirty tissues and food wrappers.

"Hey! Give that back!" I protest. I swipe at him, futilely. He's practically a foot taller than I am, even without his trademark high heels.

Anthony's dark eyes move across the page and his eyebrows dance on his forehead. "Is this a love letter?"

"No."

"Yes it is. I know a love letter when I see one."

"Anthony," I practically whine.

"Are you *still* pining over that bartender?"

I'm finally able to pry the notebook away from him. "It's nothing," I insist. I defensively press the notebook against my chest. "It's a writing exercise for a play I'm working on."

"Let me guess—it's a romantic comedy about a stubborn playwright who pines her days and nights over a lost love." The corner of my mattress depresses as he sits down. "But seriously, girl.

What's up with the baditude?"

"Baditude?" I repeat.

"Bad attitude—*baditude*. It's going to be a thing, just you wait."

"You're ridiculous."

He presses his lips together. "This is about that girl, isn't it? Charlotte the Magnificent."

"It's about a lot of girls, not just her."

"Scandalous," he smirks.

"Not like that," I scowl. I sit up in bed and rub my hands over my face. "Today's Tuesday," I mumble into my hands.

"Thank you for the calendar update."

"Tuesday is the day my mom has coffee and an apple tart at a coffee shop in Bunker Hill."

"Your mom?" he echoes. "I thought all your people lived in igloos?"

"She might. I don't know anything about her life. I haven't talked to her since I was five."

"Then how do you——."

"I paid someone to find her, and he did."

"People really do that?"

"I did, apparently. But I'm too chicken shit to actually talk to her. I went to see her this morning, but I ended up hiding among the self-help books in the bookstore."

"Oh, child. You really are hopeless."

I flop back on the mattress and pull the covers over my head. "You're free to leave whenever you want."

A stiff tug has the sheets yanking off of my bed. "You need to get up, girl, and stop feeling sorry for yourself," Anthony ordered. "You've got money in your pocket and a roof over your head. Plus, you've got *me* in your corner."

"You're right, Anthony. What more could I possibly want?"

Anthony's pep talk has me feeling moderately better about myself and my life—so much so that I actually decide to brush my teeth. I'm in the bathroom, cleaning up, when I get a call from Claire. We haven't spoken since she drove me to the detective's office earlier in the week, and I'm sure she's curious how the meeting with my mom went.

"Y'ello," I greet around my toothbrush.

"Are you dissatisfied with the work I've been doing as your literary agent, Abigail?" Claire's tone is precise and clipped.

I spit the toothpaste into the bathroom sink. "Huh? Of course not. Why would you even ask?"

"Because I got a call from Harper Publishing this morning as a professional courtesy to let me know that you'd submitted a new play to them."

"A new play? I have no idea what you're talking about, Claire. I haven't been writing, let alone trying to get something published."

"So you didn't write a play called *The Girl with the Cotton Candy Hair*?"

The name tumbles out of my mouth without my permission. "Charlotte."

It takes me a moment to think about that day at the airport. I'd tried to push it out of my head, not wanting to subject myself to perpetual humiliation. Charlotte had thrown the manuscript in my face, but had she taken it back? I can't remember putting it in my carry on bag before going through TSA security.

"The bartender? What does she have to do with this?"

I rub the back of my neck and grimace. "I wrote a play for her daughter when I was there. But she practically threw it in my face after she read it."

"Your writing isn't *that* bad," Claire deadpans.

"You're hilarious."

"Harper sent me a copy of the play. The little girl who makes friends with a firefly, but everyone else thinks she's talking to her invisible friend? It's charming, Abby. I didn't know you had it in you."

"Yeah." I sigh and lean against the bathroom sink. "I was feeling particularly inspired."

"Do you want me to set up a reading?" Claire asks. "I know children plays aren't your usual genre, but it's good. I think we go for it."

"I wrote it as a present. It's not for sale."

"You wrote an entire play as a *present*? Did you win the lottery or come into an inheritance I don't know about?"

"It's just money," I murmur. "It won't make me happy."

"Is this about that girl? You've been noticeably off since you got back from Minnesota."

"The trip shook me up," I admit. "Emily losing Adam . . ." I trail off. "It made me rethink my priorities."

"Are you ready to talk about what happened out there?"

I've already told Anthony everything. There's no point in keeping the information from Claire. "I cheated on Kambria with Charlotte, and they both found out."

"Oh, Abby," Claire sighs.

"I know." I rub my face with my free hand. "It's really bad. I wrote the play to apologize to Charlotte. I gave it to her the day before I came back to LA."

"Why would she submit it for publication under your name?"

"I have no idea," is my honest reply.

"Well, if you change your mind about selling the play, let me know."

"I won't, but thanks."

I know better than to look for Charlotte's home number online—she practically lives off the grid—but I've still got the bar's number in my cell phone from the night she called me to come over.

Before I can psych myself out, I pull up the Grand Marais number and hit the redial function. I hear the sounds of a working bar in the background when someone answers my call: "Roundtree's Bar and Grill, this is Charlotte."

I almost lose my nerve when I hear her voice.

"Hi. It's Abigail. Abigail Henry."

I hold my breath, expecting to get cursed out or at least hung up on. Instead, all I hear is quiet breathing and the muffled chatter of background conversations.

"Charlotte?"

"I'm here."

I audibly swallow. The words I've wanted to say to her for so long threaten to come up, but this phone call isn't supposed to be another useless apology. "You sent my play to a publisher."

"I thought it was *my* play," she corrects me.

"It is, I just, no one else was supposed to see it."

"I don't have time to talk about this right now. I'm at work."

"I know, I'm sorry. I didn't know how else to reach you. How did you even know how to get the play published?"

"I might not own a computer, but I know how to use Google,"

she states.

"Right. Sorry," I awkwardly bumble. "I was just surprised you'd done it."

"The play's good, Abby," she says. "Like really good. And I didn't want you to not publish it because of my temper."

"I broke up with Kambria," I blurt out, unable to keep the words to myself anymore. "When I realized my feelings for you were more than just a silly crush, I called her to end things. But she had lost her cell phone, and I could only leave voicemails. That night when she showed up at your bar I had already broken up with her. She just didn't know it."

There's a pregnant pause on the other end of my call, but I can still hear the background noise of music and conversations, so I know she hasn't hung up on me.

"I don't know if that makes me feel better about what happened," she finally replies. "I'll have to think on it."

"Can I see you again?" I ask. "Or at least talk to you on the phone?"

"Isn't that what we're doing right now?" she points out.

"I meant after. When we hang up."

I hear her deep sigh. I know I'm being unfair, especially considering she's at work. "I need time to figure things out, Abby. I'm a single mom; I have someone else whose happiness has to come before mine."

"Does that mean you think I could make you happy?" I cautiously ask.

"I really have to go." She doesn't answer my dangerous question. "You can call me later if you want, but not at work. At my house." She rattles off her home number, and I scramble to find something to write it down on. There's a grease-stained pizza box on the coffee table, and I scribble down the seven digits with a black sharpie pen.

"Thanks for not hanging up on me," I say in earnest.

"Sure, whatever," she sighs before she actually does.

CHAPTER FOURTEEN

After the past few disastrous weeks, I'm more than ready for a little Ben & Jerry's therapy. I have no plans for the rest of the day except to binge-watch HGTV and eat my emotions. When I unlock my apartment door, arms encumbered with grocery bags and the day's mail, I notice something different, but it takes a full minute of me standing in the front foyer before I figure out what it is.

"What the . . ."

I would say that I've been robbed, but the only thing the thief took was the garbage that had been strewn about my apartment. Gone are the dead potted plants, replaced with new green shoots of promising life. The overflowing garbage can has been emptied, the dirty bowls and spoons in the sink are now clean and air-drying on the dish rack, and the stack of pizza boxes on the coffee table has disappeared. My apartment is clean.

"You're welcome," comes a voice from the living room. Anthony sits on my couch, one leg crossed over the other.

"What did you do?"

"I hired someone to clean your filthy hole of sorrow and despair," he grins. "You're welcome."

"No, no, no," I immediately panic. "My pizza boxes. Where are my pizza boxes?"

"On their way to a landfill so your apartment doesn't turn into one. Honestly, Abs, it was getting disgusting. I could smell you all the way out in the hallway."

I drop the grocery bags on the kitchen table and head straight for the living room. I can still smell the scent of glass cleaner in the air. The pizza box with Charlotte's phone number is gone. I had been waiting to call her, stupidly not wanting to appear too eager to reconnect.

"You're lucky the neighbors didn't start to complain," Anthony continues. "They probably thought you died in here and that rank stench was your rotting corpse."

"I needed that pizza box."

"Unless Jesus's face appeared to you in a grease blob, why in the world would you need to keep that old foul thing around?"

"I wrote Charlotte's number on it."

His lips purse. "I didn't know you were talking to her."

"Just once."

"So isn't her number stored in your phone?"

"No. I talked to her at work. She gave me her home phone number and told me not to call her at the bar anymore."

"You're an idiot."

"How was I supposed to know you'd go all hoarders intervention on me?" I growl in defense.

"Why not message the woman on Facebook, Instagram, Snapchat, Twitter," he lists off on his fingers, "or whatever new app the kids are using nowadays?"

"It doesn't work like that. She doesn't even have a cell phone."

Anthony raises a skinny eyebrow. "Excuse me? Are you dating an alien?"

"We're not dating," I'm quick to correct.

"Semantics."

"Life is different up there. The pace of life is slower, cell service is spotty, and people still have dial-up Internet. People say hi to each other and make eye contact when they pass each other on the sidewalk."

Anthony pretends to shudder. "It sounds horrible."

"It's nice," I defend.

"Girl, I've dated nice men before. They're also *B-O-R-I-N-G*."

"Charlotte's not boring."

Anthony makes an amused humming sound. "Oh, we're back to the bartender again?"

"Bar *owner*," I correct.

"A regular old sugar mama, I'm sure."

I slam my clenched fist against a couch cushion and release an exasperated noise. "Why did she have to be so amazing? I was perfectly content living my life until she showed up with those legs and that smile. And why does she have to be the world's most perfect mom?"

"Is this you working out your Mommy issues?"

"Don't be disgusting."

"You really don't know anyone who could get Miss Amazing's phone number for you?"

"My sister, maybe. But I'm sure I'll get her old lady lecture about how I need to leave Charlotte alone, and that I need to move on and that's what's best for the both of us."

"Is she right?"

"Probably," I admit with a frown. "It's not like we're in a place where one of us could or should move for the other one. I mean, hell, we barely went on a date together."

"You lesbians and your U-hauling," Anthony censures.

"And she's not even gay," I add.

"Wait, what?" Anthony's features take on a sharp, confused look. "I thought you all did the horizontal mambo."

"We did," I confirm, "but that doesn't mean she's suddenly gay now."

"Are labels really that important to you?"

"No, but I'd at least like to know if she was interested in dating a girl before I moved there to be with her."

"You would really do that?"

"Why not? It's not like there's anything keeping me in Los Angeles anymore."

Anthony presses a hand to his chest, right above his heart. "I'm crushed."

"You know what I mean," I say, making a face.

"We're going dancing tonight, Miss Mopey."

"You know I don't dance."

"Fine. *I'm* going dancing and you're going to drink and pretend to be having a good time. I won't take no for an answer."

"All I want to do is eat my feelings."

"Speaking of feelings." He pulls a stack of envelopes out of his man purse. It takes me a moment to realize they're mine. "Do you mind explaining these? I thought there'd be at least a little sex, but it was only feelings, feelings, feelings."

I snatch the stack of unsealed envelopes out of his hands and press them against my chest, over my heart. "You had my apartment cleaned without my permission, *and* you read my letters? That's private, Anthony," I practically growl.

Even though Anthony's one of my closest friends, it's wildly embarrassing that he's read the letters meant for Charlotte. I was never going to mail them, but I've had too many feelings in my head lately. Physically writing out my thoughts was the only way to stay sane.

Instead of responding and defending his decision to invade my privacy, he's breezing into my bedroom and pulling clothing off its hangers in my closet. I have no choice but to follow.

He holds up a black blouse in front of his chest and makes a face before tossing the item onto my bed, which has been meticulously made. "Your wardrobe is making me depressed."

"If this is how you plan on cheering me up, it's working wonders." I flop down in the center of the bed and the fresh scent of laundry detergent billows up around me.

Anthony continues to raid my closet, tossing the discarded clothing on top of my reclined body. "Save that sarcasm for the ladies at Club Charlie tonight."

"No, Anthony. I hate that place," I whine. "The music's obnoxious and the drinks are overpriced. And you know Kambria will probably be there."

"Which is exactly why we're going, and you're going to look fabulous."

"*I'm* the one who did the breaking up, Anthony," I remind him, sitting up. "I don't have anything to prove."

"Not according to those letters you don't."

"I can't believe you read those," I complain. "Do you want to read my diary while you're at it?"

"You're just lucky I don't know where that woman lives, or I would have mailed them to the North Pole myself. I was half tempted to address them to Sexy Blonde Bartender, Nowhere, Minnesota."

"You wouldn't."

"Oh, I would," he returns. "Either you're an incredibly convincing writer, or you've got it *bad* for this girl."

"They're nothing. Just emotional fuel for the writing machine."

He makes a noise that sounds both unimpressed and unconvinced. "Prove it."

Club Charlie is within walking distance from my apartment, which is probably one of the only reasons why I agree to go. It entertains a mixed crowd, but most nights it's largely a queer clientele. It makes me miss the laid back, low-pressure ambiance at Roundtree's. This place has never been my scene, but after recently spending so much time at the hometown watering hole, the differences are even more dramatic.

Anthony leans across the bar, showing off more cleavage than I've got. He's in full-on Drag Queen mode: tight sparkly dress, fake eyelashes, and skyscraper heels that would break my ankles if I attempted the look. Even though he convinced me to wear a dress tonight, standing next to His Radiance, I look practically butch.

"Hey cutie," Anthony purrs to the bartender working our area. "Get me a gin and tonic. And this beautiful, rebounding lesbian will have a beer with the highest ABV you have."

"Actually," I interject, leaning over the bar to be heard, "can I get a brandy Old Fashioned, muddled?"

The bartender crisply nods. "Sure thing."

"That's an interesting choice," Anthony remarks as the bartender begins to make what is sure to be a twenty-dollar drink. "I don't think I've ever seen you order one of those."

"New Look Abby, right?" I deflect. If he knew the truth—that the drink reminds me of Charlotte—I'd get an earful.

"Cheers to that. And speaking of New Look," Anthony leans closer so he can speak directly into my ear, "that mousey little librarian type has been eyeballing you since we got here."

He points unobtrusively near the line for the bathrooms. I scan the small bunches of people until my focus stops on a girl with black framed glasses. Her bangs are bluntly cut across her forehead and the rest of her dark hair is pulled up into a ponytail. She's cute, and she looks nothing like Kambria or Charlotte, which is a bonus. We briefly make eye contact before she turns and adverts her gaze.

"She's probably looking at you, Miss Fabulous," I dismiss.

"I can guarantee I'm not her type," my friend retorts.

"I'm really not looking for anything," I say, turning back toward the bar when my drink is placed in front of me. As I bring the well glass up to my mouth, I smell the familiar sting of alcohol.

"Does Miss Fancy Playwright have too many friends and can't make room in her life for one more?" Anthony needles me. "Go talk to her."

I drink down half of my Old Fashioned in one thirsty gulp. It burns on the way down, but I don't cough and sputter like an amateur. "Fine," I grunt. "Why not? I've got nothing better to do tonight."

Anthony slaps me soundly on the back, and the second half of my drink threatens to slosh over the rim's edge. "That's my girl."

I linger longer at the bar to finish the rest of my drink and get a refill. Then Anthony shoos me away in the direction of the woman who has continued to sneak glances in my direction.

"Hey," I greet.

She looks up from her drink. Her pink mouth is puckered around a plastic straw. The moment she sees me, she spits the straw out. "H-Hi."

"I'm Abby."

"Carlie."

Her hand is wet from the condensation on the outside of her glass and her handshake is limp. I'm instantly unimpressed. I glance back toward the bar to where I'd left Anthony, but he's already onto his next target. I see him smiling with too much teeth and unnecessarily touching the tattooed forearm of a tall man in skinny jeans. The object of his attentions is wearing a three-quarter-length cardigan over a t-shirt with a deep v-neck that shows off a spattering of coarse chest hair.

I've officially been abandoned.

"What kind of work do you do, Abby?" Carlie asks, making conversation.

Name. Occupation. It's the same wherever I go. And those more versed in this game than myself are able to wiggle in what kind of car they drive and if they own or rent where they live.

"I'm a playwright. I write plays for the stage."

"Cool. Like Shakespeare."

"I guess," I shrug. "I'm not a big deal or anything, so don't get your hopes up."

I'm always careful with how I introduce myself and how I make my money. These clubs are loud and miscommunication is easy. I don't want to lead on someone who thinks I work for a movie studio and can get them a job.

"Don't take this the wrong way," I continue, "but this doesn't really look like your scene."

Her dark eyes widen behind the thick lenses of her glasses. "What do you mean?"

"You look like the kind of girl who'd be more comfortable in a coffee shop talking about Jane Austen or the Brontë sisters rather than dancing to EDM at the club."

Her shoulders slump and her head falls forward, and I instantly regret saying anything.

"Damn it," comes the quiet curse.

I rest my hand on the top of her shoulder and squeeze. "Shit, don't listen to me. I've been a real jackass lately. I don't know what I'm talking about."

"No, you're right. I don't belong here." I hear her sharp intake of air and her chin tilts back up. "My ex-girlfriend said I was boring. I guess tonight was to prove her wrong."

"I'm really, really sorry," I apologize again. "This isn't my scene either. I just got out of a messy relationship and my friend dragged me here to cheer me up."

She continues to stare into the bottom of her drink. The ice cubes are nearly gone.

"Do you maybe want to ditch this place and have a real conversation over coffee?" I meant what I said to Anthony earlier; I'm not looking for anything except for an excuse to leave this club.

"I don't know," she hesitates.

"I promise I'm not a psycho," I say with a small laugh.

"I'm pretty sure that's the exact thing a psycho would say."

"Fair enough."

Carlie stiffens beside me and makes an audible squeaking noise. "Oh no. My ex. She's here."

"Where?"

"Five foot, seven inch strawberry-blonde goddess who just walked in."

I turn my head in the direction of the front entrance, but the club is too crowded and the lights are too dim for me to see anyone matching that description. It's a wonder Carlie was able to notice her, but I sympathize with the heightened awareness that comes with a fresh breakup. I've been on the lookout for Kambria all night. We haven't spoken since she left my dad's house for the airport.

"That's perfect," I remark. "This is what you wanted, right? To have her see you out having fun and not being boring."

She doesn't seem to hear me. "Abby, will you do me a huge favor?"

I don't have time to respond either way before she's grabbing me around my waist and kissing me. My eyes widen, and I don't exactly kiss her back, but she keeps her lips attached to mine until she's satisfied her ex-girlfriend has looked in our direction.

She ends the kiss nearly as abruptly as it began. I lick my lips, tasting the orange juice and vodka of her screwdriver.

"I'm pretty sure your ex doesn't know what she's talking about," I note, "because a boring person doesn't do that."

Her laugh is light, and she ducks her head demurely. "Do you still want to get that coffee?"

We're in a pretty walkable neighborhood, so when we leave the club, we seek out an all-night diner on foot. It's a nice night and we walk slowly, neither of us in a rush, but both clearly relieved to no longer be in the nightclub.

"My ex-girlfriend used to drag me to a different club nearly every night," Carlie says, arms wrapped around her torso even though the outside temperature is warm. "I thought I'd like it better over time, or at least get used to it, but that never happened."

"Kambria loved to go clubbing, too," I say. "She said it was for 'networking' purposes."

"Is that the messy relationship you just got out of?" she asks.

"Kind of." I make a face. "It's a long story."

"It's a long night," she counters.

"Yeah, but I'm pretty sure that after this story you won't like me very much," I reveal. "It's not a flattering reflection of my character. How did you and the strawberry-blonde goddess meet?" I ask, detouring our conversation.

"I'm a barista, and she was the hot girl with the complicated coffee drink. I memorized her order after a few times of coming in; I guess she thought it was sweet or something," she shrugs. "I should have known it wasn't going to work out based on her coffee choice though."

"Is there a connection between drink choices and personality traits or something?"

"Exactly. And in my experience, the simpler the better."

I pause in front of a window display at a bookstore. The lights in the store are all turned off because it's well after business hours, but the books in the window are lit up under spotlights. One of the featured books is a children's picture book about an insect family. I don't spy any fireflies on the cover, but I'm pretty sure this is a sign that Charlotte and Amelia have ruined me. I can't even look at a cartoon rendering of a bumblebee without thinking about them.

Carlie stops when she notices I'm no longer walking beside her. "Everything okay?"

"I live around here," I find myself announcing. "How about I make us some coffee there instead?"

No more writing children's plays, no more books about fireflies, and no more drinking Old Fashioneds. I've got to do something to get them out of my head.

My apartment is on the eighth floor of a high-rise apartment complex. There's not much of a view, the floor plan is minimal, and the rent is high, but the location is convenient and the doormen are all friendly.

"I have to admit," I announce when we're in the elevator. "I'm kind of intimidated."

"Intimidated?" Carlie echoes. "Why?"

"I'm just realizing that you make coffee for a living. You're probably into all those frou-frou coffee drinks with fancy foam designs."

"I actually take my coffee black. Hot chocolate is about as frou-frou as I get."

The elevator stops on my floor and the doors open. "I think I can handle that."

I try to not psych myself out as we enter my apartment. I haven't had a girl over since I got back from Grand Marais, and before Kambria it wasn't like the girls were knocking down my door. But everything is tidy inside my place and it smells good, and I find myself actually indebted to Anthony for going to the trouble of having my apartment cleaned.

"Bathroom?" Carlie asks as we linger in the foyer taking off shoes and hanging up purses.

"Down the hall, first door on the left."

While she's gone, I find a playlist on my laptop for background noise, and I search among the lower cabinets to find the coffeemaker that I rarely use.

There's a stack of unsorted mail on the kitchen countertop, taking up valuable real estate that I need for the coffeemaker. A quick glance tells me it's mostly junk mail, but a card-sized envelope draws my attention. There's no name in the top left-hand corner, but the handwriting is my sister's and the return address is my dad's house. Inside the envelope is a thick piece of cardstock with the words *You're invited to a party!* printed in a black cursive font at the top. It's an invitation for a grand re-opening of my dad's store, which the text informs me has been renamed to Henry Family Handicrafts. I set the card to the side and make a mental note to call my sister in the morning. Something is happening in Grand Marais, and the invitation has me worried.

A second envelope is buried amongst the magazines and free mailers. It has no return address, but the stamp on the right-hand corner is covered in the postal code for Grand Marais. Inside, I find a single piece of notebook paper. It's the kind that comes in a spiral bound notebook. It even still has the ragged edge from where it was torn out of the book.

I don't recognize the handwriting, but after one sentence in, I realize whom the letter's from:

Your dad gave me your address so I could thank you for the book. Amelia makes me read it to her every night before I leave for the bar, although at this point she could probably read it to me from memory. She also won't let me fix the light on the front porch—the one that keeps flickering. She calls it our lightning bug light.

I wasn't supposed to have feelings for you. You were leaving for California, and I thought we could have some fun and that would be the end of it. But when I found out you'd had a girlfriend the entire time, it hurt all over, and I hated you for that. It made me realize that I felt something for you; it's been a really long time since that's happened. It gave me hope that maybe I wasn't completely broken.

You can write back or not; I think part of me just needed to write out these thoughts and send them into the world like a message in a bottle.

"Is that a handwritten letter?"

I'd been so focused on Charlotte's words that I didn't hear Carlie walk up behind me.

"Yeah." I quickly fold the letter in half.

"I haven't seen one of those in years," she remarks. "It reminds me of having a pen pal in the fourth grade."

"She's not much for technology," I explain.

Carlie makes a humming noise. "Is that the rest of the messy situation you were talking about?"

"Uh huh."

"What happened?"

She's asked me that question once before, and on the second time I feel my resolve slipping. I want to talk about this to someone. I need to. And maybe Carlie is the impartial stranger to do that with.

I make a face between a grimace and a grin. "How much time do you have?"

She smiles warmly. "All night."

Coffee cups are emptied and refilled until we've drained the last of the coffee I have in the apartment. We talk all evening and into the morning about relationships past. I tell her about the mess I created with Kambria and Charlotte and she doesn't judge; she listens. She tells me about her own insecurities with women. She leaves when the sun is just beginning to come up and we hug before she goes out the front door. I don't think either of us sees a romantic connection with the other, but Anthony had been right about one thing; it feels nice to have someone to talk to.

CHAPTER FIFTEEN

One of the benefits about being a full-time writer is getting to make your own schedule. I can sleep for how much or how little my brain and body needs. After Carlie leaves, I sleep for a few hours. When I wake up, I've got no place to be and nothing to do, but I'm not quite ready to mentally process everything I've been feeling lately. That's sure to happen the moment I set pen to paper, so I procrastinate on dealing with those emotions for a little while longer. I turn my phone off entirely, not just to vibrate or even to silent, pull a mindless mystery novel off a shelf, and cuddle up on the couch to read.

Very often it's not the content of the book that brings me peace and resolve, but the simple act of solitary reading. It's an emotional and mental vacation from the daily grind to acknowledge that I deserve time to myself. I control the pace, and if I want to read another chapter, I do.

My monastic life is short lived, however, when I hear the sound of a key in my front door followed by the clicking of heels.

"So you *are* alive." It's Anthony. "I was texting you."

"I had my phone off."

Anthony picks up my discarded book from the coffee table like it's a dirty diaper. "I haven't seen one of these in years. It's practically an antique." He sets the book down and puts his hands on his hips. "Where did you disappear to last night? Did you and the librarian hit it off?"

"Kind of."

"What happened?" He sits down on the couch with his hands on his knees and leans forward. "I want all the sordid details."

"I invited her back here for coffee and we talked."

"You talked?" Anthony is aghast. "That's it?"

"I told you I wasn't looking for anything."

"Kambria came in not too long after you disappeared with your new librarian friend."

"She's a barista," I correct. "And her name is Carlie."

"I'm still going to call her The Librarian."

"Did you talk to Kambria at all?" I ask.

"Her mouth was attached to that same redhead's, so I'm afraid I never got the opportunity."

"I feel like I should reach out to her and properly apologize," I think out loud.

"Why? That ship has sailed, honey. It's time to move on to the next."

"Did you ever even like her?" I question.

"Not really, but I'd never tell you that when you were in a relationship. She's a cute little thing, so I understand the attraction, but she was a little dull for me."

My phone, now on, rings its annoying hip-hop ringtone. "Saved by the bell," I breathe out. "I should take this. It's my sister."

Anthony waves me off.

"Hey." I'm filled with trepidation. The last time she called when I was in California, it was to tell me that her husband had died. I instantly expect the worst.

"Did you get the invite?"

"I did." I relax a little bit, but I'm still expecting her to drop some bomb on me.

"What do you think of the new name? We had the hardest time coming up with something for the store. Handyman Henry wouldn't work anymore, and Henry & Daughter didn't have the right ring to it."

"Slow down, Emily. What's going on over there?"

"We're re-opening the store."

"I can see that from the invitation, but why? I didn't realize it had closed."

"Dad and I thought it was time for a little rebranding. And we can't very well keep the Handyman name if I'm going to own half of the business. I'm clearly not a man."

"Wait." I sit up straight on the couch. "You're doing what?"

"I'm investing the insurance money from Adam's accident into the business. Dad wants to slow down and not work so many hours, and I'll be picking up the slack." There's a hopeful energy in her voice that I haven't heard in a long time.

"What do you even know about being a handyman? Handyperson," I correct myself.

"I know how to do things. I've watched Dad fix gadgets all of my life. So can you come to the party?"

She continues to talk when I hesitate with my answer. "Is a funeral the only thing that can tear you away from your life in California?"

"Let a girl talk, huh?" I complain. Her passive aggressive question has me annoyed, but more with myself. I had been away from my family for too long before Adam's funeral.

"What does a person wear to the grand re-opening of a hardware store? Is it black-tie only?" I ask.

"More like business flannel."

"Well luckily that's all I have in my wardrobe. Can I bring a friend or is this like a family-only event?"

"A friend or a *girl*friend?" Emily pointedly asks.

"I'm single."

"For real? Or is this your different-area-code-single like before?"

"Keep it up, and I won't come."

"Sorry. I'll behave."

She's being a nag, but I'd rather have this annoying little sister version of herself than the woman who refused to get out of bed.

"Charlotte wrote me a letter," I reveal. "Like a real letter, not an e-mail."

"Cursing you out for being a despicable human?"

"Kind of." It doesn't really matter the content of the letter. I'd found it to be both hopeful and sad.

"Is this your way of asking me if she'll be at the party?"

I clear my throat. "Is that ridiculous of me?"

"Yes."

"Emily—" I start.

"Charlotte Johansson's not on the guest list," she cuts me off. "*Now* will you come?"

The news is a relief, but I discover it's also a disappointment.

I hold my hand over the receiver and turn to my friend. "Hey, Anthony, wanna go hang out with some moose?"

There's just one more thing I need to do first.

+ + +

<u>ACT 3</u>

<u>Scene 2</u>

SETTING: The café of a bookstore in Bunker Hill.

AT RISE: ABIGAIL HENRY hides behind a book display, regarding an older woman who sits by herself at a table, reading from a well-worn paperback book and sipping hot coffee. The woman is unaware of her silent audience, but even if she had been, she wouldn't recognize ABIGAIL as her estranged daughter.

LINDA HENRY

(looking up from her novel)

Can I help you?

ABIGAIL HENRY

(sits down in the chair across from LINDA)

My name is Abigail Henry. I'm your daughter.

I say to her the words I've practiced over and over again in the bathroom mirror once I decided I was going to find her.

"Is this some kind of joke?" My mother's eyes flick around the busy coffee shop like she's looking for the hidden cameras. Her gaze dashes everywhere except to my face.

"I've been looking for you for a very long time."

She finally looks directly at me. "Why?"

"Why?" I echo. I don't expect her question. *Shouldn't it be obvious?*

"Do you need money or something?" she asks. I see her gaze flick to the floor where her purse resides. "Are you in trouble?"

"No, nothing like that."

"Then why have you been looking for the woman who abandoned you over twenty-five years ago?"

When she says the words out loud, it forces me to sit back in my chair. *Twenty-five years.* God, that's a long time.

"I wanted to see you."

She continues to stare shrewdly at me. It's so reminiscent of Emily, it's eerie.

"I wanted to know who you are," I try again.

She folds her arms across her chest and repeats her earlier question. "Why?"

Her question bothers me in a way I couldn't have expected. I stand up so quickly, my chair nearly topples over. It lurches back on its two rear legs, hovering, threatening to fall, before to comes slamming back to the earth. I feel a lot like that chair.

"You're right," I grunt out. "This was a mistake and a waste of time." She hasn't said those words, but they seem to be hovering in the air around us.

Why? *Why?!* Fuck her.

I grab my bag off the floor and stride purposefully out of the bookstore, moving my legs as fast as they'll go without breaking into an all-out sprint.

I suck in a deep breath once I get outside. My shoulders, once rigid and proud, now slump forward in defeat. I feel like a fool and I've no one with whom to share my embarrassment. I slide my sunglasses over my face to hide the tears that threaten to spill down my cheeks.

"Abigail, wait."

My head and my heart tell me to keep walking, but my feet disobey their silent command. I stare straight ahead with my chin tilted up. I can feel the coming quiver of my lower lip.

"I'm sorry," I hear her say. She's standing in front of me, but my eyes are closed behind the dark lenses of my sunglasses. "You ambushed me. I wasn't expecting to run into my daughter when I left the house for coffee this morning."

I suppose that's fair, but I don't admit it out loud.

"Can we start over?" she pleads. "Maybe get something to eat?"

I adjust my glasses on my nose, but I don't remove them. "Why?" The monosyllabic question bubbles up my throat, and by the time it rushes past my lips, it's become a snarl.

"I'm guessing you went to a lot of trouble to find me."

She doesn't know the half of it. I've gone through multiple agencies and a handful of investigators who all told me to give up.

"One cup of coffee," I finally allow.

Her things are still at her table for two, which is where we end up sitting. There's a small square of paper on the table announcing upcoming events at the bookstore-coffee shop. I fold the paper in half and repeat the motion until the paper is so small and compact that it can no longer be folded. I'm agitated—not the best emotion under which to be entertaining a reunion like this. I wonder if Daniel Hanson suggested a public meeting like this because he knew propriety would force me to keep my emotions in check.

"You have a granddaughter named Emily."

"How do you—." My mother cuts herself off and starts again. "You found me; I shouldn't be surprised that you know about them, too. The name is a coincidence," she reveals after taking a drink of her coffee. "I had nothing to do with that. I even encouraged Samuel to pick another name, but his wife was stubbornly stuck on the name Emily."

"Do they know about us?" I ask.

Her manicured fingernails tap against the side of her ceramic mug. "No."

"Why not?"

"Because it's embarrassing. Besides, how do you even start that conversation? 'Guess what, Family, I was married before and had two little girls whom I abandoned.'" She shakes her head. "That's not very flattering."

"But it would be the truth," I note.

"If you say a lie enough, it becomes your new truth."

I visibly flinch, and she apologizes.

"I'm sorry, Abigail. I speak without thinking sometimes."

I fiddle with the handle of my ceramic coffee mug. "I do that, too."

She smiles and the crow's-feet at the corners of her eyes deepen. The lines on her face tell me she's smiled a lot in the past twenty-five years. "You're beautiful."

I rub the back of my neck. The compliment doesn't sit well with me. "Good genes, I suppose."

Her face takes on a look of concern. "How's your father doing?"

"He's great. Wildly successful. Business is booming. New girlfriend every other week," I breeze. "I've stopped bothering learning their names by now."

I don't know why I feel the compulsion to lie. A better one would have been to say he'd happily remarried not long after she left. But it's too late to say that now.

I'm sure she can tell I'm lying. She smiles softly instead of calling my bluff. "I'm glad he's well. And your sister?"

"She's great, too." I leave it at that without elaborating.

I hadn't really thought this through. I knew I had questions for her, but I never took the time to reflect on the fact that she would probably have questions about how we had turned out, too. I'm not going to tell her that my dad hasn't been on a date in nearly three decades and that Emily's back to square one now that her husband had died.

"What about you?" she moves on. "Job? Married? Any kids?"

I can't handle her questions. "Can we not do this right now? It's a little much."

Her smile tightens. "I understand." Her hands open on the table, palms up. "Whatever you feel comfortable telling me."

I'm an author who can't write unless she's ruining someone's life. I can't hold onto steady relationship because I've got too many walls, and it's probably because of you.

"I'm fine," I settle for.

What a disaster.

"This was ... interesting," is the word she decides on.

My sunglasses, like reflective armor, are back on the bridge of my nose. "Yeah, we probably shouldn't do it again."

The wounded look on her face makes me angry. "No?"

"Let's not kid ourselves, Linda," I say, finally reverting to the only name Emily will refer to her by. "We share DNA and a few other mannerisms, but that's about it. And to be honest, even just talking with you makes me feel guilty about Dad and Emily."

"I understand. If you change your mind though . . ."

"Don't worry," I cut her off. "I won't."

CHAPTER SIXTEEN

Anthony has had his face pressed against the passenger side window of our rental car for the past hour. "This place is adorable, Abby," he says as we slowly drive down Main Street. "It doesn't look real."

"Does that mean you're going to stop picking on me about where I'm from?" I ask.

"Never."

It's my second time of the short summer visiting Grand Marais. In a few days the town will be celebrating its annual dragon boat festival, always popular with tourists and locals alike. As we drive past the harbor I can already see a few of the long boats out in the water.

"Where's your dad's store?" Anthony asks.

"Just a few shops up on this street." I pull the vehicle over to the shoulder when we get closer. The hand-painted signage outside the store is gone, and the new name—Henry Family Handicrafts—is printed on an updated awning over the main entrance.

"Cute," Anthony remarks.

"Do you mind waiting in the car for a second?" My eyes are locked on the new storefront.

"Sure, but crack a window for me, child." He waves himself with a hand. "I didn't know it got so hot in Iceland."

I leave the car and hop up the concrete stoop that leads to the store's entrance. The glass pane windows at the front of the store are covered with tan butcher-block paper. A computer-generated sign promises the store's grand re-opening the next day. I try to peer through the small window cutout in the front door, but my vision is blocked by more of that construction paper.

I don't expect the front door to be unlocked, but I try the handle and the latch pops free. The door swings open—no bell ringing above my head—and I walk inside. The store smells different. I'm overpowered by the scent of fresh paint and sawdust. The worn wooden floors have been sanded and refinished, and the walls have received a fresh layer of white paint. The products on the shelves are the same, but the shelves themselves are different as is the layout of the store. The register is now by the front door instead of the back, and an advanced, touch-screen register sits atop an empty glass display case.

"She changed everything," I speak aloud.

My head tilts up and my eyes travel to the ceiling when I hear noises coming from upstairs. Anthony is waiting outside in the car, but I continue my investigation. It's been years since I've been in the upstairs apartment. No one has lived in it since my parents moved to my dad's current house, not long after I was born. I imagine it covered in grime, serving as storage for things that wouldn't fit in the shop downstairs.

A poorly lit staircase at the back of the building leads up to the second-floor apartment. On bad days growing up, I used to threaten that I was going to move out of my dad's house and live above the store. They were always empty threats, however. The upstairs apartment was unlivable, too hot in the summer and frigid in the winter with no running water or cable television.

The door to the apartment is ajar, and I can hear banging noises and the sound of a radio coming from inside. I tentatively push open the door wider.

"Hello?" I call out. "Dad? Emily? Are you in here?"

The door opens into a small mudroom that's currently stuffed full of rolls of pink insulation. I wiggle past the materials and follow the sounds of the continued banging. My ears lead me to a small galley kitchen. The appliances are outdated, but the room is filled with natural light. An open window over the kitchen sink allows a cool cross breeze through the apartment.

It takes me a moment to realize that the banging noise is coming from the sink and that there are two legs sticking out from underneath the cabinetry below the porcelain sink. A baby blue flip-flop taps in time with the song on the radio.

"Emily?" I tentatively guess.

The legs stiffen, followed by an even louder bang. Two hands and arms appear and the person beneath the sink crabwalks out.

"Jesus, Abby!" my sister exclaims. "You scared me!"

"I called out your name, but nobody answered."

Emily's hair is up in a ponytail and the top of her head is covered in a bandana. She looks a little like Rosie the Riveter. "Did you just get here?"

I nod. "Literally just driving into town. I saw the new sign out front so I stopped to check it out."

Her grin is wide and excitable. "What do you think?"

"You changed a lot of things."

She bobs her head. "I know. But I figured if we're going to have a grand re-opening, people will want to be able to see a difference." Her smile falters momentarily. "Do you not like it?"

I shove my hands into my pockets. "It's different."

Her smile is gone. "You sound like Dad."

"Hey, it doesn't matter what I think. You're the one sinking all this money into the store or whatever."

"We needed a sign that's actually visible from the street. And the new cash register means Dad can actually accept credit cards now."

"Yeah, but did you have to take the bell down?"

"It's getting polished."

"What about the Popsicles?" I question.

"They're still in the freezer. But I bought a second freezer for all of dad's venison so the meat and the ice cream don't have to live together anymore."

I nod once. It's acceptable. "Okay."

"God, you and Dad are like the same person—terrified of change."

"Hardly," I scoff. "I'm the one who lives in Los Angeles." I don't want to fight, but it's so easy to fall into this pattern when I'm around her. We revert to our child-like selves. "What's up with the baditude?" I ask.

Her eyebrows pinch together. "The what?"

"Not important," I dismiss. "What's with the nag job?"

"I know. I'm totally stressed. I think I underestimated how much work this would be."

"Are you second-guessing moving back?"

"Not yet. But ask me again this winter when there's nothing to do except count the snowflakes."

"That doesn't sound so bad."

"Are *you* second-guessing being in LA?" she asks.

"I'm losing myself out there. Los Angeles," I say aloud. "I know it's supposed to be a place where you can re-invent yourself, but maybe who I used to be wasn't so bad. The girl that grew up in Grand Marais never would have cheated or broken up with someone over voicemail," I explain. "Being back here reminded me of who I used to be. Grand Marais hasn't changed; *I* have. And I don't know if that's a good thing anymore."

"Then why are you still out there?"

"I found Mom."

Emily looks up sharply at me. The movement is so abrupt that she nearly hits her head under the sink. "I must be getting high off of these fumes because I could have sworn I heard you say you found Mom."

I lean against a countertop and sigh. "I hired a private investigator to find her, and he tracked her to LA."

"Why in the hell—." Emily stops herself and shakes her head. "Never mind. I know why you did that."

"Do you? Because for the life of me I still don't know why I did it. I've been asking myself that very question ever since I had a stupid cup of coffee with her."

"Look at yourself, Abs. Look at your life. Everything has been shaped by Linda's abandonment. Growing up you escaped into books and later the theater. Now you write plays about people whose lives you'd rather be living. And don't even get me started on your love life."

"I haven't found the right girl," I bluster.

"Or you're afraid to let anyone get close to you because you don't want anyone to hurt you," she counters. "And yet you're terrified of being alone."

I chew on the inside of my cheek.

"Wrench," she sticks out her hand.

"It was a mistake. A big fucking mistake." I rummage around in the metal toolbox on the floor and find the tool Emily needs. "I can't believe how much time and money I wasted trying to track her down."

"So that's the real reason you've been in Los Angeles? Because you knew she was there?"

"I guess so."

"And now that you've had your grand reunion, what now?"

"I don't want to see her again. I should probably move."

"It's a really big city, Abs. I'm sure you won't bump into each other."

"It's tainted now. She's there, and I won't be able to stop thinking about that. I'll see her at every grocery store and coffee shop."

"What about moving back home?" Emily suggests. "You can write wherever you want to. Take a plane to LA if you have meetings or read-throughs."

Emily's partially right. I can write anywhere, but to be a working playwright, I have to be near a city large enough to have a vibrant theater community. That means Los Angeles or New York or Chicago, maybe even Minneapolis.

"I don't think I could live here fulltime, away from civilization. It might drive me crazy."

"But you'd have me. You'd have dad," she points out.

"I know, Em. But I don't think I'm cut out for small town life anymore. Plus, there's the gay thing," I add.

"Stop with the excuses," she scolds. "Nobody cares that you're gay. People in this town only know you as Abigail Henry, not Abidyke Henry."

I arch an eyebrow. "Did you come up with that all on your own?"

She makes what I can only describe as a pleased smile. "Pretty good, right?"

"Not too shabby," I concur.

"I can't see Charlotte living in a big city, sis."

"I wasn't thinking about her." I avert my eyes, afraid they'll give away too much. "How about you? Any new love potential?"

I hear my sister's muffled snort under the sink. "Yeah. They're knocking down the door."

"Have you put yourself out there?" I ask. I don't even know how a person would do that in a town the size of Grand Marais. Most people have to consult their genealogy before they start dating to make sure they're not related.

"I'll get there," she says. "I want to start dating again eventually, but you've got to let me work through these emotions in my own way, on my own time."

I give her a wistful smile. "So you're saying another long weekend won't cut it, huh?"

"Probably not."

When I return to the car, I'm appropriately chastised by Anthony for leaving him for such a long time. But soon we're back on the road towards my dad's house, which unfortunately has us driving past the one place I'd most like to avoid on this second trip home.

"There it is," Anthony breathes in reverence. "Like Mecca itself—Roundtree's Bar & Grill."

"No."

"Pretty please, Abby? I'm *so* thirsty." He smacks his lips together as though parched.

"There's a big ol' lake out there I'd be more than happy to throw you into."

"She's probably not even working right now," Anthony reasons.

"She owns the bar," I remind him. "She's always working."

"How about I go in and you wait in the car this time?" he proposes.

"No," I say again.

"I'll behave!" he promises. "I just want to see this woman."

"So do I," I murmur as we drive past the bar.

"Then why are you being so stubborn?" he demands. "Turn this car around and let's go see if she's there."

"There's no point, Anthony. We're only in town for three days. Seeing her would only make things harder."

"What things?"

"Going back to LA? Trying to move on?"

"I think you're being dumb, Miss Abby."

I slink down in the driver's seat and continue to steer us in the direction of my dad's house. "Yeah, well nobody asked you."

+ + +

I spend my first night back in Grand Marais sleeping on the pull out couch in my dad's den. The apartment above the hardware store isn't ready yet so Emily's still sleeping in her old bedroom, and because he's a guest, Anthony gets my room. The den had once been an ambivalent room to me, possessing no real emotional currency, but now it holds recent memories of guilt and regret. Even without the stiff, squeaky mattress, it would have been an uneasy night.

The room is dark except for the periodic glow of my cell phone. My thumb hovers over the touch-screen display. The number for Roundtree's Bar & Grill is still in my list of recent contacts. I could call and see if Charlotte's working. I could drive over to the bar. I could sneak out of the house, and no one would ever know that I was gone. But to what purpose?

I think about Charlotte's letter. I've read it so many times, I have it memorized, word for word. I know the color of the ink pen she used, and I can visualize the elegant swoop of her cursive writing. I imagine her drafting multiple versions, or at least weighing each word before committing it to paper. She didn't have to write me. She didn't have to thank me for the book, let alone share her feelings about me. It was different when thousands of miles separated us, but now it's only a short drive. I push a long, frustrated breath from my lungs. It's going to be a long, sleepless night.

The next morning I'm up before the rest of the house, mostly because I never went to sleep in the first place. The antique roll-top desk in the den houses an old computer that probably hasn't been turned on since Emily graduated high school. I wince when the dial-up modem shrieks, determined to wake up everyone in the house. I've forgotten how loud the Internet used to be. I've also forgotten how *slow* it used to be.

"You've got to be kidding me," I mumble to myself as I wait for the website to load. The spinning hourglass on the screen mocks me. I don't get very far before I hear footsteps creaking in the hallway, which has me swiftly turning off the computer monitor.

"It's a little early to be watching porn, don't you think?" Anthony remarks as he stalks into the room.

"I wasn't," I deny.

"Oh really?" His tone lifts in disbelief. "Then why did you shut down your computer so fast?"

I bite my bottom lip. "No reason."

"I don't believe you."

Anthony is much taller and stronger than me; he easily wedges between me and the computer like a basketball player boxing out to get a rebound.

"Don't, Anthony!" I try to grab his arms and pin them behind his back.

He sticks his butt into my gut, blocking me from the computer. "Nuh uh," he denies me. "I wanna know all your dirty little kinks."

I swipe at his hands to no result. "It's nothing, I swear."

My dad pops his head into the room. "Everything okay in here?"

We immediately stop hitting and slapping each other.

"Yeah, Dad. We're fine."

"Try to keep it down," he says in his stern, paternal tone. "Your sister's still sleeping and today's a big day for her."

"Okay, Dad," I agree.

"Yes, sir," Anthony adds.

With a final, doubting look between the two of us, my dad leaves.

When he's gone, I slap Anthony's arm, but I can't help my giggle. The moment makes me feel decades younger. "Stop getting me in trouble."

"Don't try to blame me. You get yourself in trouble all on your own," Anthony chides. "Now let's see what you were trying to hide."

All I can do is cover my face as he turns the monitor on to discover what I've been looking at.

"This is the lamest porn ever," he complains. "Why didn't you want me to know you were looking up an online newspaper archive?"

I peek through the space between my fingers. "I was hoping there'd be a story about Charlotte. Maybe when she played volleyball in college or bought the bar."

"God, you're a glutton for punishment."

"I know," I sigh.

"Do you think there's a picture?" he asks. "I want to see what she looks like."

"I didn't get that far before I was rudely interrupted," I huff.

Anthony's eyes don't leave the computer screen. "Put a sock on the door handle next time," he says. "What's this girl's last name?"

"Johansson. Two s's."

"Good Norwegian stock," he says as he types on the keyboard.

"I think it's Swedish," I correct.

"Same thing," he dismisses. "Roundtree's Bar and Grill under new ownership," he reads aloud.

"Move over," I order.

Anthony continues to deny me access to the screen. "She's cute." He scrunches up his face and leans closer to the monitor. "Or at least I think she is. This photo is horrible quality."

"Let me see." I shove against his shoulder, but he still won't move.

"No." He continues to read: "There's a familiar face behind the bar in downtown Grand Marais, but instead of being a bartender, now she's the owner. Charlotte Johansson, daughter of MaryAnn and Frederick Johansson, is the new proprietress of Roundtree's Bar & Grill, long-time watering hole for the residents of the city. 'When we decided to retire,' says Curt Roundtree, who has owned the local pub with his wife Veronica since 1973, 'the obvious choice was Charlotte.' The local woman bartended during summers when she was home from college at the University of Minnesota." Anthony stops and quirks his lips. "Well, that was wildly unremarkable."

"It's a weekly town newspaper, not award-winning journalism."

"Maybe you could move here and write for them," he suggests with a teasing smile. He finally moves out the way so I can see. "So what now, stalker?"

"Googling someone is hardly stalking," I scoff. "If it were, you'd be on America's Most Wanted." I take one last look at the grainy black and white image of Charlotte that accompanies the story before shutting down the computer.

"What should I wear to the party today?" He crosses his legs and clasps his hands over his knee. "I've never been to a hoedown before."

"I thought you were going to stop with the small town jokes?"

"I said no such thing. You lived here, so own it."

"When do I get to see where you grew up?" I realize that I don't know where Anthony's originally from.

"Child, there was no growing up," he dismisses. "I was born fully formed and fabulous."

"I'm sure."

"Should I butch it up at the party? Am I supposed to be your boyfriend?"

"Not unless you want to confuse the entire town. They already know I'm gay."

"Why didn't you say so? Miss Fabulous could have been your

date."

"I could only be so lucky."

+ + +

I can't find a single working pen in the entire house.

All of the letters I wrote to Charlotte are back in my apartment in Los Angeles, but I can't let myself leave town without at least leaving her a note. I don't know what I'll write yet, but first I need to find something to write with. Every pen I find has dried up or run out of ink. It's probably the Universe telling me to back off again, but this time I'm ignoring the cosmic message. I pull open the junk drawer in the kitchen and rummage among the rubber bands and random envelopes. Nothing.

At the bottom of the deep drawer is a book I'd nearly forgotten existed. The local phone book. Thank you, Universe. There are a number of listings under the last name of Johansson, but I find the one I'm looking for: *Johansson, C. 208 Prospect Avenue.*

I glance up at the ceiling, hearing the sound of the upstairs shower turn off. Anthony's getting ready and my dad and Emily are already at the hardware store setting up for the party.

I grab the cordless phone in the kitchen and dial the number before anyone can walk in and try to talk some sense into me.

"Hello?" I hear her voice.

"Charlotte?"

"Speaking."

My throat tightens and I'm barely able to get out the next few words. "It's Abby. Henry," I clarify, not knowing if there's more than one Abby in her life.

"Oh, uh, you caught me at a bad time. I'm just out the door."

"I saw my mom on Tuesday." The words rush past my teeth.

"What? How?" she asks. "I didn't know you guys were in contact."

"I hired someone to find her, and he did."

"Oh. Wow. How did it go?"

"Not well. Actually, pretty horrible. I kind of wish I hadn't done it."

"I'm sorry, Abby. That couldn't have been easy."

Her words make my heart ache. She's far too kind. I've been an asshole and yet she still shows me compassion.

I internally debate if I should say anything about the party later or the fact that I'm in town. "Well, I suppose I should let you go."

"It's okay."

"I thought you were running out the door?"

"I am. But, I have a little time. I only said that because it gave me an out in case I changed my mind about talking to you."

"Have you? Changed your mind?"

"Keep talking," she says. "I'll let you know."

"How's Amelia?" I ask. When I say her name, I picture that untamable blonde hair, the same as her mother's.

"She's good. She's really excited for first grade. School doesn't start until after Labor Day, but she made me go to Duluth last week for back-to-school shopping."

"That's adorable."

She makes a noise in agreement. "Her backpack is filled with Trapper Keepers and pencils, and she's already picked out her outfit for the first day."

"Uh oh," I chuckle. "Is it a pink tutu and her rain boots?"

"Actually, it's pretty sensible. I was impressed."

"And how's Reggie?"

"He's still hanging around, still eating half of the food on my daughter's plate."

"I can't blame him. You're a good cook."

"That's a leap," she protests. "You've only had my eggs."

"I wouldn't mind some more."

There's a quiet cough, and I wonder if I've said too much.

"Are you writing again?" she asks.

"I've been dabbling, but nothing really serious. I should probably do that though before the bill collectors start knocking on my door."

"What do you do all day if you're not writing?"

"I think about you."

I hear her sigh. "Abby…"

"I'm sorry," I jump in, immediately regretting trying to flirt. "It's too much too soon, isn't it? This is our first time talking since…"

"I know. And I've thought about this—what it would mean to start talking to you again. It's probably not healthy or fair to either of us."

"What do you mean?"

"A long-distance relationship? Those never work out. Someone's going to get bored, or frustrated, or distracted by the next pretty girl."

"Someone," I repeat. "You mean me."

"Maybe I mean myself," she counters.

"We can't be friends?"

"Can we even do something like that—be friends?" She says the words as though they're the most preposterous thing she's ever heard. "Just talk with no flirting or emotions or words of endearment?"

"You mean talk about the weather and sports? I can do that."

"Really?"

"Sure. How do you think the Vikings are gonna do this season?"

"Are you asking me for real?"

"I don't know. But are you willing to give it a try?"

There's a pregnant pause. "I'm sorry, Abby. I really do have to go. You called at a bad time."

"Okay. Maybe … maybe we can talk later?"

"About sports?" I hear her soft laugh, and I immediately feel better about the impromptu phone call.

"I'll start looking up random sports trivia right now."

CHAPTER SEVENTEEN

"You'd better get a move on," Anthony scolds. "Your sister's party starts soon."

There's a damp towel around my head and my face is makeup free. "I was planning on being fashionably late."

"Being 'fashionably late' to a family party is tacky, Abigail Henry," he scolds. "I thought I taught you better."

Despite Anthony's rushing, we're still late getting to the grand reopening. Emily had said jeans and flannel were appropriate, but I want to look nice. I don't often have occasion to wear a dress to events I actually want to attend.

The butcher-block paper has been removed from the store's front windows and there's practically a line waiting to get inside. It looks like the opening of a hot new club in Hollywood, not a hardware store's rejuvenation.

Inside, the store is packed, and Emily is surrounded by well-wishers. It's a far more comforting view than when she'd been circled by mourners. A lot can change in a month.

"Nice dress," Emily approves when we finally have a moment to talk. "What's the occasion?"

"Haven't you heard? My little sister is crazy." I raise my plastic wine glass in salute.

She sticks her tongue out at me. "Thanks."

"So, you're really doing this, huh? Staying in Grand Marais, working at the hardware store, and fixing up that old apartment yourself."

"Yup. I'm gonna gut the bathroom, get new appliances in the kitchen, update all the electrical, and the wood floors will get refinished like I did downstairs. After some fresh paint on the walls, new light fixtures throughout, and hardware on the kitchen cabinets, it might actually be livable."

"Sounds like you'll be busy for the next five years," I quip.

"Just in time for your next visit," she counters.

I take a sip of my wine. "You're hilarious, Em."

Anthony sticks close to my elbow during the party except to get food. "There are some tasty morsels here, and I don't just mean the food," he remarks when he returns with a plate stacked high with snacks. "We need more Lumbersexuals in LA."

I'm about to warn him not to fall for a local when I notice the graphic on the plate under the stuffed mushroom caps and cherry tomatoes. It's the logo from Charlotte's bar. "Where did you get that?"

"By the giant stack of paint cans," he says, nodding his head toward a back corner of the store. "Your sister ordered quite the spread. I guess Midwesterners actually eat at parties."

I spot a collapsible table set up near the painting supplies at the rear of the store. I haven't had a chance to wander that deep into the room yet. A woman in a cap-sleeve dress stands behind the table, carefully arranging finger-foods and bite-sized desserts on elevated serving dishes. Her blonde hair is tied up in a bun, accentuating her high, chiseled cheekbones. A denim apron with the logo for Roundtree's Bar & Grill protects her clothes and cinches her lithe waist.

"You told me she wouldn't show up," I hiss in my sister's direction, "but she's the damn caterer."

Emily shrugs, unaffected by the venom in my voice. "I never said she wouldn't be here. I said she wasn't on the guest list."

"You knew what I meant! Why the hell would you do this to me?" I lament.

"Because I love you, Abs. And sometimes you need to get out of your own damn way."

Anthony looks puzzled. "What did I miss?"

Emily and I speak at the same time: "Charlotte."

"Where?" he gasps. He stands on his tiptoes and cranes his neck to see over the partygoers. "Oh, this ought to be good."

Despite the room's moderate temperature, I can feel my body begin to overheat. I don't know what to do or say, but the store is too small and there are not enough people at the party to avoid her the entire night. I can either walk out the front door and pretend like I never saw her, or I can be brave and finally confront her.

Emily nudges me in the rib cage. "Go talk to her," she urges.

"Why?"

She rolls her eyes. "Because you like her, duh."

"And if you don't," Anthony piles on. "*I* will."

"Okay, okay."

I drink down the remaining wine in my glass, but it's not nearly enough to give me a false sense of bravado. I shake out my hands at my sides. This isn't the organic reunion I was looking for, but I can't let this opportunity pass me by.

Charlotte's focused on re-stocking food and doesn't look up when I stop in front of her. The scent of warm food co-mingles with the hardware store's natural perfume. I stand for a moment with the food table between us and watch her at work. She plucks lollipop drumsticks from rectangular metal trays and arranges the food on the serving plate. I'm transfixed by her fingers, long and tan.

She's beautiful—even more so than the mental picture engrained in my head. I want to kiss her red mouth and make her forget about all the shitty things I've done.

Finally, I clear my throat. "Hi."

"Is there something I can get you?" She still doesn't look up. Other guests reach around me and grab the complimentary offerings nearly as quickly as she can lay them out.

I rub at the back of my neck. "I'm hearing rave reviews about the food, so I had to check it out for myself. Are those mini quiche?"

When she eventually looks up, her features reveal her surprise. She looks a little like a deer in headlights, and I can't blame her; I'm feeling the very same way.

She ignores my compliment and question: "Emily told me you weren't coming back for the party."

"Yeah, there seems to be a lot of subterfuge happening," I note wryly. "I think she's trying to play matchmaker."

I steal a glance in Emily's direction, but she's currently involved in an animated conversation with Anthony and doesn't seem to notice me, or else she's doing a good job of pretending like she's not watching us.

"Why didn't *you* tell me?" Charlotte asks.

"I don't know. I didn't want to complicate things, I guess. I'd just barely extended the olive branch."

She nods, understanding. "I like your dress."

"Thanks." I absentmindedly touch the hemline of my outfit. It's a blue cotton halter dress with a skinny orange belt at the waist. Anthony told me the color compliments my dark chestnut hair, and I trust his judgment more than my own. "It's probably a little much for a hardware store re-opening, but it's kind of fun to get dolled up sometimes."

"It looks good."

"You're the one with legs born for skirts," I feel compelled to add.

Her hazel gaze falters, and she looks away.

"Um, how about those Twins? Think they'll win the division?" I clear my throat. "I just mean ... you look really nice, too."

"I'm a sweaty mess. I've been cooking all day." She brushes a few chunks of hair that have fallen out of her bun away from her face.

"The spread is impressive," I compliment. "I haven't eaten yet, but it all looks really good."

"You should fix yourself a plate," she suggests. "Emily's paid the bill."

I exhale, long and low. We're conversing civilly, which is encouraging, but she may just not want to make a scene in front of half the town.

"How long are you in town for?" she asks as she begins to make a plate for me, piling it high with deep-fried foods.

"My flight's tomorrow afternoon."

I notice the hitch in her movements when she hears my answer. She licks her lips and nods, but doesn't say a word.

"I don't have to," I blurt out. "I mean, I could always postpone it."

"Why would you do that?"

"I just thought that maybe ... maybe we could spend some time together."

"Do you have writer's block?"

I know what she's referring to, but I'm not going to let her derail my efforts. I know there's something greater than bad blood between us. "No. I want to spend time with you."

"For how long?"

I stare at her with intent. "For as long as you'll have me."

"Pretty words from the writer."

"Charlotte ..." I've run out of those pretty words.

She makes a disgruntled noise and unties her apron strings. "We should talk about this someplace else. People are starting to stare."

"I don't care."

"Well, *I* do," she says sharply. She removes her apron and discards the garment on the buffet table. "I have to live in this town, and I'd rather not be the center of another gossip tornado."

There's a room in the back of the hardware store that serves as my dad's office. It was also Emily's and my playroom growing up. The scent of wood and oil and nails is even more pronounced in the little room. It looks untouched by Emily's upgrades.

I close the door behind me to give us more privacy. Charlotte walks to the center of the room and turns on her heel to face me as the door clicks shut.

"You never called," she says in a voice more matter-of-fact than accusatory. "You write a play about Amelia, you track me down at the bar, and then you never call. Until today," she snorts, "when you're actually in town."

I grimace at the truth in her words. "Would you believe me if I said I lost your number?"

"I don't think it really matters if I believe you or not anymore."

Beyond the thin door the muffled sounds of the gathering continue. I wonder if Emily or Anthony has noticed we've disappeared.

"I got your letter."

She sighs loudly and her fingers grip the front of her hair near her forehead. "That was dumb of me," she speaks to the ceiling. "I wanted to take it back as soon as I sent it, but my arms weren't long enough to get it out of the mailbox."

"I wrote you a letter every day I was back in California," I admit. "I wanted to send them so badly."

"Why didn't you?"

"I guess I didn't see the point. I was in California, and you were here, hating my guts."

"I didn't hate your guts," she's quick to rectify. "I was confused. And hurt."

"I'm so very, very sorry, Charlotte," I say with devoted sincerity. "I'll apologize until the end of days if that's what it takes."

"I don't want more apologies."

"Then what do you want?"

"Something you can't give me."

Her words cause my stomach to stir uncomfortably. "What makes you say that?" I don't wait for her answer because I know what she'll say. She won't do long distance, and she's not going to move. "I really like you, Charlotte. A lot. You're smart and funny, and not to mention, sexy as hell."

"I'm also a single mom," she adds.

"I know. And I adore Amelia." I latch onto her hands. I've gone long enough without touching her. I'm encouraged when she doesn't pull away. "I think we could be good together."

"Nothing has changed, Abby. I'm too old to do long distance, and I've already told you I'm not leaving Grand Marais," she sternly insists. "Amelia's got enough to deal with without me ripping her away from her home."

"I'm not asking you to. I can write anywhere."

"You'd really want to leave your glamorous life in California for the chance to date a single mom?" She looks unconvinced.

"She's not just any single mom," I boast. "She happens to be a successful business owner who makes the best scrambled eggs and brandy Old Fashioneds in town."

My attempt at levity is lost on her. "Grand Marais is too small for you," she says with a shake of her head. "It'll never last."

"Maybe I don't live in Grand Marais. Not right away, at least." I hadn't seriously considered a move before, but now that the words are out, it doesn't sound like such a bad idea. Los Angeles was never a forever city for me. "Maybe I have a place in Duluth or the Twin Cities, and we see each other whenever we want. Give it a chance, Charlotte," I implore. At this point I'm not above begging. The phone call was important, but seeing her again, in the flesh, has solidified how much I want to be with her. "Give *me* a chance."

She tucks her lower lip into her mouth, and my heart feels like it's stilled in my chest as I wait for her answer.

EPILOGUE

ACT 4

Scene 1

SETTING: A high school football game in small town America. It's near dusk, but the stadium lights haven't turned on yet. The sky is filled with light pinks and purples.

AT RISE: ABIGAIL HENRY and EMILY HARVESTER sit together on metal bleachers. Before them the local high school football team competes in a match against a rival city's team. A line of cheerleaders shout out practiced routines and other fans sitting around ABIGAIL and EMILY root on the local team.

Emily and I don't know any of the kids on the field, but that doesn't dampen our exuberant cheers. It's nearly halftime and the Cook County Vikings are up by a touchdown.

"How's business these days?" I ask.

Despite my earlier misgivings about Emily becoming partner in my dad's business, it's actually been going really well. It's kind of a relief actually. Now my dad might actually consider retiring one day, and the business will stay in the family for at least another generation.

"Really great." Her head bobs with enthusiasm. "Dad's finally figured out the new cash register."

"Only took him two months," I remark with a chuckle. "I'm impressed."

The hard metal of football bleachers vibrates beneath us each time someone climbs up them. More than a few people stop to say hi and most at least make purposeful eye contact and say hello on their way to their respective seats.

"We've got a big job coming up," she notes. "The sports boosters want a new concession stand with heat. Are you interested in a little part-time work?"

"You don't want to trust me with power tools." I shake my head and laugh. "Besides, I'm actually getting some good work done on my new play."

"What are you working on right now?"

"A love story."

"Does it have a happy ending?"

I stare at a leggy blonde in light blue skinny jeans climbing up the bleachers, her hands occupied with two Styrofoam cups. The polished brass buttons on her fitted army green jacket gleam under the fading sun. She's wearing a scarf that my grandmother made me; it looks better on her.

"That remains to be seen."

Charlotte sits beside me and passes one of the cups to Emily and the other to me.

Emily sniffs the contents of the Styrofoam cup. "Did you put booze in this?"

"I'm a bartender, aren't I?"

"Drinking on school property?" Emily's voice lowers sternly. "Abby, keep your girlfriend in line. She's gonna get us all in trouble."

I arch an eyebrow. "I'm pretty sure she does what she wants."

Charlotte leans towards me and nuzzles her nose against mine. "And you wouldn't have it any other way."

As happy as I am, I can't help feeling guilty that I've got Charlotte, but Emily no longer has Adam. The three of us hang out a lot when

I'm in town, and we do our best not to make Emily feel like a third wheel. The prospective suitors in Grand Marais are lacking, but I'm always on the lookout when I'm in Duluth.

The timing worked out well; Emily had a condo in downtown Duluth that wouldn't sell, and I needed a place to stay after I let my lease run out in Los Angeles. Duluth is a midsized city, the second most populous in the state behind the Twin Cities. It's only a two-hour drive from the city to Grand Marais, which is manageable, especially knowing whom I'm driving to see. My writing schedule lets me visit for extended long-weekends and the Minneapolis airport is only two hours from Duluth if I need to fly out to Los Angeles for a reading or to workshop a new play. It's been a compromise, but it works for now.

"Thanks again for re-wiring my front porch light, Em," Charlotte says. "It's too bad I'm dating the Henry sister who can quote Chaucer but knows nothing about electrical work."

"I could have fixed it," I protest. *Not without electrocuting myself*, I keep to myself. "But I didn't want to kill Amelia's firefly light."

The girl in question stampedes up the bleachers with two friends tagging behind. She started first grade a few weeks ago and everything seems to be going well. She loves her teacher and the school, which is coincidentally the same building where Emily, Charlotte, and I also went to elementary school. Mother and daughter came up with a compromise about the clothes Amelia wears to school. Like casual Friday at a business, Charlotte lets Abigail choose her own crazy outfit for Fridays, which means that for tonight's home football game she's dressed herself in overalls, a red jacket, and her green rain boots. She looks a little like Christmas come early or maybe Paddington Bear.

"I like your shoes, Amelia," my sister compliments.

Amelia's face brightens. "Thanks, Mrs. Harvester!"

"You've really got to make her stop calling me that," Emily complains under her breath. "It makes me feel like a dinosaur."

"Amelia would probably like you better if you *were* a dinosaur," I respond.

"Mommy, can I have money for a licorice rope?"

I jump in before Charlotte has time to respond. "I've got it." I dig into my jacket pocket and find some change. I drop a handful of silver coins it into her cupped hands like she's hit the jackpot on a slot machine. "Don't spend it all in one place, kid."

Her tiny fists curl around the change. "Thanks, Abby!" she grins.

Without having to look in her direction, I can tell Charlotte is probably glaring at me.

"You spoil her."

"I'd rather spoil you," I counter, "but you're stubbornly independent, just like your daughter."

"Hey, Abby," Amelia chirps, trying to garner my attention.

"What is it, kiddo?" I snap my eyes to her round, smiling face.

"Did you know that there are over two thousand kinds of fireflies? And they're not really flies at all; they're beetles."

"I did know that," I say, leaning forward. "And did *you* know that some fireflies light up at the same time? They're called synchronous fireflies."

"Did you know that some female fireflies pretend to be another kind of firefly so they can eat the boy fireflies?"

Beside me, Emily nearly spits out her boozy hot chocolate. On my other side, I can feel Charlotte shaking with laughter.

"That wasn't in the book I got her," I mumble to my girlfriend.

"You really did create a monster," she replies with a good-humored chuckle.

Amelia bounds away to her friends waiting for her at the bottom of the bleachers.

Charlotte leans her head against my shoulder and my arm reflexively goes around her waist to pull her closer into my side. We're the same height and build, but I love it when she cuddles into me. She's stubborn and proud and self-reliant, which makes me appreciate these soft moments even more.

Charlotte hasn't shied away from the inevitable whispers or the gawkers. But then again, she's always been stronger and braver than I could ever be. She's had to be like that because of Amelia. She also eventually convinced me to publish the children's play I'd written for her and Amelia. I'd balked at the idea for a while, but between Charlotte and Claire's joint cajoling, I finally gave in. The promise of royalties didn't hurt either.

"You guys are so cute, it makes me want to puke," Emily speaks up. "Seriously. Stop being adorable."

I know she considers herself responsible for this reconciliation, and for once, I agree with my sister. Without her subterfuge and the family store's re-opening, we probably would have been too scared and too stubborn to talk to the other person.

I stick out my tongue at Emily, but I don't pull away from Charlotte. I never could have expected to be this comfortable with a girlfriend out in public in my tiny, remote hometown. I'd always thought I'd never be able to be myself, to be Out in this town where I grew up, but Charlotte pushes me outside of my comfort zone every day. It brings my friend Julie's words to mind: I should have trusted these people who had been part of my life for so long to love me no matter what. But I had been invisible for so long, I'd been afraid that people would start to notice me for all the wrong reasons.

Looking around the stands of the high school football stadium, seeing so many familiar faces from my past and my present, and surrounded by the people I love most in this world, I realize that maybe I had it wrong all along. Maybe you can go home again.

I press my lips to the top of Charlotte's head. Her body's warm and she smells like sunscreen even though our beach days are over until next summer. She slips her hand into my jacket pocket where my other hand currently resides. Our fingers seek out the other's, tangling naturally as if we've been doing this our entire lives. All of my previous relationships were only dress rehearsals preparing me for this role—the most important and significant of my life.

ABOUT THE AUTHOR

Eliza Lentzski is the author of lesbian fiction, romance, and erotica including *Winter Jacket 3: Finding Home, Fragmented, Don't Call Me Hero, Winter Jacket 2: New Beginnings, Apophis: A Love Story for the End of the World, Winter Jacket, Second Chances, Date Night, Diary of a Human, Love, Lust, & Other Mistakes*, and the forthcoming sequel to *Don't Call Me Hero* (Winter 2015). She also publishes urban fantasy and paranormal romance under the penname E.L. Blaisdell. Although a historian by day, Eliza is passionate about fiction. She calls the Midwest her home along with her partner and their cat and turtle.

Follow her on Twitter, @ElizaLentzski, and Like her on Facebook (http://www.facebook.com/elizalentzski) for updates and exclusive previews of future original releases.

http://www.elizalentzski.com

Printed in Great Britain
by Amazon.co.uk, Ltd.,
Marston Gate.